He was listening to her thoughts

Sandy seemed so intent on reading her expression, in that way he had that Victoria liked so well, of peering into her eyes with a look of total absorption and anticipation. As if whatever she might be thinking could be so important. As if he cared so much.

How much did he care?

It was as though her eyes had posed the question and his had answered, *I care a lot.*

I'd like to believe you, she told him.

Believe me, he was saying.

And then the last chime of midnight died away and she was struck by what a long silent conversation they'd managed to have in such a short amount of time. Victoria looked at him standing there, so close. There was so little distance between them, and it suddenly seemed silly that there should be any at all....

ABOUT THE AUTHOR

New York is home for Leigh Anne Williams, who lives in picturesque Greenwich Village. In addition to being a romance novelist, Leigh Anne is a lyricist and scriptwriter.

Books by Leigh Anne Williams
HARLEQUIN AMERICAN ROMANCE

232–GOLDEN DREAMS
265–KATHERINE'S DREAM
269–LYDIA'S HOPE
273–CLARISSA'S WISH
300–LOVE ME LIKE A ROCK
343–SPIRITS WILLING

Don't miss any of our special offers. Write to us at the following address for information on our newest releases.

Harlequin Reader Service
901 Fuhrmann Blvd., P.O. Box 1397, Buffalo, NY 14240
Canadian address: P.O. Box 603,
Fort Erie, Ont. L2A 5X3

LEIGH ANNE WILLIAMS

MAGIC HOUR

Harlequin Books

TORONTO • NEW YORK • LONDON
AMSTERDAM • PARIS • SYDNEY • HAMBURG
STOCKHOLM • ATHENS • TOKYO • MILAN

Published January 1991

ISBN 0-373-16376-2

MAGIC HOUR

Chapter One

Ed Baskin stole another look at his Rolex watch, glanced guiltily at the empty chair between them at the table and sighed. "I can't apologize enough," he said, adjusting the bridge of his aviator glasses for the umpteenth time.

"You don't have to," said Victoria, giving him one of her nicest smiles. "The food's very good here."

"He's not usually like this," Ed said, looking now from Victoria to Maxanne.

Maxanne nodded sympathetically. "At least he called," she said, ever diplomatic. She and Ed exchanged a look, agent to agent, that seemed to speak volumes.

Victoria caught the drift. Writers and artists were irresponsible kids, forever creating problems for their long-suffering parent-managers. But she didn't bridle, because she was the good child today, anyway. *She'd* shown up. And if Sandy Baker never did, that was fine with her.

All things considered, this luncheon meeting was turning out to be even better than she could have imagined. The food at Le Café Rouge really was good, and if Mr. Baker didn't arrive, she'd be relieved of the responsibility of telling him "no" in person. Because despite the Oscar-winning director's reputation and his studio's generous offer, she had no intention of selling the movie rights to *Jumpers Creek*.

Victoria took another sip of the white-wine spritzer she'd allowed herself this afternoon. She savored the tart carbonation on her tongue, happy to survey the main dining room of the chic downtown bistro while Ed and Maxanne traded stories about The Biz. She liked the atmosphere here and it was full of interesting people, like that man at a window table she'd noticed earlier.

Three hundred pounds of gourmand, he seemed to be methodically eating his way through the entire menu. She noted for her mental character file the look of the cloth napkin tucked beneath his chins and the shine of the pinkie ring on his manicured little finger. She didn't know where she might use this in the new book, but it was a nice baroque detail.

The new book. Where she really should be was at home working on her second chapter, but Maxanne had insisted on this meeting. Her agent thought she was crazy to nix a deal with Sandy Baker, and Victoria understood that turning down such an offer would probably seem like madness to most authors in her position. Well, maybe it was crazy, but she had her reasons. And she had enough faith in her talent to gamble that it wouldn't be the only offer of its kind to ever come her way.

Not that she wasn't flattered by the attention and unaware of what it signified. Thirteen years ago, her first and very autobiographical novel had made her a literary bridesmaid, known as a writer of "promise", but not a bride. Now the critics, even the infamous Devon Gibson of the *Times*, had pronounced that promise fulfilled. The public, after showing general disinterest in her three subsequent novels, was at last chiming in with the agreeable ring of bookstore cash registers. *The Folly of Wendy Goode* had reached the lower rung of the *Times*'s hardcover best-seller list this past month.

Which was why Hollywood had called. The film rights to *Wendy Goode* were already being sought by a major studio. But this interest of Sandy Baker's in her first novel had taken Victoria by surprise. Maxanne had been surprised, too, and eager to sell the rights. Wasn't Sandy Baker one of the hottest directors in America? And wasn't that novel, Victoria's personal favorite, the only one that had never received proper attention, never made her any money? So wasn't this a dream come true?

More like a nightmare, Victoria mused. She shifted uneasily in her seat, stealing another glance at that mountain of a man by the window. He was on his fourth or fifth course, going slow and steady, looking marvellously content. She envied him his absolute calm, a man in his element—born to eat.

And she was born to write, she supposed, but the consequences of that livelihood were only now catching up with her. Victoria had never told her faithful agent, but she was secretly glad *Jumpers Creek* hadn't instantly catapulted her to the top of the best-seller list those many years ago. The book hadn't been meant for that kind of attention—or scrutiny. It was literally too close to home.

Mother, she was sure, hadn't even read it, though she said she had. That was just as well. Dad had read it and overpraised it, as of course he would, and Cissy had damned it with faint niceties. As for the other residents of Silver Spring, people who'd shown up in the pages of it only thinly disguised, Victoria wasn't sure to this day what they thought. But since she'd never gotten letters of ire or affection from any of them in the years since, she had a sense that she'd gotten away with it.

Gotten away with what? Being too honest. True, that was the way first novels were supposed to be: filled with fictionalized facts snatched from the fledgling author's true day-to-day existence. She hadn't done anything wrong, hadn't betrayed anybody's awful secrets, or caricatured people she knew in mean-spirited ways. Still, an uncomfortable feeling haunted her about that book even to this day. Maybe it was because she was the one who'd been exposed in it, her disguise thinner than the others'.

Or maybe she liked to think she'd become a better writer since. In her more recent work, certainly in *Wendy Goode*, she'd perfected a certain ironic tone, a "coolness that bespoke a new maturity," as one reviewer had put it. The young woman who'd written *Jumpers Creek* in a passionate heat of self-revelation all those years ago had been anything but cool.

Victoria was proud of that younger self, of course, and still felt as protective of that book as any mother would be of her firstborn child. But she was wary of having that child held up to possible ridicule. And she'd heard enough horror stories about books ruined by moviemakers to make her balk at putting her work in some unscrupulous screenwriter's hands. After more than one sleepless night this week, in spite of Maxanne's arguments, she'd made her decision.

This meeting with Sandy Baker was really more of a courtesy, a formality. The director was in town briefly to oversee a "post-dub sound mix," whatever that was, on his latest film, and he'd insisted on meeting Victoria even after he'd been told through his agent that she wasn't interested in selling the film rights. Maxanne had said it was a good idea, politically, to at least hear the man out.

If Victoria was going to be stubborn about this and persist in her folly, as Maxanne termed it, the agent was willing to play bad cop to Victoria's good one. She'd be the bearer of the bad news to Baker and his agent, while Victoria could be as friendly and charming as she wanted. That way, if Baker was interested in any of her other books, or if

Victoria had a later change of heart, good relations would still be maintained.

As it was, Sandy Baker was the one who seemed to have had a change of heart. If he couldn't even manage to get to the meeting he'd set up—

"Victoria, this is a little embarrassing," Ed Baskin was saying. She began to politely demur. "But my daughter is a big fan of yours," he went on, and she realized, as he removed a copy of *Wendy Goode* from his leather satchel, that he wasn't referring to Baker's nonappearance now. "Do you think you could . . . ?"

He was uncapping a silver Cross pen for her. "Oh, sure," she said, opening the book. Good move, Ed, she thought. Keep the author's ego massaged to cover your client's faux pas.

"Her name's Janice," he said.

Victoria snuck a glance at Maxanne, who was clearly registering the same thought she'd just had, then dutifully scribbled best wishes to Janice Baskin on the inside cover. She handed the book and pen back to Ed, who thanked her profusely, then checked his Rolex one more time. She felt bad that he was obviously upset. She had to restrain herself from putting a sympathetic hand on his tanned wrist and telling him everything was fine, really. She hadn't wanted to meet Sandy Baker anyway.

Ed began telling Maxanne another show-biz anecdote. Relaxing in a growing sense of well-being, Victoria took another sip of her spritzer and looked around the sunlit interior of Le Café Rouge for that splendiferous dessert cart she'd seen wheeled by earlier. She was tempted to indulge in a pastry, as long as she was here. The pâtisserie on wheels had been loaded with provocative desserts, and if the giant gourmand by the window didn't get to it first... Maybe just a little one, as a reward for good behavior. She'd ask the waiter when he returned.

She and Maxanne had arrived pretty much on time, although reaching the restaurant's front door had been a minor ordeal. The San Gennaro street fair, one of many such Italian festivals that erupted in the streets of Greenwich Village and Soho during spring and summer, was in full swing on Sullivan Street. Its boisterous panoply of booths selling sweet sausage, ices and other scrumptious Neapolitan specialties alongside shooting galleries and gambling wheels lined the usually quiet street, now closed to auto traffic but filled with tourists and locals.

Le Café Rouge was smack dab in the middle of this tumult. Although it was quiet in here, with soothing French Renaissance music piped through unobtrusive speakers, Victoria, gazing out the window from their table, caught glimpses of the parade of people out there and heard the muted sounds of their occasional gales of laughter and revelry. Even on a weekday, lunch was a busy time for Sullivan Street during the fest.

As a longtime Village resident, Victoria tended to avoid the street fairs. It was hard enough just navigating her own neighborhood, Bleecker near MacDougal Street, which was still a city tourism attraction. But beyond the crowds and noise, it was the food she was wary of. Those cannolis, zeppoli and éclairs! Sinful delights, and horribly addictive, all of them. She'd gone on a sugar binge after she and Doug had finally parted ways, and she was now still in the midst of a penitential diet.

Ed had left her novel facedown on the table near her elbow. Victoria stole a glance at the publicity head shot that filled its back cover. The photo was over two years old, when she'd been thinner. She'd certainly had more prominent cheekbones when that shot had been taken.

She studied the glossy face with an objective eye, looking for signs of "coolness that bespoke a new maturity." No way. The blue-green eyes had a vulnerable warmth, the slightly pursed lips an almost childlike pout. Nearly every feature on her face, it seemed, had some idiosyncratic quirk that made her look both younger than her years, thank goodness, and an unlikely candidate for a Serious Writer canonization.

Her nose was straight, but for the tiny bump at its peak, her skin fair but blemished by a small brown mole near the corner of a mouth which always struck her as oh-so-slightly lopsided when she smiled. Cindy Crawford, the model, had made beauty marks like that so fashionable that Victoria had seen a woman at a book-signing soiree last week with one painted on. Life was unfair. Where had Cindy Crawford been when Victoria was thirteen, and it felt like that little mole was bigger than half her face?

Well, she'd accepted her face by now, even if it did look a bit thinner in the photo. The main difference between the woman on the back of the book and the one studying it, Victoria noted, was her hair. Cropped short when the photo was taken, it was now a casual cascade of lightly brushed curly ringlets. She liked it better that way. The style made her look less tomboyish, she decided, more the thirty-seven years she was.

"Mr. Baskin?" The maître d' was hovering by the table. "Another call for you."

Ed Baskin put down his napkin. "That must be our boy again," he said with a rueful smile, rising.

"Send our fond regards," Maxanne said wryly.

She watched the tanned, gray-haired agent move off to take his call, then turned back to Victoria with a frown. "This really is a shame," she said. "He's okay, Baskin. We could've worked with him. Well, maybe we still can."

Victoria cleared her throat significantly, as Maxanne prepared to light up another cigarette. An inveterate smoker, the matronly blonde of sixty years had no intention of giving up "her favorite vice," despite Victoria's many attempts to get her to stop. But she understood that for Maxanne, the ever-present cigarette dangling from her lips was more than habit. It was a prop. It transformed her appearance from that of a motherly-looking lady into someone faintly gangster-like, especially when she stabbed the air with the cigarette to make a point, or blew a sharp jet of smoke out of the side of her mouth for punctuation.

Victoria made a mental note to use Maxanne's smoking rituals for Lura, the mother in her new book. It would give Lura more of the edge she wanted for that character. "We don't have any intention of working with Mr. Baskin, remember?" she reminded Maxanne. "Listen, the way this lunch has worked out is fine with me."

Maxanne tapped her cigarette at an ashtray and shook her head. "I just hope he's not going to ask us to wait around," she said. "One quick cup of coffee and we walk out of here with our dignity intact, okay?"

"Okay."

Victoria felt all the more buoyant. Soon lunch would be over, and she could go back to work on her novel. Sandy Baker and his offer would be history, and that was a relief. Still, she was a bit curious about the absent filmmaker. She wondered if he would've been the kind of man who wouldn't take "no" for an answer.

Victoria had made it her business to steer clear of such men. She was no fan of macho types. On the other hand, the problem with Doug had been his inability to say "no" to her. Funny, but there'd been times when she'd secretly wished her ex *had* been more tough and assertive. But that was all academic by now.

Sandy Baker was probably one of those L.A. airheads who didn't understand the word "no" at all. He'd want to talk "concepts" and "vision," while his agent talked points and percentages. The whole idea gave her the creeps. What did anybody in the movie business know about literature?

All they knew about were teen movies, slasher movies, sequels and prequels. And selling popcorn.

Someone new had walked into the restaurant. Victoria was aware of it suddenly by some second sense. Or maybe it was the way other people at nearby tables seemed instinctively to be aware of it, the women in particular shifting their eyes toward the doorway, their antennae bristling. She turned to follow their gaze and saw the man in the black-and-white cardigan.

He was tall, and handsome was an inadequate word for that face, with its hawklike nose, dark eyebrows, the penetrating dark eyes that radiated an acute intensity even from a distance, the high cheekbones and chiseled jaw, lips that gave a surprising soft fullness to a visage that was resolutely angular, all male. His hair was chestnut brown, on the longish side, with a streak of silver at the crown.

His manner of dress, with the overlong cardigan, the striped button-down shirt and pleated trousers seemed both flippantly casual and absolutely stylish. Nothing about him suggested money, yet one could sense immediately that the man belonged in surroundings like this, where the maître d' would gravitate to his side, as the Café Rouge's was doing now, and greet him with the familiarity of a friend.

And there were others. A couple at a table close by were waving a greeting. A drop-dead beauty at the bar was already sliding a graceful long-nailed hand along his arm, bestowing on him a smile radiant with perfect teeth as he turned to say hello. *She's not your type,* Victoria found herself thinking. And sure enough, the man gave the beauty a warm but perfunctory greeting and moved on.

Victoria smiled, continuing her silent appraisal. The man was inspiring similar reactions in women all over the restaurant, along with the narrow-eyed study of their male companions. It was as if he owned the room only moments after entering it, and everyone knew this.

He was slowly making his way down the bar. The smile that suddenly illuminated his face as the bartender made some remark was the capper, Victoria decided. There was a warmth there, unexpected in its openness, its complete lack of self-consciousness, that took years off the man's face in an instant, not that he looked a year over thirty-something to begin with.

And there was more, she noticed with her trained eye for detail. His two front teeth were slightly crooked, indented. That gave his smile and his whole face a boyish sexiness that was captivating, offsetting the almost brooding intensity of those sensitive eyes.

"Lord," Maxanne muttered. "I want one of those."

Victoria laughed. She was watching the man now to see what table he would join, curious to know what kind of woman might have captured this kind of man. His eyes had been scanning the room, and at the sound of her laugh, louder than she'd intended, they met hers.

There you are, his eyes said. It was as if the room had fallen silent and he'd murmured it into her ear. She felt her own smile freeze on her lips as the hint of a smile hovered on his. He was coming over to their table.

Of course, she should've known. Not what she'd expected, true, but this had to be the infamous Sandy Baker. He was right in front of her, bending, a hand grazing her shoulder. "Don't hate me," he said, his voice a low, warm rumble. "This was unavoidable."

He paused long enough to gauge her reaction. Victoria gave him her best deadpan gaze of practiced cool, to let him know that his mesmerizing good looks weren't going to make her melt. She saw him receive the subtle message, saw his smile broaden slightly with an insouciant lilt that seemed to telegraph a reply: *Oh, really? We'll see about that.*

And then he was sliding into the empty chair next to hers, turning to her agent with his hand extended. "Maxanne?

Sorry, we had a major crisis up there. Nearly lost a half million dollars' worth of sound mix. Ed been talking your ear off? Where is the guy, anyway?''

''We thought he was on the phone to you,'' Maxanne said. For once, the officious agent looked entirely undone, her eyes more that of moony schoolgirl than a steely-willed agent.

Victoria retained her mask of polite indifference. She wanted to hold onto that resentment she'd been harboring only minutes earlier, her aversion to all things Hollywood. Sandy Baker had a charismatic presence. She instinctively understood that he routinely used his high-wattage charm to get past people's resistance, and she wanted her resistance to hold up. And that was a bit of a struggle as he turned back to her, his dark eyes caressing her face with an interest that was palpable.

''Victoria,'' he said. ''You're the soul of patience. I hope the food was good, at least.''

''It was fine.''

Oh, good. There was a scintillating comeback. What had happened to our rapier-sharp wit? She'd have to do better than that if she wanted to hold her own against a man practically every woman in the restaurant wanted to sleep with, including her.

Had she really just thought that? She didn't mean it, of course. But from the subtle shift in his expression as he continued to look at her, she almost thought she'd *said* what she'd been thinking. Sandy was smiling again.

''I like the long hair,'' he said.

His tone was so familiar that she wondered if they'd met before, even though she knew they hadn't. Then as he turned away to greet the returning Ed Baskin, she remembered the book jacket. He was a slick one, all right. She sat back and studied Sandy Baker in action.

The two men were already immersed in a rapid-fire paragraph's worth of technical terms. She gathered that something had gone awry with the complicated sound track of his film in progress. She noted that he wasn't apologizing, only reporting. The assumption here was that complication concerning his film, equivalent to a car accident or a death in the family, would be tacitly understood to eclipse such minor matters as business meetings, lunches. Or her.

But it was hard to be miffed. Baker was a good storyteller. She listened more to the sound of his voice than to the words themselves, as he began sketching a vivid picture of an inept technician in a pressure cooker of an uptown editing room. There was a delight in his telling of it that struck a resonant chord in her. She'd done this so often herself, taken an incident that in the actual experience had been emotionally horrendous, then recounted it to a friend and rendered it hilarious instead.

"And the reel's already been demagnetized, blank tape now, five hundred thou and months of blood, sweat and tears down the tubes in the blink of an eye, and the man is standing there, scratching his head, saying, 'Safety? What do you mean, safety reel? We were supposed to have one?'"

Ed Baskin laughed. "That's like the old, 'Ready whenever you are, C.B.'"

Sandy nodded. "Exactly. So if it hadn't been for old Tom from Magnasound..."

They were talking in that fraternal way men who worked together so often did. You either knew the code or you didn't. Much as she was interested in what he was saying, Victoria felt herself bridling at the way this lunch had suddenly turned into the Sandy Baker show. The guy had kept them waiting for over an hour. And now that he'd arrived, wasn't she the one who was supposed to be the focus? Again she scanned the room for that pastry cart, and found it, parked over by the window, with no attendant waiter in sight.

"Had dessert yet?"

She turned, startled by his voice so close at her ear. "No, actually," she began. "But—"

"Come." He was rising from his chair, guiding her up along with him, a hand at her elbow. "Let's pick out something." He turned back to Maxanne and Ed with a smile. "You'll excuse us. French pastry is calling."

She shouldn't be letting herself be coaxed along like this, she mused, as he politely motioned for her to lead the way. But the man was unusually adept at keeping her off balance, whether he intended to do that or not. He'd been talking a mile a minute, but he'd somehow sensed both her boredom and her yen for sweets. Her rising annoyance had been deftly quelled, as the pasty cart loomed before them.

"I've been looking forward to this for days," he said, as they paused, taking in the two tiers of confections.

"You have a sweet tooth?" she asked.

"No." He smiled. "I mean looking forward to you."

"Oh." She looked away, concentrating on the éclairs and napoleons. Time to perfect that "mature coolness."

"Not days," he corrected himself. "Years. Ever since I read your book."

"You've read it—then?" Her determination to be cool faltered as her voice broke slightly. She still wasn't used to people being familiar with *Jumpers Creek*, and she'd assumed that Baker had read it only recently, after her more current success.

"Twice," he said.

She looked from the marrons glaceés to Sandy Baker's eyes, which sparkled with an even more alluring gleam. She wasn't sure she believed him entirely, but she was grudgingly impressed. "I didn't think Hollywood directors spent much time reading first novels by obscure authors."

Sandy Baker looked amused. "Well, I couldn't speak for Hollywood directors," he said. "I only know a few of them."

"But aren't you . . . ?"

"Born and bred in Brooklyn," he said. "And you know, you're not required by law to check your I.Q. into an airport locker when you arrive in Los Angeles. Some of us actually do continue to use our minds out there."

He was smiling. "I didn't mean—" she began, embarrassed.

"Don't look now," he murmured. "But there's a man behind you who's been systematically eating everything in the restaurant. And he's eyeing our pastry cart."

"Oh, him." She nodded, not turning. "A very neat diner, though."

"Not a crumb on the suit," Sandy agreed, his eyes still on the pastries. "And I particularly like the pinkie ring."

Now, that was interesting. Sandy Baker had managed to sit there, "schmooze" with Ed and Maxanne, bat his eyes at her *and* register the kind of details in the environment that she had, all at the same time. "Yes," she agreed quietly. "A very distinctive sort of vanity, there."

"Say, did you notice the elderly woman at the round table near the door? Reminded me of your Mrs. Grell."

Victoria glanced past Sandy, glimpsing the gray-haired matron in a suit whom he was undoubtedly referring to. Funny, but something about the woman had caught her eye, earlier, and now that she thought about it, the lady did bear a passing resemblance to the English teacher from *Jumpers Creek*. Victoria looked back to see Sandy watching her. *You're good at this*, she thought, surprised.

"It's my job," he said. "Or at least, part of it."

And was mind-reading, too? "I see," she said warily.

"Not unlike yours. I mean, we're both after the same thing."

She folded her arms. "Which is . . . ?"

He shrugged. "I like to think of it as prospecting. I do it with a camera, your shovel's a pen. But we're both in the business of digging up the lode. Mining. Looking for those little nuggets of truth."

Victoria nodded. He certainly didn't waste any time with small talk. "I suppose," she allowed.

He smiled. "Cautious, aren't you."

"Maybe I have my reasons."

"Maybe you should let go of some."

She stared at him. "And what's that supposed to mean?"

"I'm not the enemy, Victoria," he said quietly. "I'm on your side. I'm not interested in making a mess of your book. I'm interested in mining the treasures that are still buried in its pages."

A provocative remark, and couched in a challenging tone she couldn't ignore. "There's no buried treasure there," she scoffed. "It's just a simple little story."

"Yes, but rich with implications. And it would make a fascinating film. One that would touch people. The truths you found in *Jumpers Creek* certainly moved me. And I have a feeling there's even more to be found there."

Victoria held his gaze, feeling a shiver of apprehension that was tinged with a strange excitement. His eyes were probing hers with an arrogant directness. She wasn't sure if she liked that, but she did find it oddly arousing. "Oh, you know what they say," she said. "All that glitters . . . ?"

Sandy Baker chuckled. "We'll see about that. You know what I'd really like?" he asked abruptly. "One of those cannolis."

A cannoli? The very word made her involuntarily wet her lips, a vision of the cream-filled confection dancing before her eyes. "I don't see any," she said, glad he'd changed the subject.

"I passed some on the way in." Sandy was gazing not at the pastry cart but out the window, where the street fair was in full swing. "From De Roma's."

"The best," she said automatically.

"Better than the San Remo bakery's," he said. "Which are actually—"

"Overrated," she agreed.

"Come on," he said.

"You mean—?"

"Our gourmet friend can have this whole cart to himself," Sandy said. "Let's go."

Caught up in his impulse, she followed him as he turned and started for the door, feeling like a kid playing hooky. It was only a short distance from the window to the entrance, just long enough for her to make a token protest.

"What about—?"

"Ed and Maxanne'll do fine without us," he said, holding open the door. "I'm sure they'd rather talk to each other, anyway."

She caught a glimpse of Maxanne's startled expression across the room as Sandy guided her into the sunlight, and then they were swallowed up by the activity on the street.

Chapter Two

"It's at the end of this block," Sandy said, casually sliding an arm round her back for a moment to maneuver her expertly out of another pedestrian's way. People milled down the center of the street in a steady stream, carrying cups of fresh fruit salad or munching on jumbo shrimp.

Victoria blinked in the sunlight. Dazzled by the street life, she let herself be escorted through the crowd, conscious that Sandy's breezy familiarity was presumptuous, but unable to fend it off. At least not while he was telling her things that were honey to any author's ear.

"Incredible accomplishment for such a young writer," he was saying. "I didn't know it was a first novel."

"The critics did," she demurred.

"Critics," he said, in a tone that made the two syllables sound like the worst of swear words. "That book has flights of pure fantasy in it. Magic. And so true to life at the same time. That's the kind of combination I love."

"I ... Well, thank you," she said, uneasy. Maybe this hadn't been a good idea, letting him whisk her away from Maxanne. She didn't want to lead the man on. But at least he was no longer alluding to still-buried truths being hidden in her book.

"I guess Ed didn't really convey to you how important this project is for me."

''Well, he did say you had strong feelings about it,'' she said warily. ''But, you know, Mr. Baker—''

''Sandy.''

''Maxanne's already told Mr. Baskin that we're not interested in—''

He stopped her in mid-sentence, turning her firmly but gently to face him, with a hand on each shoulder. ''Victoria, I've been carrying this film around in my head for a long, long time.''

''Well, that may be, but—''

''I know how to do it,'' he said, his eyes looking into hers with an intensity that was unnerving. ''I know you don't know me, you don't trust me, you may not even *like* movies, but there's one person alive in the world who knows how to put this story of yours on the screen, and you're looking at him. You want one with cinnamon or without?''

''What?'' They were in front of the booth from De Roma's, she realized. The cannolis in question were lined up on dainty white doilies on the counter, and a rotund man with a mustache was waiting expectantly, chubby-fingered hands poised over the pastries. ''Plain,'' she said.

''Two,'' Sandy told the man, and added, ''Two espresso.''

How did he know she wanted an espresso? She did, actually, but she didn't have time to even register the formality of a protest as the fresh cannoli was put into her hand. And Sandy Baker was off and running again.

''We shoot on location,'' he was saying, over the gentle roar of the De Roma booth's espresso machine. ''None of this studio nonsense. We cast with an unknown for the lead, that's vital. We don't want the audience bringing in any preconceptions about Sarah. They should discover her, as she's discovering herself.''

That's *me* he's talking about, she thought. And ''on location?'' What location? And wait a second, what shooting? The man was way, way ahead of things here, and she wanted to tell him she didn't want to hear about this. But he was nudging her hand to her mouth, which was now suddenly full of delicious sweet ricotta and sugar dough, heaven in a single bite, and she couldn't say a word. Just savor and listen.

"It'll have to be fall, that's essential to the piece. You bring in that color and tone on your first page, and that's what we need to establish in the first shot. I just hope the town hasn't changed all that much in twenty years."

The town? Victoria finally managed to find her voice. "Silver Spring?"

"Of course. As long as the Glen is still intact, and the high school itself, we're fine. If we have to construct a new doughnut shop, that's not too expensive—"

"Wait, wait," she said, waving her palm. Sandy was taking a paper cup of espresso from the man behind the counter, and he promptly put it into her hand. She had no choice but to take it. "You can't."

He looked startled, pausing in the act of biting into his own cannoli. "Can't?" he echoed, as if testing a word from some foreign vocabulary.

"You can't film in Silver Spring. You can't film anything at all!" The espresso maker died down as she practically yelled this last bit. A couple bearing twin toddlers in a double stroller looked at her askance, backing away from the De Roma display. "You don't have the rights," she said, in a more reasonable tone.

"Maxanne and Ed'll work that out," he said, all nonchalance, his tongue licking at the edge of his cannoli's cream. "That's their job."

"You don't understand," she said, exasperated. "There isn't anything to work out. I'm not interested."

He looked at her as if she'd announced that the earth was flat. "*Jumpers Creek* was meant to be a movie."

"That's funny," she told him. "I never would have thought of it as a film, not in a million years."

"Now *that's* funny," he said. "Because your style is so visual. That opening paragraph of yours—it's like a long crane shot in a Bertolucci picture, or Hitchcock."

"Crane shot?"

Sandy nodded, starting to walk her to the periphery of the crowded street as he gestured in the air with his free hand. "We're up as high as the treetops, those fiery blurs of autumn color you describe. We start with an overhead view of Elm Street, people like stick figures on the sidewalk below, houses like toys until we slowly descend..."

That *was* the sense she'd conveyed in the beginning of the book, a kind of floating down from a large perspective to single out her one small heroine amidst a bigger landscape. In spite of herself she couldn't help seeing it, this picture he was painting in thin air.

"...and now we're picking up one of those figures, who's walking slower than the others, turning off the sidewalk, across this vacant lot, and we're closer now, close enough to see how she's dressed, she's different from the others somehow..."

"The coat," Victoria reminded him.

"Of course, the coat," he said. "The rips in the elbows, the patch in the back, the way her hair is, and we can't see her face yet—"

"Why?"

"Because," he said triumphantly, "she's reading her notebook as she walks, totally engrossed."

Victoria opened her mouth to dispute him. Her Sarah didn't bring her notebook into the story until many pages later, almost at the end of the first chapter. But she instinctively understood and appreciated the logic of his construction. This little shortcut made sense. It said something about

Sarah immediately, in a way that worked visually. "Doesn't she look where she's going?" she asked instead.

"Her feet know where she's going," he said. "To quote Victoria Moore."

"You mean she's on her way to the Glen?" This, too, wasn't supposed to happen right there, at least, not the way she'd written it.

"Of course. And we hear—what? The distant sounds of football practice . . ."

"From the back of the high school," Victoria said, understanding now. "I see. You're combining my second chapter—"

"But not losing anything important," he admonished her. "And the best thing is, the way this shot ends—we're talking tour de force, by the way, one long single take that's already covered a quarter of a mile in maybe forty-five seconds—is when there's the sudden blare of a motorcycle engine, and we see Sarah's face for the first time."

He turned to her, eyes aglow, his own face transported in the sunlight as he conjured this vision before them. "She looks up, startled from her reverie. And we see it all—the innocence, the vulnerability, and that instant glint of mischief in her eye as she recognizes . . ."

"Rocko's bike," Victoria said slowly. "Yes."

"Yes," he repeated, finally silent, letting the ephemeral images hang in her imagination as she took it all in. He'd done it, taken the essential elements from the beginning of her story and woven them together in one seamless sort of . . . cinematic sentence that was absolutely faithful to the tone of the book, even if it abridged and reconstructed its actual sequence of events.

"That works," she allowed, more impressed than she wanted to let on.

"Of course it works," he said lightly. "I told you," he said, tapping his forehead. "It's been with me. For years."

Victoria, never at a loss for words, fell silent. She munched on the end of her confection, aware that Sandy was watching her. They'd been strolling toward the periphery of the fair, where the stalls thinned out to a few at the corner of Broome Street. She absently licked some cream from the end of one finger.

Sandy's dark eyes seemed to savor the little gesture. She retracted her tongue, suddenly self-conscious. She felt as if she'd just been photographed. It dawned on her then that this man was as much a writer as she was, in his way. He was a constant observer, always focusing in on the smallest details, fixing them in his mind for future reference.

"Look," she said abruptly. "Maybe you can understand this, then. You may have carried your film around, as you said, but I'm the one who carried that book—like a baby, only it took twice as long to birth. Years. It's a very precious thing to me."

"Of course." Sandy was nodding. "All right, I shouldn't say this, but I could try to get you script approval. I doubt the studio will go for it, but we can try."

Victoria sighed. "Sandy, the point is, I don't want the film made."

"I don't believe you." He gave her a penetrating look. "I could see the excitement in you just now, when we talked about those shots. The bug's already bitten, only you won't admit it."

Victoria couldn't help smiling. "Well, it's a fun fantasy, that's all. Still, I don't—"

"Okay, okay, you're forcing my hand," he said with a frown. "We'll go beyond script approval. You want to write a draft with me?"

Victoria stared at him, shocked. "Lord, no," she said. "I don't know the first thing about writing screenplays and besides, I wouldn't have enough objectivity to do the job right. You know that."

"True. I was sort of hoping you'd refuse." He gave her a rueful smile. "I'm just looking for a way to make this work."

In spite of herself she was already wavering, caught up in his intensity and, yes, a little excitement of her own. "I suppose if there was a way I could participate," she mused. "Not in the actual writing, but in the process, somehow. If I could have some say in how the film was made..."

Sandy ran a hand through his hair. "You realize that most directors don't allow writers within a mile of the set."

"Maybe so," she allowed. "But then I guess we don't have anything more to discuss."

Sandy narrowed his eyes at her. "I'm a loner in this business," he said. "I write them myself, I direct 'em myself. I've never collaborated with another writer because I've never felt the need. But just this once..." He shook his head. "Ed will have my head for even thinking of such a crazy thing," he said grimly, staring past her into the haze of sausage smoke and balloons, as if seeing his agent be-yond it.

"What?" she asked. "I've already told you I'm not in-terested in writing a screenplay, with you or without."

"We'll put you in the package," he announced. "Call you...creative consultant—it's just a title," he said quickly, before she could say anything. "But what it would amount to is that you would have your say in what we did. You'd have access to the shooting script, you'd be involved in pre-production, you'd be on the set, for as long as you like." He shook his head again. "I can't believe I'm offering this, to a..." He stopped.

"A what?" she asked sharply.

"Anyone," he said, frowning. "I must want you more than I even thought I did."

Me? she thought. No, he wanted her book. She could see the idea was causing him real distress—and in truth, that was okay with her. She'd finally succeeded in stopping his smooth machinery, putting them on equal footing. If she was going to take a risk like this, then he'd have to sacrifice something, too. "What kind of a 'say'?" she asked.

"We'd communicate," Sandy told her. "What we'd be doing is making an agreement, artist to artist, that I won't intentionally violate the spirit of your work. And you'll be there to see to it that I don't."

The whole idea was fantastical. Even hours ago, she wouldn't have considered such a proposal. But Sandy's energy, the sheer persistence of his vision, still had her in his thrall. She'd seen it, for the first time, her Sarah Campbell, alive and walking down a real Elm Street, larger than life. It was a heady concept.

"What if we can't agree on anything?" she asked.

"You like my opening shot, don't you?"

"Yes, but—"

"Look, there are a lot of other writers who wouldn't have gotten it, or would've balked at the liberties I took with their precious prose. You were right with me. That's the reason I'm suggesting such a risky proposition. We're already working as a good team."

He smiled at her. His eyes seemed to caress her face, drinking in every feature with an appreciative alertness that made something inside her respond with subtle arousal. The word "team" had never struck her as having a particularly erotic undertone, but somehow, coming from the lips of Sandy Baker, it did.

Wait a second. What in the world was she getting involved in, here?

"We haven't discussed . . . figures," she said, and felt the heat rise in her cheeks, comprehending the unintentional second meaning of the word as his gaze flicked ever so lightly from her face to her feet, giving her figure the briefest of interested appraisals.

"We don't have to discuss that at all," he said, his smile mischievous as he paused just long enough to let the idea's sensual implications linger in the air. Then his expression immediately turned serious. "The business people can take care of all the paperwork," he continued. "But rest assured, if I go through with this—if Ed and the studio let me—I give you my word, you'll get whatever you want."

Again, she couldn't shake the feeling that he wasn't only talking about deals and contracts. "And what if we don't want the same things?" she countered.

"That's the risk we take," he said. "But we may surprise each other. And I like surprises." His eyes searched hers as he held out a hand. "So what do you say? Shake on it?" Victoria hesitated. "You'd better," he said wryly. "Before I come to my senses."

Before *he* did?

"Here's a nice couple!" crowed a voice behind her. "Take ya picture? Only a buck fifty!"

It was a tanned and beaming teenager operating a Polaroid camera at a concession booth, already motioning his assistant, a little girl in pigtails and a parochial-school frock, to point the lens in their direction. Victoria started to shake her head, but Sandy was nodding enthusiastically.

"Yes, this is perfect," he said.

"Sandy—" she began.

"We'll get this moment on film for posterity," he told her, smiling at the three-foot-high camerawoman.

"Here, just stan' against the sheet heah..." The young man had stepped out to guide her into position next to Sandy.

Victoria let him set them up, feeling both nervous and triumphant. He was making a compromise, yes, but she was the one who'd completely reversed her original decision. Everything was happening so quickly. They were standing side by side in front of the camera now, and Sandy was holding out his hand again.

"You're getting what you want, and you're forcing me to give up what I usually want—total control," he said.

Sheer madness. She told herself that he couldn't be serious, striking deals like this with a handshake in the middle of a street fair. But something told her he'd hold her to it. There was a seriousness in Sandy Baker behind his flip manner, that she could already sense ran deep.

Maybe that was the thing that pushed her. That and the undeniably compelling look on his face as he awaited her response. *Risk it*, he seemed to be saying. *Risk me—risk yourself.* To go along with him felt like jumping blindfolded off a cliff, right after deciding you had no intention of jumping anywhere. But as dangerous as she knew such a step might be, she thought she might be able to trust him.

"The spirit of your work," he reminded her. "We're going to be absolutely faithful to it. So do we have a deal?"

Victoria sighed. "I suppose," she muttered, and shook his hand. The camera clicked. She felt a little jolt that had nothing to do with that, though. It was the feel of his warm skin against hers, the gentle pulse she felt in his hand, the strength in it. A shiver ran from her fingers up her wrist and through the core of her.

She started to pull away but he held her grip. "One more," he told the girl with the camera. "We need two," he informed Victoria solemnly. "One for each of us."

She didn't know how long she could hold his hand like this. Her stomach was doing odd flip-flops. She looked away from his glimmering eyes and forced a smile for the camera as the little girl squinted one eye with an archly professional detachment, then took a second picture.

"No kiss?" asked the grinning proprietor.

Sandy smiled. "Just a hearty handshake," he said. "It's only our first date."

"Hey, ya guys look great together," the young man said. "I bet youse have a long and happy life."

THE WOMAN IN THE PHOTO looked perfectly poised, the man calm and confident. You'd have thought they were old friends. The contrast between his olive-dark skin and her fairer tone, the few inches of height he had on her, these insignificant details often absorbed her attention in the days that followed. The photo was the proof of her folly. It was also the only glimpse of Sandy Baker she was to have for six months.

In that six months, she had regretted her impulse of the moment a hundred times. Now more than ever, as she clutched the already weathered and worn Polaroid photo in her free hand, she wondered what in the world had possessed her to agree to this thing, this thing that was taking over her life. It might even mean the death of her, she mused morbidly, as she clutched the arm of her window seat. The seat-belt sign was blinking on again.

They'd been experiencing "a little turbulence" as their laconic pilot had informed them earlier, after the first jolts had given Victoria a minor heart attack. It wasn't that she feared flying, it was just that she rarely flew. So she didn't have the jaded, unperturbed air of her fellow passengers, who paid scant attention to the plane's dips and shakes.

It's your fault, she told the grinning guy in the Polaroid for the umpteenth time. But she knew better. It was her fault. She was the one who had let that manipulative eel of a man get her into this mess.

A wave of self-righteous anger went through her as she thought about the unbound sheaf of papers in the bag beneath her seat. Sandy the Snake. How could he? How had he brazenly written an entire draft of *Jumpers Creek*, the movie, before even meeting her to ask her for permission to do such a thing? Easily, was the answer. That was the way he was.

She held onto the anger. It was better than the panic she'd been feeling as the plane continued to bump and shudder in the air. It still smarted, knowing that Sandy Baker had been so certain she'd say yes that he'd gone ahead and written the script, worked out a deal with his studio and even pre-cast the movie, practically, before having lunch (no, a cannoli) with her that day in New York.

She stared at the photo in her lap through narrowed eyes. What a con artist. It hadn't all been "in his head," it had already been on paper. But that wasn't the worst of it, not by far. No, the horrible thing was . . . it was good.

It was *too* good, actually. There were things he'd done with her material, subtle shifts in tone, adjustments in emphasis, that made her extremely uncomfortable. It was uncanny, how close his version was veering toward the very truths she'd willfully had to distort. And there were a few scenes she simply couldn't allow him to film, not the way he'd written them. She wouldn't let him, not even if she had to bodily tackle the camera and rip out the celluloid.

"It may come to that," Maxanne had told her at their last meeting, with a wry smile. "Because honey, legally, you're in an area that's very, very gray."

"He's not allowed to violate the spirit of my work," she said, using the phrase that had become a private mantra of sorts in her moments of high anxiety.

"Define spirit," Maxanne said.

Victoria merely glared at her. "You're the one who worked out the contract," she reminded her grimly. "You tell me."

"It means whatever you two decide it means," Maxanne said, blowing a perfectly formed smoke ring at the ceiling of her office. "But when it comes down to the bottom line, you don't have final say. He does."

"I don't believe this," she sighed, slumped in the leather chair by her agent's desk. "In other words, I can yell myself blue in the face, but if he doesn't want to listen, he doesn't have to?"

"Oh, he has to *listen*," Maxanne said. "That's what your 'creative output' is all about. But Vicki, what he *does* is up to him. You don't have final approval on the shooting script—nobody does, no writer I know of, not even Stephen King, who could certainly ask for it."

"Why did I agree to this?" she asked Maxanne's shag carpeting.

"Checked your bank balance lately?"

Victoria looked up to frown at her agent. "You know that wasn't the reason."

Maxanne held her gaze with a knowing smile. "No, though it sure should take the edge off. If I remember correctly, the reason had more to do with . . . what did you tell me? His understanding of your work."

Victoria nodded balefully. "Right."

"And maybe that come-hither smile of his."

"Max!"

Victoria looked at Sandy Baker's smile now. It brought back a vivid memory of the way he'd looked at her, and the way she'd felt when he first took her hand. She shifted uneasily in her seat, gazing out at the cloud banks as the seat-belt sign finally, mercifully, blinked off. Much as she didn't like to admit it, Maxanne hadn't been entirely wrong.

She'd been attracted to Sandy Baker, sure. But she hadn't taken his flirtation and flattery seriously. She'd assumed he was that way with most women, and especially one that he wanted something from. She figured that as a director, as someone whose job it was to coax emotional responses from actors and actresses, he was very adept at manipulation.

In the half hour she'd spent with the man, she'd been able to sense a lot about the way he worked. She'd felt a kinship to his self-awareness, understood the leaps his agile mind took. She'd recognized in him some things she knew about herself. Maybe that was why they'd seemed to click so easily.

The oddest thing about that encounter, when she thought back on it, was the way both of them had cut right to the core of the issues between them. There hadn't been any small talk. In fact, there hadn't been any preparation or pussyfooting, at all. He'd started out talking to her as if she was someone he already knew, and she'd responded in kind. She wasn't used to that happening with a man.

And whether it was part of his general modus operandi or not, Sandy Baker had made her feel, from his very first glance in her direction, that to him she was the most important woman in the world. That what she thought, wrote, had to say, was of vital interest. Which made the arrival of this script, only days before, seem all the more like a betrayal.

Well, not a betrayal, exactly. Yes, she'd been angered initially months ago, when word leaked out that a draft existed, predating her meeting with Sandy. But even in her annoyance she'd had to laugh at the man's arrogance, and respect it. He believed in himself and his films with a sureness that brooked no obstacle. It wasn't a bad quality for an artist to have. In fact, it was an essential one.

No, it was the script itself, this more recent rewrite of his original draft, that made her feel uncomfortably exposed. There were things in it that reflected her "input," as the movie people obnoxiously termed it. He'd incorporated some suggestions she'd made in one of her letters, even used a line of dialogue she'd sketched out, verbatim. But the changes he'd made from novel to script showed he had certain ideas about the characters that gave her pause. He seemed to know things about them she *hadn't* told him, not in conversation, and certainly not in the book itself. And they were things she didn't want known.

Victoria looked out the window, her brow creased with apprehension. Somewhere down there, a film crew had already invaded the little town of Silver Spring. People who'd never set foot there were already traipsing up and down the paths of her private memories, ready to set her creations in motion, larger than life, and feed them to the monster camera lens. Somewhere down there, Dad was awaiting her arrival, along with hordes of people she didn't even want to think about running into. And what would *they* think, when they found out what was going to go up on the screen?

What would Mother think?

She shoved that thought, with its attendant black cloud of worries, aside. Not thinking about Mother had been a necessary requisite for going through with this. She'd deal with those emotions when she got there. On second thought, maybe staying aloft in a bouncing airplane wasn't such a bad thing, after all.

"Miss Moore?"

She'd been absorbed in inspecting the airport lobby for any signs of the distant past. It had been so long since she'd flown into Dayton, and now the place looked wholly unfamiliar to her. She was trying to remember when, exactly she'd been here last, when a young man with his hair in a ponytail, wearing blue jeans, a red T-shirt and red sneakers came bounding over to her, extending a hand to take her bags.

"Hi, I'm Scott. Is this everything?"

"Yes, thanks. No, I'll keep this," she said, holding onto her shoulder bag.

"We're right outside," he said, waving her on as he headed for the glass doors.

The sun was still bright in the sky, and it was when she stepped outside that the memories started flooding in. The air was the thing that did it, a certain autumnal crispness that conjured up back-to-school feelings, thoughts of burning leaves, scents of pastures and fresh-baked doughnuts. She got into the car as Scott held the door open for her, feeling like a dog whose nose was already sniffing out the direction home.

Scott explained that he was a P.A., or production assistant, a low man on the technical totem pole, who'd been given the task of picking her up. The red Datsun he was driving was one of many rented by the crew, and it would become hers to use for the duration of the shoot as soon as they arrived in town.

"You're just in time to catch the tail end of our first day's shoot," Scott informed her, easing into the thin traffic on the highway proper. "We've been up since dawn, working downtown, but I'm sure we'll go past sunset."

"Where downtown?"

"Walnut and Grove. The doughnut shop."

A shiver went through her, excitement mixed with fear. *Her* doughnut shop. Or at least, her heroine's. Sandy Campbell worked there, three afternoons plus one night a week, just as young Victoria Moore had. The idea of seeing this surrogate self of hers in the actual location made her feel strange. She hadn't even met the actress, Grace Sullivan, yet.

"How is it going?" she asked.

"Great! Baker got two shots in the can already."

Victoria looked at her watch, noting that it was nearly four in the afternoon. "Only two?"

Scott chuckled. "Hey, for a first day on the set that's quite an accomplishment. We'll pick up speed as we get settled in. And once Silver Spring gets used to us. We've had a bit of traffic control to deal with."

"Traffic?"

"Pedestrians, mainly. Kids from the college and the high school."

Victoria nodded. She could well imagine the uproar on Walnut Avenue, which was the central commercial thoroughfare in town. If a film crew from Hollywood had come to Silver Springs when she was in high school, she would have cut classes all day just to be close to it. She probably would've tried to be in the movie, and failing that, tried to run away with the film crew. It was the kind of romantic notion that would have appealed to her, like running away with the circus.

It was nice to hear that the contemporary Kennedy High kids were duly impressed. In New York City, film crews were as common as traffic jams, practically. The arrival of another star on the set didn't occasion much excitement anymore. People who lived in the neighborhoods where films were being shot tended to regard the crew members as mere nuisances who kept asking them to walk on the other side of their own block.

But Silver Spring, apparently, was star-struck. "We had to double up on security," Scott went on. "The set was crawling with kids. You know, for a small town, they seem to have like a dozen schools."

"Only three, really," Victoria told him. "There's the elementary, the high school and Anteus College. The junior high isn't in Silver Spring, technically. It's one town over, in Cedar Hollow."

"Oh, right," Scott said. "I forgot you're the expert." He glanced over at her, curious. "Do you come back here a lot? I hear your folks still live in town."

Victoria shook her head. "It's been a few years," she said.

"Must feel strange, then, huh?"

"I'll tell you when I get there," she joked. She didn't know *what* to feel, besides nervous, not yet.

"Do you want me to drive you straight over to their place? Carey didn't give me any specific instructions."

"Carey?"

"The A.D.—Baker's assistant."

"Oh. Well, no, you can drop me at Walnut near Elm."

"The hotel?"

Victoria nodded. "Sandy thought it would be more convenient," she said, feeling a need to justify a choice that she was already having second thoughts about. "I mean, in terms of me having access to the production. And who knows what kind of hours I'll be keeping, if I try to hold my own with you guys," she explained. "I thought my parents would appreciate some peace and quiet while I'm here."

Scott nodded, eyes on the road, seemingly satisfied with her explanation. "I don't even talk to my folks," he said. "Want a soda? There's some cold ones in that cooler behind you."

"No, thanks." This was silly, anyway. Why did she have to justify her decision to anyone, let alone this kid?

Because Dad's feelings had been hurt. He hadn't said anything, directly, on the phone, but his quiet surprise when she told him about her plans had spoken volumes. She'd assured him that she'd be over there every day, and guaranteed her presence at as many dinners as she could manage. That seemed to make him feel better. Mother, she was sure, would be just as happy not having her "underfoot," as she used to put it.

Familiar landmarks passed by as Scott rattled on, telling her names of crew members and their various functions. She wouldn't remember any of this, she knew, as she watched a distant trio of cows stroll lazily across a field near a giant billboard advertising some night spot in Dayton. She'd have to learn everyone's name and his or her reason for being there as she went along.

As they drew closer to Silver Spring, she tried to keep anxiety at bay. She'd go one step at a time, facing Mother, then the rest of the town, then Baker and company. Her own function amidst what was sounding like an army of technicians was so vague. She'd have to make sure she didn't get shunted to the sidelines, an ineffectual literary traffic cop who yielded little power.

"No, it's the next one," she told Scott as he slowed, approaching a turnoff.

"Oh, right. Thanks."

Funny how it all came back. The landscape hadn't changed that much since her teenage years. And now, as they came around the winding curve of highway toward the familiar green sign that indicated Anteus College, Silver Spring, Xenia ahead, she could almost fantasize she was seventeen again, out for a spin in Melinda Griffin's car. The two of them groaning, she more than Melinda, that there were still such things as curfews, parents, homes they had to return to. Why not just pass this turnoff and keep going, barreling west to California, or north to Alaska, for that matter?

She'd have to call Melinda as soon as she got in. She was looking forward to seeing her childhood friend again, with a mixture of eagerness and apprehension. To her, Melinda represented the road not taken. Melinda had stayed behind. For all their plans and fantasies, she'd never left Silver Spring for that great wide world beyond.

From the letters they periodically exchanged, Victoria sensed that staying put in the center of Ohio was fine with Melinda. She had a husband and two children and a job she liked, teaching at the high school. But her friend's letters did betray a wistful envy for Victoria's comparatively bohemian life-style. Victoria hoped it would be easy to pick up their friendship where they'd left it, after not having seen each other for so long. She was counting on Melinda, in a

way, to be there for her if things got too strange with
Mother. She'd always been there in the past.

Here was the old dairy. There, a billboard announced a
McDonald's, which was unwelcome news to her. But what
did she expect? Silver Spring was no Brigadoon, untouched
by time and progress. She'd been surprised to hear that Logan's Bakery, as the doughnut shop was formally named,
was still standing. She'd half expected it to have been replaced by a Dunkin Donuts by now.

The road twisted sharply past Collier's field, with more
suburban-looking houses replacing the occasional old
farmhouse. They passed a few students on bicycles. More
and more of them, many with the Anteus logo on their
sweatshirts, appeared as the car wended its way into town.

Victoria had a brief pang, feeling her age. So young! Was
it possible that she'd looked up to these fresh-faced unkempt and unformed boys and girls as sophisticated demi-
gods, when she was a high-schooler and they were college
students? Good Lord, she at thirty-seven probably looked
like an ancient adult to those kids.

"Here we are," Scott announced, forgetting again that
she knew as well as he, or better, where they were. Walnut
stretched before them, lined with trees, every parking space
occupied, the sidewalk alive with students and the occasional "townie" adult. She nearly laughed as she considered that this had once been her concept of "downtown."
Even at its busiest, the street looked more like something out
of a Norman Rockwell painting than a modern metropolis.

Except for a few blocks down, where traffic was being
diverted left and right by a red-faced policeman standing
behind blue barriers set across the street and sidewalk. Scott
was already turning off, going the back way down Birch, she
surmised. She couldn't see past the heads of the crowd
gathered there. But that had to be the film in progress.

A feeling of exhilaration rose in her, and though she hadn't seen it coming, she understood why. It was the rush of pride, bordering on conceit, she'd been suppressing all day. Hey, Silver Spring! the adolescent girl in her couldn't help crowing. It's me! *I* brought this here, me, old geeky Victoria Moore! What do you think about that?

So much for feeling old. She'd already regressed. Scott paused at the stop sign at Birch and Ninth. "I guess I'll take us all the way around," he said. "So we can get your bags up to the hotel."

"You know," she said suddenly. "If it's all right with you, I'd love to get a peek. At the set, I mean."

"Sure," Scott said.

"Just to let Sandy know I'm here," she added, but again, the P.A. didn't need explanations.

"I tell you what. I'll drop you at the next corner, take the car down to the Walnut Arms and leave it there in the lot for you, how's that? Someone from the hotel will help you with the bags."

"That'd be great," she said, her heart beating furiously. What had her original plan been? She was going to check into the hotel, take a leisurely stroll around town, and then maybe, just to say hello, pay a casual visit to the set. Oh, sure. Although an hour ago she'd wanted to be anywhere in the world but here, she was now filled with an urgent desire now to be in the center of that action at Logan's Bakery. She couldn't imagine waiting. I guess you can take a kid out of Silver Spring, she mused, but you can't take the Spring out . . .

Scott dropped her at Grove. "Here," he said, flipping open the glove compartment. "You'd better hold onto one of these." He handed her a sticker that had *CREEK CREW* emblazoned in green lettering on a black background.

"Thanks." He pulled the door closed after her with a cheery wave. She was on her own. Sticker in one hand, shoulder bag clutched to her with the other, Victoria strode down Grove toward the tumult on Walnut.

Chapter Three

She stole a look at her reflection in Woolworth's window as she approached the corner, glad she'd worn her pale blue dress from Diane B. with flat sandals. It struck the right note of casually fashionable New Yorker, she thought, not dressy, but definitely not local. She thought of putting on her sunglasses for the sense of anonymity they'd allow her, but that might seem too much. Too Hollywood. She was a writer who lived on Bleecker Street, after all.

As she turned the corner she had her first glimpse of the crew in action. From here, it seemed total chaos. There were vans lined on the opposite side of Walnut, the kind she recognized from those ubiquitous location shoots in Manhattan, and cables of all shapes and sizes snaking across the pavement. A young man who looked like a duplicate of Scott had a bullhorn to his face, barking incoherent instructions to unseen crew members. Harried-looking technicians were adjusting a huge klieg light on the sidewalk, as others set up strange-looking sheets of canvas on either side of it.

Well, here she went, Victoria Moore, former undistinguished townie, now celebrated author, into the midst of this glamorous set. How would Sandy greet her? she wondered.

"Sorry, miss, you can't walk this way."

The man in front of her, a bandanna round his neck, walkie-talkie at his ear, was waving an impatient hand in her direction. Victoria held up her new sticker. He peered at it, then her. "You with wardrobe?"

Victoria smiled. "No, I wrote it." His squint deepened. "The book."

"Book?" He look confounded. "What book?"

Victoria was momentarily at a loss. Not exactly the welcome she might've imagined. Fortunately a short, slim woman in khaki shorts and a man-tailored shirt and bearing an overflowing clipboard had stopped in mid-stride to see what the trouble was.

"Bryce, you dimwit, it's Victoria Moore!" she said, extending a hand. "Hi, I'm Susan Jacks, loyal script girl extraordinaire to the great sahib Baker."

"Who?" Bryce was asking Susan, as Victoria gratefully shook her hand.

"Bryce, I know the last thing you read was the new issue of *Penthouse*," Susan said, "But this woman wrote *Jumpers Creek*, along with four other most excellent novels." She flashed Victoria a smile. "Just get in?"

Bryce was already moving off, muttering into his walkie-talkie. "Yes," Victoria told her. "I thought I'd stop by and say hello, tell Sandy—"

"S.O.B. is deep in conference," Susan said, guiding her through a labyrinth of equipment that lined the sidewalk. She caught the expression on Victoria's face and laughed. "That's an affectionate nickname, although he can ride a crew pretty hard. Sandy Owen Baker—the initials just happen to suggest other meanings. Watch your feet there."

She pointed at a tangle of cables in Victoria's path. "Actually, there are some who'd say that S.O.B. stands for *sob*," Susan continued, as they wended their way closer to the bakery's entrance, where more technicians could be seen manning light stands.

"Sob?" Victoria echoed, curious.

"As in Mister Heartbreak," Susan said. "Baker's been involved with some of the most beautiful actresses in the world, but none of them could keep him." She slowed, casting Victoria a wary sidelong glance. "I shouldn't be saying any of this, of course."

Victoria shrugged, remembering that she had seen Baker's name coupled with a popular star in some supermarket tabloid once. "I hardly know the man," she said, realizing that this was true.

"Ah," Susan said with apparent relief. "Well, you'll get to know him, if you stick around. How long are you planning on being with us?"

"Most of the month," Victoria said. "I understand the location shooting's supposed to take at least three weeks."

"Could be more," Susan murmured. "But don't quote me. Okay, here we are." She peered around the stocky figure of an electrician who was blocking the front doorway, adjusting the position of a huge mounted floodlight. "Sandy's over there with the D.P. If you want to watch us do a take, slip around the side here and stand back of that sound table, there. It's okay, Rob," she told a tall, gangly man in a sweatshirt at the door. "She's here to work with Sandy. Let her stand back where Ted is."

Rob nodded, pointing her toward a corner where a man in headphones was bent over a plethora of recording equipment on a folding table. "Let me know if you need anything!" Susan called after her, and disappeared outside the shop.

No one paid Victoria any attention as she stepped around the sound man and took up a position against the wall. The counter area was ablaze with light, and there as so much activity around it that it took her a minute to comprehend what was going on. She identified the camera, which was the center of attention, a large gleaming silver machine mounted on a wheeled platform in front of the counter. And then she saw Sandy Baker close beside it.

There was a gray-haired man in animated conference with him, gesticulating from the camera lens to the counter and back again. Sandy was sporting a rather incongruous baseball cap and a stopwatch around his neck, which gave him the look of a sports coach. But he had on a baggy cardigan, less flashy than the one he had been wearing when she first met him, and a clipboard under his arm stuffed with a thicker sheaf of papers than Susan's. That made him seem more like a film director.

The gray-haired man laughed loudly at something Sandy said, then turned away to confer with another technician. The men who'd been milling around the mounted camera suddenly sped into motion, attending the machine, shifting its wheeled platform. Walkie-talkies buzzed and crackled, more and more people emerging from the doorway behind the doughnut counter like circus clowns from a Volkswagen. The sound technician at the table in front of her barked instructions to a lanky young man carrying a long metal pole with a microphone attached.

In the midst of this melee, Sandy was walking toward her. Victoria steeled herself, wanting to hit the right note of professional decorum. He was smiling now, a welcoming grin on his handsome face. He wouldn't be smiling if he knew how many problems she had with his script.

No handshake this time, she saw. He had his arms outstretched, apparently prepared to give her a friendly hug. How did one keep bearing a grudge at a man like this? She started to smile as he sauntered closer—

Sandy wrapped his arms around the woman who had just materialized at Victoria's side, a beautiful, tall redheaded woman who laughed happily as she threw her hands around the director's neck, then kissed him full on the lips. Victoria stood her ground, unnerved but unable to keep from staring. An actress, she intuited from the woman's flamboyant gestures.

They were already moving off, back toward the camera, but before Sandy turned he peered in Victoria's direction, perhaps conscious of her gaze. He looked right at her without even the slightest sign of recognition, then turned away, his arm around the redhead's waist.

Her practiced cool had to work overtime as she felt a surge of outrage. Irrational or not, she felt intensely slighted. True, Sandy Baker barely knew her, but she *had* flown sixteen hundred miles to meet him here today. And it was her movie, wasn't it? Despite the blatant disregard she'd gotten from nearly everyone so far.

A hush was descending on the set, punctuated by calls for silence from yet another blue-jeaned man with a megaphone. She gathered that they were about to actually film something. Jaw set, determined not to give into her resentments, Victoria stepped closer to the sound table to get a better look at the action. Ignored though she might be, she had a right to see what was going on.

"Excuse me—miss—" The whispered hiss at her came from a woman in shorts with short-cropped hair and glasses. "We're clearing the set for this next take. Could you step outside, please?"

This was too much. "I'm Victoria Moore," she said evenly. "Tell Sandy Baker that I'd like to stay right where I am, if that's all right with him."

Something in her tone evidently let the woman know that Victoria meant business. She hurried off and Victoria watched as she leaned into the little circle near the counter where Sandy was in conference with his cameraman again. She saw Sandy straighten up and shoot a perplexed glance in her direction. Once more he seemed to look right at her and not see her. He murmured some words to the woman and returned to his animated discussion with his crew.

The woman didn't return, so Victoria stayed where she was, thankful for this small victory but still smarting. It was only as a taciturn technician gently blocked her from stepping to her left that she realized she was standing between two huge mounted floodlights. It dawned on her then that Sandy probably hadn't been *able* to see her, facing that glare.

Even as she was comprehending this, her pride somewhat assuaged, a true silence descended on the room and her attention was caught by the girl who emerged from the darkness on the other side of the counter, wearing an apron. Victoria stared, riveted by the actress's features. She looked about seventeen. She had the kind of face that looked almost ugly when you first saw it, but revealed its true idiosyncratic beauty the more you looked. And you couldn't help looking. Victoria certainly couldn't. Because she was looking at herself.

No, it was a more attractive young Victoria, with a very different look, she realized. The hair was different, the jut of her chin, the color of her eyes. And her shirt was wrong— she wouldn't have worn something that obviously "hip." Still, she felt a shiver of recognition as the actress stepped up to the counter's edge, staring past the counter, biting her lower lip with a pensive expression. She was Victoria, she was Sarah Campbell, and something other—herself, of course, a woman who clearly already possessed a strong personality.

"Speed. Sound is rolling," called the sound man.

"Camera."

The snap of an unseen clapboard was heard, with someone chanting a series of numbers. Fascinated, Victoria watched the actress brush a stray lock of hair back from her forehead with the back of a hand that was white from powdered sugar. She straightened up suddenly, staring in the direction of the bakery door. Fatigue seemed to fall away from her youthful face, and even from this distance, Victoria could see the reddening in her cheeks as she stepped back from the counter and self-consciously, hurriedly, wiped her hands on her apron and yanked it straight, her eyes still glued to the bakery's entrance.

Instinctively Victoria glanced over to the door, half expecting to see Rocko, the motorcycle-riding, rock'n'rolling idol of Sarah Campbell's youth, come sauntering in. But of course there was no one there but a few technicians who seemed singularly bored, not even looking toward the camera as they casually attended their equipment.

Victoria looked back to the counter. "Sarah" was still transfixed. Then, with a lightning motion so fluid it was almost invisible, she popped a wad of gum from her mouth and affixed it to the underside of the counter. Once more she stood absolutely still, awaiting the arrival of her hero.

There was a gentle chuckle from the camera area, and a murmured "Cut" that was nearly inaudible. The entire room buzzed into motion again, "Sarah" suddenly breaking character and giggling, obscured from view as technicians converged on the brightly lit counter area.

"Ms. Moore?"

Victoria, shaken from her own transfixed gaze at this re-created scene from her youth, turned to see the short-haired woman beckoning her forward. "We're setting up another angle. If you could come this way?"

Victoria followed her, too preoccupied to protest now. This was a very weird experience. She hadn't given much thought to what it would be like to see herself actually portrayed by an actress, acting out this stuff. She couldn't have imagined it. She certainly couldn't have imagined that Sandy would come up with someone for the role who had such an uncanny resemblance to the girl she used to be.

The woman was leading her past the camera and the counter, around the side and into the bakery proper. Victoria assumed she would be taken through the back entrance to the street and deposited there. In a way, that was fine with her. She'd gotten her first glimpse of life on the set, and it was plenty to start off with. She was going to have a lot to get used to, that much was clear.

Besides, she wasn't feeling well disposed toward Sandy Baker just now. If she had run into him, she might've ended up saying some things she'd regret later, criticisms of his script and his attitude. Granted, he was in the middle of shooting a film, but he could have had at least enough common courtesy to say hello.

"Sorry about the mix-up before," the woman was saying, as they entered the cooler, more dimly lit room. "My name's Debra, I'm the second A.D." She smiled and pointed to the little office that had been Pop Oglesby's. "Right in there."

Victoria paused in her stride, confused, but Debra was already moving off into the darkness. Victoria shrugged and stepped up to the office door, which was slightly ajar. She knocked, and a voice called out, "Come in!"

Sandy Baker was pacing in a tiny circle within the cozy office space, the wall phone's receiver at his ear. Smiling broadly as Victoria took an uncertain step inside, he mimed a greeting, nodding in response to whoever it was talking at his ear. "Yes. Absolutely. We can't afford it. So ask for it anyway."

He was pulling out the chair from the old rolltop desk for her to sit in as he continued manically pacing, rustling papers on his clipboard, phone tucked between chin and shoulder. "No. Yeah. More than that. We need it yesterday."

Victoria sat. This was typical Baker, she decided. Throw her off guard by being casually rude, mollify her by having her meet him in a private, off-the-set conference—then make her sit and wait while he talked to someone else.

As if aware of her thoughts, he silently mouthed "I'm sorry" at her while he continued listening to the person on the phone. Victoria nodded, giving him what she hoped was an understanding but slightly put-out smile. "Hold it," Sandy said. "Run that by me again." He paused in midstride to jot something down on his clipboard.

Victoria looked around her, surprised to see that Pop's little domain looked remarkably the way she remembered it. The rolltop desk was just as cluttered, the wall just as full of faded WWII pinups, the air still a musty combination of familiar sweet, doughy smells and ink. Memories hovered in every corner. She remembered vividly that time Pop had called her in here, to reprimand her in his kindly, awkward way, for . . .

Good grief, that scene was in the script, wasn't it? And what if Pop himself was still around? What would he make of seeing that incident played out by actors, a little bit of what was his private life as well as hers, exposed to a popcorn-munching public? Her earlier discomfort at her predicament resurfaced as she thought of the script in her shoulder bag.

And there was the true culprit, trading quips with Hollywood, no doubt, as he wore a circle in the office's already faded carpet with his loafers. Victoria sat up straight in Pop's chair, bag gathered in her lap as she prepared to lock horns with this cinematic seducer. He'd gotten her into this mess, but she was about to exert some of the creative control he'd promised her.

"No, call tomorrow. Or don't call, just FAX it. Right. Yeah, you, too." Sandy Baker hung up the phone with a bang and whirled around to face her. "So! What did you think?"

"Think?" she muttered, caught off guard. The intensity in the searching gaze from his dark eyes was disconcerting at this close range.

"Grace! She's incredible, isn't she?"

"The actress? Yes. She's..." Victoria tried to find the proper word.

"You," Sandy supplied, smiling. "Or Sarah. Bit of both, actually, and a lot more. I knew you'd like her."

"Well, I do," she allowed. "From the little I've seen."

"I've got to get the two of you together," Sandy said. "She's dying to meet you. I could've set it up sooner, but I wanted her to get her own sense of the character first, her own voice."

He settled back against the desk, putting his clipboard down and running a hand absently through his tousled hair, now without the baseball cap. "She'll be good," he murmured. "The camera likes her, as they say, and people will, too."

Victoria didn't doubt it. "Are you going to shoot Rocko now? I'm curious to see what *he* looks like."

Sandy chuckled, shaking his head. "Rocko won't be with us till next week," he said. "We're skipping his stuff today, going on to that next-to-last bakery scene. Besides, he's too young for you," he added, a mischievous twinkle in his eye.

"I'm over the Rockos in my life, thanks," Victoria said dryly.

"I'm happy to hear that," Sandy said, his gaze holding hers. Weird. She felt herself sort of sinking into the velvet darkness of that gaze, despite her intention of playing this cool and controlled. Sandy Baker, hypnotist-filmmaker?

"We need to talk," she announced, forcing herself to look away. What had happened to all that resentment she'd been feeling?

"You're upset about the script," he said.

Victoria stared at him. One step ahead of her again. "Well, yes," she began. "There are a few changes you made—"

"I want to go over the whole draft with you," he said, waving an impatient hand. "Now that you're with us for a while, I want to be able to get everything out of you I can."

"Oh?" she managed.

"That didn't come out right." He smiled. "What I mean is, you're my main source and resource on this project, Victoria. So far I've only been able to work with you in the abstract, through the book. But I'm really excited about the two of us teaming up in the flesh."

His tone was absolutely sincere and he seemed unaware of the more erotic implications of his chosen metaphor. She was the one who felt an inner blush as he barreled on, rising from the desk, caught up in his own enthusiasm. "Those notes you sent me a few months back were priceless. I used all of it, you must've seen."

"Yes," she said. "And it's not that I don't like—"

"You wrote it all down?" he interrupted. "Notes on the scenes that didn't work for you?"

"As a matter of fact, I did," she admitted.

"Good," he said, and gave her shoulder a quick squeeze that made her feel like a hail fellow well met. "Because now isn't the time to get into all of this. I just wanted to say hello and welcome you aboard."

"I appreciate that. When do you think—"

"We should be wrapping things up by dinnertime. Maybe you'd like to join us then? Might be a late meal, but I'm sure we could get an hour's worth of talking in before I have a production meeting."

"I'm sorry, but dinner isn't good for me."

"Oh, of course," he said. "You're seeing your folks."

"Yes."

"That should be . . . interesting," he said. There was an expression on his face she hadn't seen before. Head slightly cocked to one side, he was gazing at her with an undisguised interest that made her feel like he was reading her features, not merely looking at them. "How *is* your Mom?" he asked. "What's she make of all this?"

"I don't know," she said uneasily, then forced a smile. "Guess I'll find out."

"I look forward to meeting the whole family," Sandy said, his eyes still searching hers, his alert expression making her think he was listening not to what she'd said, but what she hadn't. Then he straightened up abruptly, glancing at his watch. "I'm sorry we couldn't hook up sooner," he said. "I've been over my head in work. And as it is, right now I've got another shot to do, a faulty film magazine to get replaced, and—"

There was a knock on the door. "Stanford?" came a singsong voice. "Are you hiding in there?"

"And the press," Sandy said in a lowered voice, grimacing. "No one's supposed to be covering us, this early in the shoot, but Catherine's an old friend. Coming out!" he called, striding to the door.

It was the redheaded woman who'd lavished such theatrical affection on Sandy before, the one she'd mistaken for an actress. Catherine gave her a quick, desultory smile as Sandy introduced them, shepherding both women through the darkness and back toward the set. Victoria wondered if the pretty journalist and Sandy had been romantically involved. Something told her they hadn't, despite Catherine's obvious hopes to the contrary.

Why was she even thinking about such stuff? It was none of her business. "I'm going to be in the thick of it from here on out, so this is goodbye for now." Sandy paused in the shadows at the counter's end, turning her around to face him. "Tell you what. When you get back to the hotel after your dinner, give me a call, okay?"

"Okay," she said. There was a subtle note of concern in his voice. She couldn't shake the feeling that he knew her seeing her folks tonight might be a touchy situation.

Catherine was hovering in the background, clearly wanting to eavesdrop. "Look," Sandy said quietly, as if aware of that as well. "This shoot may put you through the wringer. And I know you don't trust me yet. But you will."

His faint smile in the dim light had warmth and a hint of self-mockery in it. "I may seem to have some crazy ideas about what's going to work, but I'm not going to harm your baby," he told her. "I'm going to make it grow and stretch and shine."

When he looked into her eyes like this she felt her defenses evaporating like so much mist. It was an unnerving sensation, so she struggled to maintain that elusive cool. "I bet you say that to all the girls," she joked.

Sandy shook his head. "Only to survivors of *Jumpers Creek*," he said.

He brushed her cheek with the back of his hand, his fingers so lightly caressing her cheek for the briefest of moments that she almost thought she'd imagined it, as he disappeared back into the chaos of the set. But no, her skin was tingling, and her hands, she noticed to her chagrin, were shaking.

Who *was* this guy?

SANDY BAKER SMILED and nodded, letting Catherine slide her arm around his waist, but her throaty chatter at his ear could've been so much fly-buzzing for the attention he paid it. His mind was on the woman he'd just bid goodbye to.

He'd done it. He'd actually pulled this off. Sandy had accomplished many a Herculean task in his career thus far, including bringing in his first two pictures under budget, and once wriggling out of an ironclad contract with a certain tyrannical Hollywood producer—this trick earning him the nickname "Houdini" Baker from his agent. But to have Victoria Moore signed, sealed and delivered to his set—this was a spectacular coup.

She had no idea, of course, but Sandy had fallen in love with her nearly a dozen years ago. He'd read *Jumpers Creek* with the fascinated awareness that he'd met the woman of his dreams. She wasn't just a kindred spirit, she seemed to *be* his spirit, a feminine version, embodied on the page instead of the screen. She had his humor, his energy, his sensitivity. The slight differences he intuited between their sensibilities made her all the more alluring. What would the two of them be like, he couldn't help wondering, together—on a project, in a collaboration . . . in bed?

Jumpers Creek was a book he wished he'd written but knew he couldn't have, which sparked his interest in the author all the more. Who was she? The book itself was intensely revealing, at least about her youth and her inner life. But it had little in the way of autobiographical information, imbuing the elusive Ms. Moore with an air of tantalizing mystery. No book jacket photo appeared until her second novel came out.

Sandy could remember when he'd first seen the glossy black-and-white photo in a bookstore. He'd stared at her features, drinking in every detail, already deep inside a private fantasy. True, he'd only made one movie at that point, but he'd be famous and powerful by the end of the decade, and when he was, he'd film *Jumpers Creek*. And Victoria Moore would fall in love with *him*.

His rapt perusal of the book-jacket photo had occasioned an argument with his girlfriend at the time, the actress Kirsten Childs. Kirsten had good instincts. She'd sensed that his fascination with Victoria Moore was more than literary, though he blithely denied it. She read the book and hated it. Come to think of it, their disagreement over Victoria's second book had led to one of the arguments that had ultimately split them up.

He'd continued his phantom relationship with Victoria over the years, always keeping tabs on her through her occasional talk-show appearances, interviews and book reviews. In a way she'd been one constant female companion through a succession of romantic relationships. He'd suffered with her the failure of her third novel and exulted in the acclaim for *Folly*. Although this last one, the fifth, had worried him. He's sensed that Victoria was getting a bit too crafty now, having learned how to skillfully hide some of her rawer emotions and instincts. Well, maybe he'd help her get back to where she'd come from.

Because in the meantime his craft had matured, as well. It was after the two Oscars, when he realized he actually could afford to turn down some multimillion-dollar development deals, that Sandy had turned off his phone and taken three months to write his *Jumpers* draft. He'd done it on spec, to his agent's bewilderment. But Sandy had been confident he could woo the rights out of Victoria Moore. After all, he'd known her, intimately, for years.

A gamble, yes, but he hadn't gotten where he was by avoiding risks. And now his dream had come true. The first day's shoot on his pet fantasy project was almost over, and the woman he'd fantasized being with for years was here. It was ironic, but he almost wished he wasn't so busy shooting, so he could spend more time with her.

"Hmm? Sorry." Catherine had been looking at him expectantly, waiting for an answer to some question he hadn't heard.

"I said, can I watch the next take?"

"Please," he said, with an encouraging smile. "Go take my chair and make yourself comfortable." And get out of my hair, he added silently, as Catherine blew him a kiss and at last departed. Sandy waved his D.P. over, ready to descend into the maelstrom of pre-camera chaos again. But one lingering perplexity stayed with him.

He had what he wanted: Victoria Moore in person. This much of his dream had come true. But he hadn't thought too clearly about the next part. He had a film to make, and when he was filming, all personal relationships went on hold. Romantic involvements became the last thing on his mind. So now that he had Victoria Moore here, what exactly did he intend to do with her?

And what, he was dying to know, might Victoria Moore want to do... with him?

"THESE BISCUITS ARE DELICIOUS," Victoria said.

"Surprised they didn't burn to a crisp," said Mrs. Moore. "Your father was supposed to be watching that oven, which is the most temperamental old piece of—"

"A watched oven never bakes," Mr. Moore said, giving Victoria a wink across the table.

Mrs. Moore sighed, fixing a baleful gaze on Victoria's plate. "You haven't touched your vegetables."

"This is my second helping," Victoria said.

"We should've gotten rid of that oven twenty years ago," Mrs. Moore said. "But your father never likes to get rid of anything. You should see the junk that's piling up in the attic. One of these days the ceiling's—"

"—going to fall right down on our heads," Mr. Moore chimed in, and chuckled as his wife glowered at him. "I think we should take to wearing hard hats around the house. I really do. Can't be too careful."

"Your father is a very funny man," Mrs. Moore said. "All we do around here is laugh. Laugh all day and night."

The phone rang in the kitchen. Victoria instinctively started to rise from the dining-room table, but stopped herself as her mother got up from her chair. She didn't live here anymore, she reminded herself, although after only two hours in the Moore household she felt as if she'd never left. The call wouldn't be for her.

"I'll bet I know who that is," Mr. Moore said, watching his wife stride quickly around the table, heading for the kitchen. He smiled at Victoria. "Your sister said she'd be giving us a call tonight."

"Oh." Victoria turned in her seat to watch her mother pick up the phone. She heard her say hello. Then she heard the telltale upward lilt of excitement in her voice. Yes, that had to be Cissy.

"I'm sure she wants to talk to you," her father said. "But they'll be on for a bit, first."

Of course. Mother was already chatting away in a lively tone of familiarity and ease, a tone Victoria only heard her use with her older sister. Cissy and Mother, the best of chums. Victoria felt the age-old jealous resentment seeping into the pit of her stomach and tried to push it back. This was silly.

"It's a shame about the baby," Dad was saying. "I know she wanted to be here for this, but you can't be too careful. A touch of flu at that age..."

"Oh, I don't care," she said, too quickly, then amended, "I mean, I understand. Maybe next time."

Her father nodded. She saw that he, too, was falling into old patterns—Dad, the peacemaker, promoter of tolerance and understanding. She knew he was more disappointed than she was that Cissy had canceled her visit, on account of her second child's having taken ill. He rarely got a chance to see his grandchildren, with Cissy and her husband living in Seattle. It was also a very rare thing to have the entire Moore family reunited under one roof.

Victoria's movie was supposed to have occasioned such an unusual event. But when she'd first arrived shortly before sundown, Dad had given her the news. In truth, Victoria hadn't entirely minded. Although she and Cissy were on good terms when they did occasionally speak, she'd thought that possibly seeing the folks alone for once might make communication easier between Mother and her. Unfortunately she'd sensed almost immediately that Cissy's cancellation had dampened her mother's spirits. Even in her absence, Victoria's older sister was absorbing Mother's attention.

She stole another glance at the kitchen, watching her mother move out of view, animatedly talking. She seemed to be in good health. Her hair was now entirely silver, worn up in a bun that made her look uncharacteristically "country." She'd put on some weight, too. But she was just as feisty and fast on her feet in her early sixties as she'd been years before.

Victoria wasn't eavesdropping, exactly. But when she thought she heard the scrape of a certain cabinet door opening in there, she had to restrain herself from getting up from her seat. Had she imagined it?

"So what was it like down there, at Oglesby's?"

She looked over at her father, wondering if he'd heard the sound, too. Maybe he was just making conversation. As she had so many times this evening, Victoria took the thought in her head and its accompanying emotion, and set it resolutely aside. Not her problem anymore. In any event, at least Dad was taking a genuine interest in what was going on with her. Mother had hardly asked her a single question about *Jumpers Creek* throughout dinner.

"It's pretty wild," she told her father, smiling as he nodded, eyes blinking behind his bifocals with keen appreciation.

"You should've seen downtown yesterday afternoon," he said. "You would've thought the Beatles had come to town, or that Bob Springsteen."

"Bruce Springsteen," she corrected him. Her father nodded, taking a sip of juice. He, too, was showing his age, hair gone white but mostly still there, lines in his face that she hadn't seen before, and a sunken look in his cheeks that gave her pause. He'd lost weight, as his wife had gained, and Victoria wasn't used to the gauntness of his face.

"Everybody's trying to get into the act, you know," he told her, and let out a wry bark of laughter. "Pop Oglesby thinks he's gonna win himself an Oscar."

"What do you mean? He's *in* it, in my movie?"

Dad nodded. "He's playing himself—the owner of the bakery."

Good grief. So much for her worries about Pop's resenting having his past exploited on celluloid. "But he's too old!" she exclaimed, then put a hand over her mouth as she saw her father's expression. "I mean, he wasn't that old when I . . . when the book took place."

Dad shrugged. "Your Mr. Baker didn't have a problem with it, I guess," he said. "He signed 'em up right on the spot, when they were first unloading a ton of equipment over on Walnut. What do they do with all that stuff, anyway? There's enough machinery in those vans to send a rocket to the moon, I'd bet."

"Vic-toria!" Her mother's voice floated out from the kitchen. "It's your sister."

Victoria rose, dutifully taking her father's plate and her own with her as she headed into the kitchen. Mother was washing a glass in the sink as she came in, phone tucked in the crook of her neck. Victoria put the dishes down and waited. "Here she is now," Mother told Cissy, and handed the receiver to her.

The muffled wails of Cissy's ailing baby boy made an appropriate background for her sister's apology when Victoria got on the line. "It's crazy here," Cissy told her, sounding so genuinely harried that Victoria felt guilty for having resented her last-minute bowing out. "I haven't even been able to find a sitter for Lucy, let alone take care of this little guy. The poor thing's still running a temperature. And worse, I think Donald may be coming down with it."

Victoria didn't know Cissy's husband well. He was a very successful corporate lawyer, as was Cissy. The two of them had met when working on opposite sides of some extensive litigation shortly after Cissy first moved to Seattle to join a prestigious firm. Their family joke was that Donald had lost the case but won a wife. "That's terrible," Victoria said. "And what about you?"

"Still healthy, knock on wood," Cissy said. "Mom sounds cheery. They must be happy to have you."

Cheery? The adjective struck her as odd. Victoria instinctively looked to the lower left cabinet below the sink. "I guess," Victoria said. "It's too bad—"

"I know," Cissy said. "Look, if this flu thing clears up within the week, maybe I could fly out there and catch the tail end of your visit."

"That would be great."

There was no point to it, but she couldn't help herself. Quietly, the phone still at her ear, Victoria stealthily bent down and slid the little door open.

Cissy was chatting on about babies and doctors, but Victoria didn't hear her, really. She was looking at the two bottles stowed behind the cabinet door. Victoria stared at them for a long moment before noiselessly sliding the cabinet shut and straightening up again. There was the freshly washed glass, drying by the side of the sink. And almost on cue, the sound of her mother's gentle laughter from the other room.

"Vicki? Did you hear me?"

"I'm sorry, Sis. You were—"

"I said, I'll call after the weekend with a progress report. Give my love to Dad, okay? I have to do something with Jordan immediately or he's going to cry my ear off."

Victoria said her goodbyes and hung up, suddenly feeling drained of energy. A part of her registered the fact that Cissy, like Mother, hadn't asked her word one about the film or anything in her life. Another part was resisting an impulse to walk out the back door right now and keep walking.

But she wouldn't do that. Victoria washed her hands in the sink mechanically, not knowing why. She could hear her father making another one of his terrible puns and this time, her mother responding with a chuckle. Cheery now, yes.

When she reentered the dining room she saw that Mother had put out a bowl of fruit. The old silver percolator had moved from a sideboard to table, with the antique sugar and milk servers. Coffee mugs she recognized from childhood were on her father's place mat and her own. "Your mother's made real coffee, in honor of your visit," Dad announced, smiling.

No coffee for Mother, she noted, who was eating a carefully portioned apple. Victoria studied her face across the table, seeing the little signs she'd known she'd find. There was the subtle brightness in her eyes, the more relaxed expression only she, perhaps, could recognize. She stole a glance at Dad, who seemed, as always, blissfully unaware of the shift in his wife's mood. Or perhaps he was so used to it by now that he didn't notice. Or chose not to.

She didn't know what he thought. When had she ever had a real talk with him about Mother? In a way, nobody in their family really did talk to each other, did they? "I was telling Victoria about Bud Oglesby," Dad said to Mother.

"Oh, yes," Mother said, smiling, with a vague wave of her hand. "They've all lost their minds down on Walnut Street." She looked up at Victoria. "Did you go over to the bakery?"

"Yes," Victoria said, and even though she found her mother's sudden interest suspect, she was still enough the eager-to-please child that she began telling her story of the day's events.

For a few minutes, it was fun. Dad was a captive audience, asking the right questions and smiling at his daughter's witticisms. But Victoria soon saw, though her mother smiled and nodded, that her mind was elsewhere. She wasn't really listening at all.

FIFTEEN YEARS, twenty, did it matter? Victoria's feet knew the way just as Sarah Campbell's had. Some of the town's geography had changed superficially, but on the outskirts of the college campus, past the turnoff that led to the forestry area known as the Glen, there was still a winding path that led to the creek. She didn't even have to think about it, though it was night. The half-moon in the cloudless sky was plenty enough light, and she'd arrived at the old wooden bridge before she knew it.

Jumpers Creek. There it was, quietly gurgling along in the ravine below, a silvery skein of water in the moonlight. Victoria stepped out onto the rickety but solid bridge, holding the rail as she went. When she was halfway across, she stopped and gazed down, elbows on the railing.

Hard to believe she'd done it, all those years back. Even now the jump seemed frightfully steep. But she'd survived that, just as she'd survived the other aspects of her childhood, and she wasn't about to jeopardize her life now with another foolhardy leap. Much as she was tempted.

Victoria listened to the water's gentle rush below, chin propped in her palms as she leaned over, looking for the moon's reflection. It was too bad that Melinda hadn't been home when she'd phoned her, before leaving the folks'. She could've used her Silver Spring friend's boundless good humor and no-nonsense approach to any problem, now.

Problem. That's what it was, that's what you called it: a drinking problem. She'd never used the dread A-word in thinking about Mother. Mother wasn't an alcoholic. No, she just took a drink now and then. And it was all very proper and under control. You might even say it made her easier to be with.

Victoria sighed, exasperated by her age-old rationalizations. Had she really thought it would go away, that "the problem" would've somehow miraculously disappeared over time? Of course not. And was there anything she could do about it, if she really wanted to?

No. All she'd done was keep it out of her book. Sarah Campbell's mother was problematic, all right, but she didn't stock a bottle of Johnny Walker under the sink. The only worrisome thing about that aspect of this situation was Sandy Baker.

He couldn't know, of course. But he'd written some things into his draft that came perilously close to the truth. And in other ways, he'd distorted things. His version of the conflict between Sarah and her older sister was a lot harsher. The Caroline character—Cissy in a not-so-artful disguise— was much less sympathetic than Victoria had intended. That worried her, too. What would Cissy think?

Worrying about Cissy, worrying about Mother, Dad, the town of Silver Spring—it all made her feel terribly tired and upset. Victoria stood up, brushing a lock of hair from her eyes as the wind rose, feeling a now-familiar knot of tension at the pit of her stomach. She'd made a mistake. She never should've agreed to let Baker do this damn film of his. The best thing she'd done was to leave this place and do her best to stay away from it. And now...

"Not again?"

The voice from the darkness startled her. Victoria tensed, looked up, and was shocked to see Sandy Baker standing at the end of the bridge, hands on his hips and a mocking frown on his face as he surveyed her position. "Don't do it," he called quietly. "I told you, you're my most valuable asset."

Recovering, Victoria gave him a wry smile. "I'm insured, aren't I?" she asked. "Surely your producers have taken care of that."

"Maybe so, but you're worth a lot more to me alive," he said, sauntering over to join her. "Besides, Sarah didn't even break any bones," he noted. "As the author pointed out, there were much more surefire ways to go."

Victoria nodded. This was strange, thinking about Sandy Baker and having him materialize like a summoned spirit. The moonlight made the bit of silver in his hair glint as he leaned back against the railing, looking her over with an air of concerned interest. "What brings you out here?" he asked.

"Me?" She laughed. "It's still my creek, Sandy. I should be asking you that question."

"I had a feeling this is where I'd find you," he said. "We missed you over at the hotel."

"Oh," she said, chagrined. In the midst of her emotional tumult, she'd completely forgotten about their casually arranged meeting. "I hope you weren't waiting for me. I mean, I didn't think we'd set a certain time—"

"Don't worry about it," he said. "We didn't. No, I just felt like taking a walk and doing some thinking. Like you. Or even better, *with* you."

He turned to gaze down at the waters as she had, and the wind whistled in the trees. Victoria folded her arms, aware for the first time that it was chilly in the Glen.

"Here." Sandy was taking off his windbreaker.

"No, you don't have to..."

She didn't want his jacket. She didn't even want him to be here, invading her privacy as he always did. It seemed to be the man's chosen mission. But her protest died. He was already putting the jacket around her shoulders, and the simple friendliness of the gesture had a tenderness about it that touched her. "Thank you," she murmured, gathering the material about her arms.

Sandy merely nodded, leaning on the railing to watch the water flow. "And what were you thinking about?" he asked softly.

Victoria shook her head. He glanced at her. "Maybe getting out of town?" he asked.

She smiled in spite of herself. "You know too much, Sandy Baker," she said.

"Maybe," he allowed. His eyes glimmered as he gazed at her in the moonlight. "But maybe not enough." He reached up to brush that same recalcitrant curl of hair away from her eye. She was surprised at the way she trembled at his touch, but even more surprised at the way something inside of her seemed to move toward him, even as she thought to move away.

"I want to know much, much more," he murmured. "Come, Victoria Moore. Tell me about yourself." He paused, a faint smile playing about his lips. "The truth, though," he added. "I'm only interested in the truth."

Chapter Four

Oh, brother. Here she'd thought that the most difficult part of the night was behind her, and now Sandy Baker seemed up for a personal cross-examination of her psyche. Victoria looked away from his inquisitive gaze, finding it easier to watch the softly glimmering water far below. "The truth is, there's not a lot to tell," she said.

"I find that hard to believe."

She shrugged. "Maybe some writers lead wild lives, but I don't," she told him. "Anything of interest you want to know about Victoria Moore you can find in her novels."

"So it's all true, then? You *are* Sarah Campbell?"

Victoria rested her chin on her hands, resisting an impulse to emit a small moan of exasperation. She'd just hopped from frying pan into fire. "No, not entirely. Look, it's been a long day," she began. "Maybe we could shelve this conversation for some other—"

"No problem."

Surprised, she glanced sideways to see Sandy's expression. He seemed affable, amused, if anything. "Go on, be a woman of mystery," he said. "I'll put up with that for, say, twenty-four hours."

She smiled in spite of herself. "And then?"

"It's over the hot coals we go," he said, with a mock piratical scowl. "We'll get every little scintillating detail out of you. Childhood, puberty, adolescence—what dolls you played with, what tests you cheated on—"

"I never," she said, straightening up.

"Not even math?" he queried, eyes twinkling. "Sarah Campbell cribbed on her math final."

Victoria sighed. "Bring on the bamboo shoots for under my fingernails," she said. "I'm pleading the Fifth."

"Okay." Sandy leaned back against the railing. They were both silent, listening to the trees rustle and sway in the breeze, accompanied by the distant hoot of an owl. When the hooting died it was almost too quiet. She felt self-conscious.

"Doesn't mean you can't talk at all," she murmured.

"Beautiful night," he said. "Hope this weather holds up."

The sardonic tone beneath his innocuous phrases didn't escape her. "We don't have to talk about the weather," she said dryly.

"Good," he said. "How were the folks?"

Victoria opened her mouth to reply, then shut it. She couldn't think of any simple reply to that seemingly harmless question. As she tried to reason out a suitable answer, Sandy gave a low chuckle.

"Okay, I give up," he said, shaking his head. "We can't talk about you, your fictional creations or your family. What do you think of the Mets this year?"

Victoria laughed, relieved he was letting her off easily. "I don't," she said. "I'm not a baseball fan."

"I won't hold that against you," he said, and turned to lean against the railing, imitating her posture. "But you're going to have some trouble with Grace."

"Grace the actress? She's into sports?"

Now Sandy laughed. "No, no. She's into *you*. She's got a million and one questions to ask you about growing up in Silver Spring."

"Oh," she said uneasily.

"She writes things down," Sandy added. "Notes for her in-depth characterization. She carries a little notebook around."

"Good Lord."

"And then there's Catherine. The reporter? She's twisted our publicist's arm in a knot to get a story on this shoot— and she'll go after you with a tape recorder," he said significantly.

"Maybe I *should* catch the next plane out."

"No way."

He'd said it with such quiet vehemence that she turned to stare at him. "I thought you told me once you weren't comfortable collaborating," she said.

"True. But we have a deal." He held her gaze. "I know this whole experience is starting to overwhelm you, at the moment. But I'm still counting on you to be my prime source material."

"We could do it by phone," she muttered.

"No, your presence is going to pay off," he said. "Even in small but significant ways. For example, there's Grace's wardrobe. Shelley—that's my wardrobe mistress—is getting lost in the eccentricities of Sarah's clothing. She's going to have her looking like a teenage Diane Keaton, unless someone who knows more about this stuff steers her in the right direction."

Victoria remembered the shirt Grace had been wearing beneath her apron at the bakery that afternoon and nodded. "I know. They don't have the right look yet."

"So, you see? You're already invaluable."

Victoria stared down at the creek. She didn't want to leave, anyway, not in her heart of hearts. It was too unique a situation to walk away from. No self-respecting writer would.

"And think of the material you'll get," Sandy said, reading her mind again.

Victoria met his gaze. Once more she was struck by the uncanny feeling that they were already old acquaintances, that they did know each other intimately, somehow. Except... "I know what we can talk about," she said abruptly. "You."

He arched his eyebrows. "Me?"

"Yes, Mr. Inquisitive. What about you? Let's have it," she continued, enjoying the bemused look on his face. "Puberty, adolescence—I want to know what games you played in the sandbox, what tests you cheated on—"

"Never." He grinned. "I was good at math."

"How about the first heart you ever broke?"

She couldn't believe she'd actually said that. It had come out of her mouth as if of its own accord, and she probably looked more startled than Sandy did. "Just kidding," she said in the awkward silence, feeling her cheeks burn with a blush that would be hard to see, mercifully, in this dim light.

Sandy cleared his throat. "Well, you certainly know how to turn the tables," he said. "What makes you think I was an early heartbreaker?"

"I wasn't serious," she said quickly, but couldn't resist adding: "You do have a reputation, though. As I'm sure you know."

"I try to avoid heartbreak," he said mildly. "Bad for one's health. And I'm sure the rumors of my prowess as a Don Juan have been greatly exaggerated."

"Oh?" Although she knew she was probably treading on thin ice, she had a perverse desire to put him on the spot, for once. Why should she be the only person whose most private past and present were subject to public scrutiny? "You mean you can't believe everything you read?"

"Victoria Moore," he said, with a look of mock consternation. "Don't tell me you read tabloids! You're the one whose highbrow literary reputation is going to be tarnished, if that gets out.''

''I'm not 'highbrow','' she said. ''And no, I don't read those rags regularly. But I do when I'm waiting in line at the supermarket.''

''Well, then I guess you know all about me,'' he said. ''Just like I know all about you from your books.''

''Wait a second,'' she said, smiling. ''Are you equating my artful prose with the gossip in those magazines?''

''No, but all of it is a pretty distorted version of the truth,'' he said. ''Wouldn't you say?''

Checkmate. He had a fairly smug look on his face as he leaned against the railing, arms folded. Once again he had her at a loss for words. Victoria gazed down at the creek. ''Nice night if it doesn't rain,'' she muttered.

Sandy laughed. ''Yes, it is. Why don't we take a little moonlight hike? This path goes around to the Glen entrance, doesn't it?''

''Um-hmm.'' Victoria straightened, smiling as he extended his arm in a gesture of mock chivalry, indicating that she should lead the way. She started across the bridge, Sandy close behind, noting that although the man was a tease and a troublemaker, he had succeeded in dispelling her earlier mood of dire depression.

In fact she felt almost buoyant as she stepped off the bridge, Sandy at her side now on the widening path. She was suddenly glad that she wasn't alone with all her conflicting feelings. Maybe she and Sandy didn't know each other well, but she felt they were kindred spirits. He, too, obviously liked to keep his emotional cards close to his chest.

She sensed that in between the words, they'd formed a tacit truce, a kind of mutual respect for each other's private boundaries. The funny thing was, she mused, that now she was relaxed enough to be more liable to open up to him.

"So what do you think of my little town so far?" she asked him, watching the play of dappled moonlight in the treetops arching over them as they walked.

"It's perfect," he said. "Perfect for what we're doing, I mean. Didn't have to build any additional sets to start, and won't have to, if the good weather holds. The town board's being very helpful."

"I'll bet," she said, thinking of the way those stuffed-shirt Silver Spring officials would gain even larger-swelling chests from their association with such Hollywood glamor. "We'll probably get half of the population involved by the time we're done."

"I hear you cast Pop Oglesby."

"How could I not?" he said, reaching out to push a stray branch from her path. "The man's a born ham. Even through he's older now than he was in the book, he'll do fine. Why, does it bother you?"

"Him being older? Or Pop playing himself?"

"Both."

Victoria shook her head. "Whatever works," she said.

"Within reason," Sandy amended her. "We haven't planned on auditioning any of your relatives."

"Thanks," she said dryly. "You're showing great discretion."

They walked in silence for a ways, the rushing of the wind in the leaves above replacing the distant gurgle of the creek as the dirt trail snaked toward a cluster of pines. "So how was it, at the old homestead?" he asked. "If you don't mind my asking."

"It wasn't so bad," she said carefully.

"Four words," he noted. "I'll consider that a minor victory."

"Oh, stop," she said. "The truth, the truth," she sighed. "All right, you want to know the truth? Everybody's pretty much the same as they always were. My father's upset that I'm not staying with them, because he'd rather I was there, and my mother's just as happy that I'm not. She's a lot more upset that my sister isn't coming.''

''I see.''

''And my sister may show up in a few weeks, but she may not—and in a way, I'd rather she didn't. There,'' she said, drawing his windbreaker tighter around her as the wind rose. ''Now you've got all the lurid details. Happy?''

''Moderately,'' he said. ''And why isn't your sister coming?''

''Jordan's got the flu. That's her baby. And you know, now that we're on this subject, one reason I'm glad my sister may not show up on the set is that she's liable to have a fit when she sees what you've done to her in this new draft.''

''What I've done to her?'' He smiled. ''Victoria, it's your character.''

''You know what I'm talking about,'' she said grimly. ''I softened her. You sharpened her.''

''It made better dramatic sense.''

''I suppose,'' she muttered. ''But it's not going to promote great sibling relations.''

Sandy slowed his pace. ''Well, how great have they been?'' he asked quietly.

She turned to face him in the little clearing where the pines rustled. ''Relatively peaceful, in recent years,'' she said. ''It would be nice to keep it that way.''

''I don't mean to sound callous,'' said Sandy. ''But my job is to make a great movie—not to preserve family harmony.''

''I know,'' Victoria said, brushing some pine needles from her skirt. ''But I still think those later scenes with Sarah and her sister could use some . . . fine tuning. If you make Caroline too much of an ogre, it throws things out of whack. In this author's considered and objective opinion.''

"We'll go over them together," Sandy said.

"So I can have my much-heralded creative input."

"Of course."

"Good," she said, somewhat relieved. Sandy was looking at her with an already familiar penetrating gaze. She met it with a challenging one of her own. "Yes, I'm completely subjective about everything, but you knew that when you agreed to do this. Right?"

"Right," he echoed.

"Look, you're the one who has the easy task here," she said. "You don't have to confront people from your past, watch somebody *be* you, and deal with your family on a daily basis—while you're worrying about all the work you're not doing back in New York."

"True," he said. "I just have to control a thirty-five-member crew, coax award-winning performances out of over a dozen unruly actors with egos the size of Ohio, fend off five interfering producers who are watching my budget like paranoid hawks, maintain good relations with the entire population of Silver Spring, negotiate with God to keep the sun shining for three solid weeks and with my Muse, to keep my camera weaving cinematic magic—while I try to convince you to take off the kid gloves and jump into the fray, so we can make an unpolished script start to shine like silver. Yup," he finished, nodding. "I'm the one with the easy task. Anybody can see that."

She got the message loud and clear, but she held her ground. "At least you don't have to have dinner with your folks every night," she said.

Sandy laughed, and she joined in, falling into step with him as they made their way out of the pines. "Where *is* your family?" she asked him, when their laughter had died down and they were on the trail again. "Still in Brooklyn?"

Sandy shook his head. "My mother moved into Manhattan a few years back. I helped her find a place on the East

Side, where she could get around easy. She's in a wheel-
chair, mostly," he added, at Victoria's inquiring look.
"Rheumatoid arthritis."

"What a shame," she said. "That sounds terrible."

"She's in good shape." She could hear the evident pride
and affection in his voice. "Strong as an ox and about as
ornery. I had a helluva time getting her to accept Martha—
this woman I hired to help out around the apartment. But
she liked it in the city."

"You bought the place for her," she intuited.

Sandy nodded. "One thing an Oscar's good for, when
you're a screenwriter. You get to show your Mom you're not
entirely the good-for-nothing she always feared you were."

"And your Dad?"

"He's gone West."

"California?"

Sandy gave a wry chuckle. "No, it's an expression he used
to use—like 'passing on.' Whenever an old crony of his died,
Dad would say he'd gone West."

"I'm sorry."

"So am I," he said, and was quiet a moment. "We never
really got along," he went on, subdued. "I guess we
could've done a better job of it, if either one of us had . . ."
His voice trailed off and he shook his head. "Should've's
and could've's," he said. "Some of the more useless words
in the language."

"I agree," she said softly. They walked up the slow rise
that led to the wooden fence delineating the Glen's boundaries, the moon full and bright now in a cloudless sky. "The
parking area's down that way, if you're tired of walking."

Sandy turned to look at her. "Oh, I could stand a little
more of your company—in this picturesque setting," he
said, with a teasing grin.

"We can take the long way around, if you'd like," she
told him.

"I'd like," he said. "Lead on."

They skirted the fence, Victoria taking the path that followed it around the edge of the forest proper. She felt Sandy's hand at her back as they ducked under an overhanging hedge and noted the ease this casual contact seemed to have, for both of them. Earlier, she would have had an impulse to pull away, but now it seemed natural.

A bit farther on, he picked a leaf from her hair and though she warmed at his touch, his fingertips brushing the edge of one ear, she told herself he was only being friendly. Friendly, she found herself wondering, or more than that?

"Is it only work you left behind in New York?" he asked.

Hmm. He had an unerring instinct for picking up on her thoughts. Either that or his mind worked in remarkably similar ways. "You mean, is there a significant someone in my life? Not really."

"Then you don't have to worry about New York. Work can wait," he said.

"And men can't?" She smiled. "What about you? Got another tabloid-worthy affair brewing?"

"Not at all," he said. "Who has the time?"

"Married to your work, is that it?"

"Exactly."

"You were married, though, weren't you?"

"I was," he allowed. "Four years."

"That's not a long time."

"Long enough to figure out it was a lost cause. Don't get me wrong," he added. "I'm not against the institution, I'm all for it. But the lady in question . . ."

"Was that actress," she remembered. "What's her name, the one who had the television show."

"What's-her-name will do fine," Sandy said, with a rueful laugh.

"It ended badly?"

"Depends on which side of the alimony payments you're on," he said. "No, Kathleen and I still get along all right. Better, now that we don't work together."

"Is that how you met?"

"I directed her in my first film," he said, taking her elbow as they both stepped wide of an upturned rock slab protruding in their path.

"Thanks," she said. "I'm sorry to say I've never seen that one. I hear it's quite good."

"*She* was quite good," he said. "The mistake we made was doing the second one."

"Why?" Victoria asked, curious. "If you were such a good team..."

"I'm not a team player, remember?" He slapped at a leafy branch in his way. "When you're a director, you're the boss, captain of the ship. When you're married, as I understand it, one person can't be the boss—at least, not all the time. And that's fine. But if you try to mix the two, well...things get pretty mixed up."

"Let me guess," Victoria said. "She wanted an equal say on the set? And that rubbed you the wrong way?"

"You know me too well," he said. "For someone who barely knows me."

"Oh, you're not so hard to read," she scoffed.

"I see." His eyes glimmered with amusement in the pale light. "And what else did I do wrong?"

"Defensive, are we?" she said playfully. "Hey, I don't know the woman. But chances are, she was equally at fault in whatever problems developed between the two of you. It does take two, doesn't it?"

"I think I detect the voice of experience," he said.

"Well, I've never been married," she told him. "But I've been involved in a few long-term relationships."

"You don't believe in marriage?"

How honest could she be? Sure, she believed in it. She just hadn't met any man, post-Doug, who'd inspired her to take that sort of landmark leap. But even as she pondered phrasing an answer to his question, she was aware that he'd once more skillfully turned the conversation back on her. "We were talking about *you*," she said. "Remember?"

"Oh, I thought we were done with my story," he said with an insouciant grin.

"No," she said. "We were just getting into your philosophy on sexual equality."

"Were we?"

Victoria nodded, not about to let him off the hook. "It sounds to me as if you like keeping women in a certain place."

"I never said that." He looked genuinely indignant.

"Well, you were making a distinction," she noted. "Vague but significant. I gather it was okay for your wife to make major decisions on the home front—"

"Of course."

"—but never on the set," she said.

"Wait a second," he protested. "You're confusing some issues here. A director-actress relationship is the same as a direction-actor relationship. Gender has nothing to do with it. In either case, in nine out of ten instances, the director is the one who has the final say."

"On your set."

"On just about any man's set."

"Or woman's," she interjected.

"Slip of the tongue," he said wryly. "There aren't that many female directors in Hollywood." He cocked his head studying her as they paused before the end of the fence. "I didn't realize I'd be dealing with a feminist."

"I'm not a feminist, necessarily," she said, smiling. "Why, are you a male chauvinist?"

"I love women," he said.

"That doesn't answer the question."

Sandy laughed. "You're a tough one, Victoria."

Victoria shrugged. "I just want to know what I've gotten into here."

"Meaning?"

"Meaning we do have to work together," she said, indicating he should follow her to the right, off the path and across the grassy knoll that led to the parking area. "And I want to know if I am going to have an equal say when it comes to decisions about my own characters—my own story," she reminded him. "Whether you've improved on it or not."

"I see."

She could see a lone gray Toyota parked in the lot up ahead. She waited for his considered reply as they strode across the grass toward it.

"Here's what I think," he said, as they approached the car. "A deal is deal. When it comes to this script, I'm willing to give you fifty percent—even fifty-one-percent decision-making power, much as it goes against my grain. But there is one condition."

"Which is?" He was standing by his car, keys in hand. Victoria paused, arms folded, facing him in the light of the solitary street lamp at the lot's corner.

"You have to give one hundred percent," he said quietly. "Of your own thoughts and feelings. We can't have secrets, hidden agendas. I can't have you screwing up a well-written Caroline because you're trying to shield a real-life Cissy. If you're honest with me and truly forthcoming, I'll meet you more than halfway. I give you my word."

Victoria bit her lower lip. "That's a quite a condition," she said. "I can't promise you I'll always be able to be objective. But I'll certainly do my best."

"Good." He smiled. "Between your best and my best we should make a damn good movie. Now will you let a gentleman—a non-chauvinistic one—give the quasi-feminist lady a lift home?"

"Certainly."

As she slid into the front seat she smiled to herself in the darkness. She'd held her ground and possibly gained some. She felt a sense of camaraderie with Sandy as he pulled the car out of the lot, but it was deeper than that.

How deep did she want it to be?

Victoria shook the thought off and concentrated on showing him the way back to the Moore house, where her rented car was parked. Sandy was talking about the shots that were planned for the next day, some small roles that were still to be cast, like the part of the mother of one of Sarah's best friends. In the familiar tone Sandy used, and the confidences he was freely sharing, she thought she could hear him trusting her a good deal more than he had in their first encounters.

"This next house," she told him, and he slowed the car, pulling up to the curb. The front-porch light was out. Her folks were already in bed, no doubt. She'd told them not to wait up, since she'd only be coming back for her car. She'd see them again tomorrow night. Sandy had turned the motor off and was looking at her across the seat.

"Coming to the set, then?" he asked.

"Bright and early."

"Good. I'll introduce you to some of the important players. And then when we break, let's have our first official script conference, in the afternoon."

"Fine," she said.

"We'll look at the problem scenes in the first act, at least, and go through them point by point. No holds barred. Truth talks, nobody walks," he quipped, smiling.

"You got it."

He was holding his hand out. Victoria shook it, smiling back, glad that the evening had ended on such a straight-ahead, upbeat note.

Then he kissed her.

She hadn't seen it coming, hadn't been remotely prepared for him to keep holding her hand and pull her, seemingly effortlessly, toward him, bending forward across the seat, his lips finding hers with unerring accuracy. She was even less prepared for how good it felt.

Soft lips, a sweet and salty taste, a heady male scent mingled with after-shave, a blossoming warmth that spread through her from lips to fingertips and toes, toes that curled as a delicious shiver stole through her body—she was conscious of all this, even as her mind threatened to melt from such a sensual overload.

She hadn't been ready for it, but Victoria had always been able to rise to occasions. On this one, her instinctual response was to kiss him back, her other hand gliding up to slide through his soft hair as his hand gently cupped and caressed her chin. His lips fit hers so nicely. The warmth of his touch was at once exciting in its newness, and enticing in its odd familiarity.

There was a brief moment of a quiet, blissful feeling that seemed to pass like a current between them, and then she remembered to breathe.

They pulled apart at the same time. She found herself looking into eyes that seemed to mirror her own undeniable arousal. Victoria sat back against the seat, still holding his gaze. "What was that?" she asked.

"What do you think it was?" he countered.

Her mind was in gear again, already backpedaling from the surprising force of the emotions she'd just felt. "I guess it was a good-night kiss."

"As opposed to . . . ?"

"Anything more," she said abruptly, and looked away, her gaze fixating on the Moore's mailbox, a few yards ahead on a post by their picket-fence gate. Years ago, in another life, it seemed, she'd sat here in a car with Bobby Ferguson, a sophomore football player who didn't know how to kiss very well but had great hair. She'd considered that summer's night a mistake, but a harmless one. This, on the other hand, could have truly dangerous repercussions.

"Are you sure?" he was asking.

Victoria drummed her fingers on the leather seat, listening to the crickets in the quiet outside, then turned to face him again. "Sandy, you don't want to do this," she said.

He raised an eyebrow. "Do what?"

"Seduce me," she said.

His smile was faint in the dim light. "I'm not sure who's seducing whom," he said. "Now, don't get that look. You're an incredibly attractive woman, and you know I'm already in love with you. On paper," he added, as her eyes widened. "I'm more than a mere fan of Victoria Moore, the writer. I've made your work my work. I'm devoting a hefty chunk of my life to it."

"That's different," she said, her voice unsteady. "As we've been trying to establish. So—"

"And though I don't mean you're the one who initiated that kiss," he interrupted gently. "You didn't exactly leap from the car."

Being coy about it was absurd. She knew how she'd responded, and she knew he knew. Victoria exhaled a deep breath. "I enjoyed it," she admitted. "And maybe that's why I'd like to make sure it doesn't happen again."

Sandy didn't bat an eye. "Bad for our working relationship?"

"Not exactly," she said. "All right, you want a-hundred-percent honesty, and real emotion? You're an attractive man, as well you know," she added dryly. "And though I'm not in love with your work, not being as familiar with it as you are with mine, I certainly like the little of you I know.''

"And why have such a good impression spoiled?" he prompted.

"Wrong," she told him. "I just want you to know who you're dealing with here."

"Maybe I do know."

"You couldn't know all of me," she said. "And here's the bottom line—I'm as much of an artist as you are. I'm just as headstrong and stubborn and willful, maybe even more so."

"So?"

"So if you have any idea that getting involved with me is going to smooth over my rough edges and turn us into a happy team with your calling the shots, you're crazy."

Sandy laughed. "No, I'm not that crazy. Smoothing over your edges isn't what I had in mind."

"What *do* you have in mind?"

Sandy shook his head. "Maybe I'm improvising. Ever heard of acting on impulse?"

"Sure," she said. "But in this situation that's not going to be good enough."

Now Sandy was the one who exhaled a long breath. "Victoria," he said quietly. "What do you want me to say? You want me to apologize? I'm not sorry."

"Neither am I," she told him. "I just want us to know exactly where things stand."

"Which is where?" he asked. "From your point of view."

She hoped she was doing the right thing. But at the risk of offending him, she had to say what was on her mind. "We're supposed to be working here as partners," she said. "You've just finished telling me tonight that being a true partner with a woman is a real problem for you. Well, until you're willing to meet me on equal ground, I'm not interested in romance."

"Really?"

"Really. I don't usually kiss on first dates, Sandy," she explained. "And at this point in my life, I don't have the time or the desire for casual flirtations. I'm a serious sort of girl."

Sandy briefly studied her in silence, his expression inscrutable. "You're being awfully forthright for someone who supposedly only reveals herself in her books."

Victoria shrugged. "I guess this is our night for getting all the hard stuff out of the way."

"I guess so." He looked from her to his hand that was still on the steering wheel, then let go of it to open his door. Victoria watched, curious, as he got out of the car, walked around to her side and opened the passenger door for her. "Come on out," he said. "It's safe."

With a rueful smile, she climbed out of the car, turning to face him on the sidewalk as he shut the door. "You're annoyed?" she asked.

Sandy looked genuinely surprised. "Not at all," he said. "Like I said, all I wanted to hear from you was the truth."

"Oh." For all her inner convictions and resolutions, she felt an irrational surge of disappointment. He was going to leave it at that? Accept her rebuff and back off without a protest? Maybe she had been wrong about the depth of his interest, in which case she certainly had done the right thing. Not that this was much of a consoling thought.

"You've given me something to think about," he said. "And I will." He smiled, then a bent a little closer toward her in the pale moonlight. When he spoke again his voice was soft and husky. "But if you think I'm going to settle for that being the only kiss we ever share, then you're the crazy one."

Victoria blinked, at a loss for a reply. He was already moving away. "Sleep tight, Victoria Moore," he called, opening his door. "I expect to see you on the set at the crack of dawn."

She stood on the sidewalk, watching him drive away, and stayed there even after his red taillights had disappeared from the dark end of the street. Once again, she was wondering what it was that she'd gotten herself into.

Chapter Five

"I want that jacket," Melinda said.

"This?" Victoria looked down at the simple black man-tailored suit jacket she wore over a white cotton blouse and jeans. "You're kidding. I picked it up secondhand at a SoHo flea market last year, for next to nothing."

Her friend shook her frizzy blond head with a mock moan of despair. "Exactly! That's what I want—I want to be able to say things like, 'I picked it up at a flea market in Soho.' You know what kind of clothes show up in a Silver Spring flea market? Overalls and granny dresses from genuine grannies—with real fleas."

Victoria laughed. "Come on, you're a better dresser than I am," she told Melinda. "Look at you."

Melinda, seated opposite her in the luncheonette booth, glanced at the dark green knit wool chemise she had on and grimaced. "Standard school teacher smock," she said, with a dismissive wave of her hand. "There must be hundreds of women wearing this dress all over the Middle West. You, on the other hand, are radiating New York casual chic, artless sophistication and . . ." She leaned forward over her burger plate. "You've been dieting, haven't you? Please tell me you're on a diet. I'll give up all hope if I hear you've looked this thin for years."

"Yes, I'm on a diet," Victoria assured her. "But you certainly don't look overweight, either."

"That's because of this dress," Melinda said, looking warily at the rest of her burger. "I couldn't fit into a pair of jeans like yours. As Jim noted, this weekend."

"How is Jim?"

Melinda frowned. "Let's keep this conversation bright and cheery, okay? It's too early in the day for me to get depressed."

"Uh-oh," Victoria said.

"Yeah, uh-oh. Are you eating your pickle? No? Good." Melinda took the pickle from Victoria's plate and munched on it, gazing moodily into space. "Give me a minute," she said. "I'll try to give you the short-form story of my marital woes, if such a thing is possible."

Victoria sat back and regarded her friend of so many years with undisguised concern. When they'd met this morning at Ernie's on Elm Street, she'd sensed Melinda was a bit under the weather, but she'd assumed that was due to the hectic work schedule she had, now that the local high school was in session again. Melinda had been teaching English and Humanities over at Kennedy for a dozen years now. She'd been with Jim a few years longer than that, and in all that time she'd rarely indicated any dissatisfaction with her married life.

Melinda had put on a little weight, true, and her usually bright and cheerful blue eyes seemed darker now to Victoria. Apprehensive, she checked her watch. She'd left the set an hour ago, with assurances that it would take at least that long for the crew to get the next shot set up. Ernie's, one of their favorite haunts from the old days, a down-home luncheonette that still served good, cheap "blue-plate specials" after all these years, and perfectly browned french fries, was only a few blocks from the set. But she knew Melinda was on a school lunch break, and this sounded like a more serious conversation than they'd probably have time for.

When Melinda had first arrived, after some hugs and tear-shedding they'd spent the whole first half hour with Melinda pumping "the world-famous authoress gone Hollywood," as she laughingly put it, for details about the film. Victoria hadn't had much of a chance to ask Melinda about herself, and she realized now that this had been intentional on her friend's part.

"Things aren't great," Melinda said abruptly, meeting the concerned looked in Victoria's eyes. "I think maybe we've been together too long, Jim and me."

"What do you mean?"

"I mean the thrill is gone, as they say." Melinda gave a sigh, and stabbed at the pool of ketchup on her plate with a long, lean fry. "Maybe it's me. It's probably me. It only *seems* to be him."

"I thought you and Jim always got along so well," Victoria said cautiously.

"We did. We do," Melinda said. "Forever and ever, world without end, amen."

She wasn't used to this caustic tone from Melinda, usually the more optimistic of the two of them. Hadn't it always been Melinda's volunteered job to buoy up "moody" Victoria, when they'd been in school together? "Well, then, what's ...?"

"We had a fight this morning." She seemed to be debating whether or not to go into it.

"About?" Victoria prompted her.

"It was over you, actually," Melinda said, with a lopsided grin of embarrassment.

"Me?!"

"Jim just couldn't wait for us all to get together, and he wanted to know when and where and everything, and who could blame him? And he was hinting about how he wouldn't mind meeting some of these movie people and why didn't we have you over for dinner, and I—'' Melinda puffed her cheeks out, expelling air. ''I got upset, for no good reason,'' she said sheepishly. ''Don't get me wrong,'' she added quickly. ''I knew it was nothing—you know, for me to get jealous about. I mean, I know Jim's not your type.''

''Melinda!''

''Calm down, Victoria,'' Melinda said, patting her hand as she saw her shocked look. ''I know you wouldn't dream of making trouble anyway. It's not that.''

''Then what?''

''I'm telling you, it's this place. It's this teensy, tiny minuscule world we're stuck in. I mean, just look at it.'' She looked around Ernie's and Victoria followed her gaze. But all she saw were familiar details that to her had a soft glow of nostalgia—the white-and-blue check curtains that hung on the bottom half of the front windows, the booths made of wood, not plastic, the old counter, edge lined in ancient chrome, that wasn't some gussied up Art Deco New York City reproduction of one, but the real thing.

''It's Ernie's,'' she said, though she knew that wasn't what Melinda wanted to hear. ''It's nice.''

Melinda shook her head. ''Nice, right. And I could recite the menu to you backward, that's how many hours I've logged in here over the years.'' Fork in hand, she idly traced lines in the paper place mat by her plate. ''Jennifer brought home a map from her social-studies class last week. It was an aerial drawing of the area, Silver Spring and Cedar Hollow, and the kids were supposed to find their own street and pencil in where their house was.

''Well, she left it out on the kitchen table,'' Melinda continued. ''And I was looking it over, picking out landmarks. I started to trace the routes I take in a normal week, from the high school to my place and the market and over to the campus when I pick Jim up or meet him for lunch. And you know what it looked like?''

"I'm listening."

"It was a circle," Melinda said. "An imperfect raggedy-edged circle with crosses and squiggly lines inside it, this line the roads I take back and forth to school every day, this one for picking up Jesse and Jennifer at the elementary, this one for when I take in the dry cleaning—and all of them, Victoria, might as well be trenches. I mean, I've walked down Walnut Avenue the same exact way so many different times I'm surprised my heels haven't worn a groove in it. And that's it. That's my world in that one raggedy circle. That's my life."

Melinda put her fork down, still looking at the table top. She looked so forlorn that Victoria wanted to somehow leap across the table and enfold her in a hug. But she knew Melinda well enough to know that she wouldn't want that kind of a display of sympathy. "But we all do that," she said gently. "I'm sure if I traced the streets I walk every day in New York—"

"It's not the same and you know it. Victoria, *you left*," Melinda said simply. "Your map's got a whole lot of territory on it I've even seen, except maybe over at the Cedar Hollow triplex or on TV. You go to book-signing parties and theater openings—"

"Rarely."

"But you get invited," Melinda said.

"Really, it isn't even half as interesting as you might think."

"Victoria!" Her tone said it all.

"Okay, okay. Manhattan has more going on in it than Silver Spring, sure. But the quality of life—"

"I never used to think I'd made a mistake," Melinda said, not listening, "staying on in Silver Spring, but these days I really do wonder."

Victoria wasn't sure what she could say. Funny, but she'd been a city mouse who occasionally envied this country one her apparent peace and serenity. But now wasn't the time to take that tack. "Does Jim feel the same way?" she ventured.

"He wouldn't say so even if he did. You know Jim. He can rhapsodize for hours about Mark Twain or Nathaniel Hawthorne. That's what they pay him for at Anteus College, he does it every day. But try asking him what he really feels."

"Try asking any man."

"Maybe so. But I know he's not as happy as he used to be. He feels like he's missing something, too."

"How do you know?"

"When he gets so fired up over anybody who comes from out of town—and they do have guest speakers at the college fairly often—I can tell. I mean, sometimes I feel like he's so used to me he doesn't see me. So when some illustrious lady poet from Boston flies in for a lecture, and I find him putting on his best suit..." Melinda's smile was a crooked line of chagrin. "Of course it wasn't you we were fighting about. I guess it's a resentment that's been building up in me and this morning set me off, that's all."

Victoria nodded. They both sat in silence while Alice took their plates. The elderly waitress, gray hair in a net, had her hands on remote control while she kept up a decades-old debate with the cashier about the amount of caffeine in tea versus coffee. When she'd moved off, Victoria leaned forward, the beginnings of an idea stirring in her head.

"Maybe you do need a change of scene," she said.

"More like a change of life."

"I don't suppose it's the time of year for a vacation," Victoria mused, and Melinda rolled her eyes.

"And what, leave the kids to run riot?"

"But there might be a way to rekindle some of your home fires in this, too," Victoria went on, thinking.

"In what? Believe me, I'm open to suggestion."

"You don't work on the weekends, right?"

"No, that's when I try to find soft, flat surfaces to pass out on," Melinda said wryly.

"How would you like to be in the movies?"

Melinda stared at her, then laughed. "You mean they're remaking *Diary of a Mad Housewife*?"

"You used to act, didn't you? You always got the leads."

"In school, sure. But what's that got to do with...?" Melinda squinted at Victoria. "Are you serious?"

"Absolutely," Victoria said. "Let me talk to Sandy, okay? Because I happen to know there are a few small parts that he's kept open, and he's interested in casting genuine Silver Spring residents."

Melinda chuckled. "Oh, yeah, local color, that's me. Come on, as Jesse would say—get real."

"I am real," Victoria said. "I bet Jim would sit up and take notice if you turned into a movie star overnight, and I know just the part that's perfect for you."

"This is the craziest—!" Melinda stopped, chin in hands, her blue eyes sparkling with mischief, more animated than she'd been all morning. "What part?"

Now that was more like it. Victoria had an intuition she'd hit upon something good. "There's not much dialogue at all. I think you'd only be in a few scenes. But believe me, you were born to play this part."

"A schoolteacher, I'll bet. What's her name?"

"Not a schoolteacher. She's Juliet Emerson, the mother of Sarah Campbell's best friend, Lucille."

"Lucille Emerson..." Melinda's eyes flashed. "Wait a second. Isn't that the character who's sort of modeled on...me?" Victoria nodded. "Oh my God," Melinda said, and sat back with an incredulous giggle. "You're asking me to play my own mother!"

"I can't think of anyone around here who could do it better," Victoria said.

"I don't know whether to be insulted or not."

"Melinda," Victoria said with a sigh. "Don't look a gift movie cameo in the mouth. If you do get the part—and I can't promise it to you—it could really give your life the kind of lift it needs."

Melinda was shaking her head. "Oh, no. No, this is too weird. I mean, it's a funny idea and everything, but there's absolutely no way I could ever..." She paused, looking up to meet Victoria's knowing gaze. "So when could I audition?"

THERE WERE SOME thirty-odd people and five truckloads of equipment sprawling over the single-block radius of Walnut between Elm and Spruce. A 35-mm Panaflex camera mounted on a crane was pointed at the entrance of the bakery, much like a cannon taking careful aim at the tent flap of an enemy's camp. At the foot of the crane, the voice of one man in a cardigan and a baseball cap rang out through the din.

"Okay, lock it up, please. Grace, hit your mark one time... That looks good. Can we have quiet?"

Dave, the camera operator, eye wedged up against his lens viewer, waved a hand from his perch upon the crane. "Hold up, Sandy, I'm getting a boom shadow."

From her seat, a folding chair set up by the curb, Victoria watched the adjustments being made, pencil poised over her pad. She wanted to get the vocabulary down as soon as possible. There was no sense in trying to communicate with Sandy with authority, if she couldn't call a thing-amajig by its proper name. So what was a boom?

She watched one of the crew members, a bearded fellow in jeans who was holding a long pole aloft, microphone dangling from its end, raise the pole higher and shift to one side. "Clear now?" he called.

Grace-as-Sarah took a few steps from the doorway to the sidewalk and looked up at the camera. "This is as forward as I get," she announced, and grinned. "At least, in this scene." Victoria could see a bar of shadow fall across her forehead.

"She's not in the clear after I pull focus," the operator said.

The man holding the pole moved to one side. The shadow went with him. "How's that?"

"Perfection," Dave reported.

Boom = microphone pole, Victoria scribbled. She watched Grace move back to her "marks"—the precise place she'd been instructed to put her feet at the start of this shot, not necessarily indicated by real chalk marks, but memorized by the actress with some visual aid. She'd talked to Grace for the first time that morning and liked her immediately.

The actress, twenty-two but easily playing seventeen with her youthful face and figure, was full of energy and sass. As Sandy had forewarned her, Grace was also full of questions, but Victoria didn't mind. She liked the way the young woman's mind worked. She wanted to know details for her character, which were quirky but incisive, such as exactly how many pounds Sarah Campbell was trying to lose before she went out with Rocko, her teen motorcycle dream. She had no airs, laughed easily and she pronounced Victoria her personal authority figure after talking to her for mere minutes.

"When it comes to Sarah, this lady is the last word," she'd informed Sandy.

"Of course," he'd said, eyes twinkling as he looked at Victoria. "Why do you think we flew her out here?"

Now she was back in the bakery doorway having a brief conference with Sandy. Two union technicians shifted a light, the director of photography barked a few instructions to Dave, and all was in readiness for the first take. But not quite.

"Dirt alert!" Victoria recognized Susan Jacks's singsong voice. "There's a candy wrapper or two down there that won't match shot twenty-one. Where's Bryce with the broom?"

Susan's prowess as a stickler for detail always drew some good-natured ribbing from the crew. But as Continuity—the person who made sure visual elements matched up from shot to shot—she was only doing her job. "We've lost Bryce," called a technician. "He's on his way to Dayton with that faulty magazine."

"Then who's sweeping?" Susan demanded.

A pale and lanky teenager who had his white shirt's top button buttoned, a passel of pens clipped in its front pocket, peered sheepishly from the shadows of the doorway. He cleared his throat nervously, looking at the diminutive red-head with eyes comically magnified by thick eyeglasses. "I've got a... You need the broom?" he asked.

Victoria recognized Edgar Oglesby, Pop's grandson, and her heart went out to him. Pop had introduced him to her that morning. He was what Melinda's kids might refer to as a classic nerd—a shy boy who was clearly ill at ease with people, preferring the safety of a science or computer lab to the athletic field.

He'd been helping out his grandfather in the early hours, moving some stock around to accommodate the crew members. Victoria had seen how intimidated he was by all this, although not entirely. He carried a small camera that seemed attached at the hip; he never put it down, and Victoria had caught him sneaking a few pictures when the crew had started on their first shot,

Now he emerged from the doorway's darkness brandishing the broom. He gave Susan an awkward smile and before one of the crew members could take it from him, pushed it along the sidewalk in front of her.

"Hey, is he union?" one of the technicians called, and he was answered with laughter from the crew.

Edgar stopped in mid-sweep, ready to bolt like a frightened rabbit. "No, go ahead, you're doing a fine job," Susan told him. "Thank you. You're...?"

"Edgar," he mumbled, head averted.

"Thank you, Edgar." She smiled sweetly at him as he finished up, his face reddened. Once he was back inside, Susan turned to make a face at the technicians and hurried out of camera range. Victoria was glad she'd been nice to the boy. She could see Melinda wasn't the only Silver Spring resident who was going to have her life affected by the *Jumpers Creek* crew.

"Okay, let's make movies!" the D.P. called.

With all technicians readied and Grace in position, the familiar slap of the clapboard was heard. Victoria watched as Sandy called for action, and after a moment Grace emerged from the bakery door.

They were shooting part of a scene that actually occurred very late in the film, but for reasons of scheduling it was being shot out of sequence. Sandy had explained to Victoria that most films were shot this way, in a seemingly haphazard sequence, endings preceding beginnings and crucial scenes often shot with only some of the actors actually on the set at the same time. Comprehending this was giving Victoria renewed respect for film actors, who often had to build their characters out of a schizophrenic patchwork of scenes done at different times and places.

In the present scene Sarah Campbell had just told Rocko, the borderline delinquent who'd captured her heart, that she couldn't run away from Silver Spring with him, and the disappointed Rocko had stormed off, never to return. The shot was of Sarah running out of the bakery, having impulsively decided to follow him after all, then realizing she was too late and walking off alone, despondent.

Victoria watched as Grace lurched out of the bakery doorway, stripping her apron off and throwing it away. She turned to stare down the street with a stricken look on her face. The actress ran a few steps down the sidewalk, and stopped, crestfallen as she felt the depth of her loss. Grace turned back to the doorway, a hand over her mouth, hesitated, then walked off in the opposite direction, as slow and aimless as an automaton.

A moment after she was gone from view, Sandy called "cut" and the sudden silence that had reigned during the take gave way to a low babble of voices. The director of photography and the camera operator conferred, the man with the mike on his boom talking to a sound technician, various other people whose jobs she couldn't ascertain swarming over the sidewalk, walkie-talkies crackling.

Victoria kept her eyes on Sandy. After a brief word with the D.P., he was huddled with Grace by some folding chairs a few yards away. Victoria would have loved to hear exactly what they were talking about. To her, the performance she'd just witnessed had been fairly effective. Grace seemed very believable. The experience of seeing someone else enact a scene from her own adolescence was still new and strange, though, so she wasn't sure how objective she could be.

Sandy evidently wasn't satisfied with some element and within minutes a second take was ready to roll. Victoria moved her chair a bit closer, watching this next performance with keen interest. The first thing she noticed was a difference in Grace's pace. The girl rushed out of the bakery, discarding her apron in a flurry, but as soon as she started down the sidewalk she slowed dramatically. The stop she made, as she realized what had happened, seemed all the more striking. It was as if Grace had literally absorbed some unseen blow.

Victoria stared, fascinated, as the actress made her way back to the bakery door. This time she put her hand on the door frame, looking as though she didn't know where she was, and stood for a moment, a lost soul staring into space, before she slowly shuffled off.

Victoria's heart gave a lurch as Sandy called "cut." She'd almost forgotten she'd been watching an actress, not a young woman in the midst of real emotional devastation. That had to be a "take." She watched, curious, as Sandy and Grace conferred again. This time she could see that Grace was unhappy about something. She was gesticulating animatedly while Sandy listened and nodded.

A third take began. This time, to Victoria's eye, Grace did everything almost exactly the same, with only one minor adjustment. When she put her hand on the door frame she looked back once in the direction Rocko had gone. It seemed a genuine impulse. Victoria liked it, and couldn't help being moved again by the actress's tearful expression. So she was taken aback when Sandy called a "cut" before Grace had even left the frame. He wanted to do it again.

This time the setup took longer. Victoria wondered if Grace would be able to work herself up like this on cue again. She also wondered how the crew was reacting to the slow progress. When she saw Susan Jacks standing near the sound table, alone for a moment, she ambled to her side. "Is this business as usual?" she asked. "Or is something wrong?"

Susan shrugged. "Sandy doesn't usually do more than three or four takes. But it's early in the shoot. He's probably cutting Grace some slack."

"Oh," Victoria said, nodding, though she wasn't entirely sure she understood.

Susan excused herself, hurrying off to help out Arlyne, the harried-looking production manager. Victoria heard the sound of Grace's laughter and turned, surprised. Grace and Sandy were standing together near the bakery doorway, he, smiling, and she, giggling, as if they'd just happened to meet there for a chat. They didn't seem at all concerned that the cinematic cannon was pointed at them, and the crew was waiting. According to what Victoria had gleaned from Arlyne, time was money on a set—the meter was running and each minute ticking by was theoretically equal to hundreds of dollars.

But as Sandy moved back to his position behind the crane and Grace turned to accept the quick touch-up administered by Kathy, the punk-bouffanted makeupwoman, Victoria surmised that Sandy had been applying psychology. Grace no doubt needed support, needed to feel at ease to go on with what was turning into a problematic performance.

And when the camera rolled again, the actress did seem looser, somehow, both more involved and apparently more spontaneous. When she threw the apron through the door she smacked her hand against the frame, and she held the wounded hand, absently, silently cursing as she continued with the shot. It was an inspired touch, whether intended or accidental, and when Victoria saw tears appear in Grace's eyes, her stomach tightened with concern and sympathy.

Then, when she was back at the doorway after her abortive run down the sidewalk, Grace did something entirely unexpected. Instead of walking off, shell-shocked and miserable, she slowly sank down on the doorstep and sat there, looking a bit like a discarded doll with her legs akimbo. Tears streaming down her face, she stared at the space where Rocko had been.

It seemed ages before Sandy called "cut," and a red light was going off in Victoria's mind. This wasn't in the script. And it was absolutely wrong.

Sarah Campbell—*her* Sarah Campbell—would never have sat down right in front of Pop's bakery and wept. She had much too much pride. Not matter how devastated she was, she'd never allow herself such a public display of emotion, especially right in the middle of Walnut Avenue and definitely not with Pop himself liable to come out and embarrass her even more. It was completely out of character, this new improvisation of Grace's.

Victoria got up, sat down and got up again, arms crossed as if she was physically holding herself back. It wasn't her place to go barging in and tell Grace what to do. But surely Sandy would see that she'd gone off in the wrong direction, wouldn't he? All she could do was watch and wait.

He was calling for another take. Victoria breathed a sigh of relief. There, they were in accord, then. She paced nervously, waiting for the shot to get underway. Grace and Sandy were deep in animated conversation again, and only with a great amount of willpower did she keep herself from joining them. But when the camera rolled once more, she couldn't help sneaking up closer to the crane itself. She watched this take practically peering over Sandy's shoulder.

Grace ran out, tore off her apron, banged her hand (nice work, it still looked accidental) and started after Rocko. She stopped abruptly, bit her lip and then suddenly burst out with a four-letter expletive that would've made heads turn from one end of Walnut to the other. Victoria bit her own lip, barely containing the "No!" she felt like crying out. This take was already looking worse.

Grace went back to the door, and, confounding Victoria all the more, gave a little laugh that sounded on the edge of hysterical. She sank down to the step, sat facing the street with a crooked tremulous smile on her face, and then seemed to notice for the first time that her hand was hurt. Cradling her hand, she began to weep, and sat there, rocking herself and crying loudly.

"Cut! That's a wrap!" Sandy called, and hurried over to comfort Grace, who was still sniffling even as the crew burst into activity around her. Victoria watched him help her up and lead her off to one of the vans, feeling something akin to outrage. How could she? How could he? Not only had Grace departed from the script entirely, her whole approach to the moment had been misconceived and, she thought grimly, putting the blame where it ultimately belonged, misguided.

Sandy was back now, but not alone. He was walking through an impromptu receiving line of crew members, each with his own question to ask about the setup for the next shot. Victoria hung back as long as she could, biding her time. There was a weak but persistent voice in her head telling her that confronting Sandy now was probably exactly the wrong thing to do. But her sense of having been subtly betrayed won out. As soon as he was in the clear, stretching for a moment in the sunlight by the bakery window, she was at his side.

His smiled as he saw her. "Hey, partner."

She couldn't match his breeziness. "Are you done with that shot?"

"It's in the can," he said, nodding and glanced over her shoulder. "We'll need more tracks laid down than that, Marty!"

"You were satisfied with that—with Grace's performance?"

Sandy squinted at her in the bright sunlight. "We got what we needed," he said, and she detected a wary undertone in his voice. But he smiled again. "Next one should be fun. We're shooting a bit with Pops."

Apparently he was determined to shrug her off, and his casual attitude was irking. Victoria glanced around to make sure no one was within earshot, and lowered her voice. "Sandy, Grace was all over the place in that last take. She wasn't even doing the script."

The smile was still on his lips but it had faded from his eyes. "It's not written in stone," he said quietly.

"But . . . It's a very important scene," she said.

He nodded. "That's why we used up so much footage on it," he said, and called over her shoulder. "Hey, Frank, show Marty where that thing's supposed to go, will you? He's off in Kansas somewhere." Sandy didn't meet her eyes when he turned back. "We can talk about it later," he said in a distracted tone, and started to walk toward the center of activity, further down the sidewalk.

"Wait," she said.

He paused, looking directly at her now, and she could feel the tension emanating from him in waves. "What?"

"I thought I was supposed to have a say in these things."

"You will."

"But that shot is in the can, as you put it. And I don't think we're seeing eye to eye on Sarah's character. Shouldn't we talk about this before things go any further?"

"It'll have to wait," he said grimly, looking past her again. "How about after lunch, okay?" He flashed that half smile at her and started to walk away.

"Sandy!" She hadn't meant her voice to be quite that loud. Victoria was suddenly aware that a number of people were looking at her. A pair of technicians in the midst of laying metal rails on the sidewalk for the camera dolly to ride on were gazing up at her. The D.P. had turned in her direction, and Arlyne, headed for Sandy with overbrimming clipboard in hand had stopped in her tracks, looking their way with undisguised alarm.

Sandy faced Victoria again, turning so that his back faced the crew as he spoke to her in a terse whisper. "Meet me in trailer number three. I'll be there as soon as I've taken care of some business here. Go there and wait, okay? *Now*." There was an edge of cold steel in his voice that she'd never heard, and an anger just barely held in check that frightened her with its unexpected intensity.

She nodded, taken aback. When Sandy turned away he was all smiles again. She watched him walk away and throw an arm around Arlyne with a jaunty, lighthearted air. Her heart was beating loud in her ears. Victoria turned, cheeks reddening, and as she looked for the trailers she saw that Grace had alighted from one, and was looking her way with open curiosity.

Victoria made an abrupt beeline for the opposite direction, her heart sinking as she got an inkling of what must have fueled Sandy's ire. Had Grace been close enough to get the drift of their conversation? She fervently hoped not. She was hanging onto that hope as she made her way to the third trailer, marked with a Scotch-taped sign, opened the door and dutifully climbed inside.

She was starting to feel like a schoolgirl who'd just been caught in a bad prank. She fought the feeling as she looked around the trailer's sparse interior. She was right, though, wasn't she? Hadn't Sandy been in the midst of violating the spirit of her work?

Working on her defense, she'd taken a nervous tour of the interior, noting bunk beds, kitchenette and VCR, when Sandy arrived. She steeled herself for facing the director's wrath, but when he sat down on the leatherette opposite her, he was actually chuckling. He looked at her and shook his head. "Oh, boy," he said.

"What?" she demanded.

"Victoria, we left out a few significant details," he said. "Some ground rules to follow."

"I should've made sure Grace was out of earshot," she said stiffly. "I'm sorry."

Sandy shook his head. "She didn't hear you," he said. "But it would've gotten sticky, if I hadn't nipped our little chat in the bud."

"Nip is right. You didn't have to snap at me."

"Sorry. But listen up, because this is important. I sincerely do want to hear whatever you have to say, except Victoria—not on the set. My crew likes to feel like there's only one pair of hands on the helm, and my actors especially can't think for a minute that there's two directors on their case. That's a surefire way to get a terrible performance. Believe me, I've seen it happen on other films."

"I understand," she said, chagrined.

"Whatever we discuss, we do it in private. Write notes. I'll debate character with you from now until kingdom come, as long as it's after the set's shut down for the day. All right?"

"Fine," she said, somewhat mollified. Still, he was sidestepping the issue. "But what about today? We can debate all we want, but what good will it do if the shots you get on film are—wrong? Sandy, that last take—"

Sandy ran his hands through his hair. "Was awful," he said. "Cutting-room floor. Won't ever see the light of day."

"Really?" She stared at him. "Well, wait, not if you like it. I mean, don't overreact just so I'll—"

Sandy looked up at her and laughed. "Victoria, don't be offended, but that decision was made long before you opened your mouth. I never intended to use that take. We're printing number two."

"But—then why—?"

"That's what I was trying to tell you. We got what *we* wanted. But I had to give Grace what *she* wanted." He smoothed his hair back. "Despite appearances, our young leading lady is horribly insecure. She hasn't 'found' Sarah

Campbell yet, to use actor-speak, and she knows it. The irony is, her instincts are right on the money, but she doesn't trust them yet, so I'm giving her some room to experiment.''

What had Susan Jacks said? Sandy was ''cutting Grace some slack.'' ''Oh, dear,'' Victoria muttered. ''I should've known.''

''What I'm doing is letting her get all the *wrong* impulses out of her system. Such as that overwrought tearjerky shtick on the doorstep.'' He grimaced. ''This way, she can feel like she's been given a chance to try out her own ideas. And she'll be much more susceptible to acting out *my* ideas.'' He grinned. ''Especially after she sees that terrible take six of hers when we screen today's rushes. She'll be so mortified by how bad it was, she'll probably underact her way through the rest of the shoot. Which is exactly what I had in mind. The beauty of it is, she'll think she came to it herself.''

Victoria stared at him. ''Sandy, how . . .''

''Cruel?''

''Unbelievably manipulative.''

He nodded. ''Welcome to the magical world of cinema, Ms. Moore, where all sorts of means justify the ends.'' His eyes had a roguish twinkle as he patted her hand. ''Now, you just stick to our amended ground rules and you'll start to really enjoy this shoot. Trust me.''

Trust him?!

Chapter Six

Victoria had always prided herself on being a film buff. For someone who traveled in literary circles, mainly, she was well-versed in the cinematic "classics" and she kept abreast of the latest releases. She liked to think she knew good direction when she saw it, inspired performances, creative camera work. But at dinner with the crew she realized she was way out of her depth.

These guys not only knew everyone and everything, they knew from a completely different inside angle. Stars were referred to by first names and nicknames, and they were judged not necessarily on the basis of their talent, but by on-the-set personality.

Between the central dirty dozen of them, Sandy's crew seemed to have worked on every major film released in the past decade. Names and anecdotes flew fast and furious over heaping plates of pasta from Emilio's kitchen. Emilio, Silver Spring's one bona-fide resident Italian cook, had retired in the years of Victoria's absence, but his son Louis had obviously been given the recipe for Emilio's secret sauces. The food at this modest, red-and-white-checkered-tablecloth establishment at the far end of Elm Street was as good as she'd remembered. Even the burly union members from New York, seated at the adjoining tables, grudgingly admitted the lasagna was better than they expected.

Sandy resided at the head of the main table, talking more than eating, eliciting gales of laughter as he recounted "war stories" about other location shoots in a running monologue. Victoria was a few seats down, between Tom, the D.P., and Jonathan, the shoot's line producer. She was impatient to get some time alone with Sandy, but chastened by her earlier near blowup with him and its aftermath, she bided her time. She concentrated on the pasta and the free-flowing film talk, and went easy on the wine.

As she watched Sandy, handsome face flushed with laughter, hands gesticulating in the air, she realized that in a sense he was still working, still the director. The filming that day had been slow, with its share of annoying technical glitches. Within their first few days of shooting, *Jumpers Creek* was already half a day behind schedule. Sandy, she surmised, was buoying group morale before it even had a chance to sink. There were myriad small dissatisfactions his teammates might have given vent to, but he was heading them all off at the pass.

He didn't neglect her, though. Throughout the meal he caught her eye, letting her know with the slightest of smiles or nods that she was on the bus, one of the gang. But there was more than that in their silent, brief communications. Every now and then she was surprised to find him watching her with a look she couldn't quite decipher. It made her self-conscious in a not entirely unpleasant way. His attention was . . . well, all right, she might as well admit it, arousing.

She'd enjoyed that one kiss they'd shared. Every now and then memories of it seeped in, momentarily making her thoughts go a bit fuzzy as she relived the sensations his brief caresses had inspired. But generally she managed to put it out of her mind, an interlude she'd be smart not to dwell on. She'd stated her case and he'd backed off, and considering the amount of work they had to do together, that was all for the best.

Still, when it seemed that the end of this family-type dinner gathering was drawing to a close, she found herself having to quell an inner rumbling of jealousy. That reporter friend of his had sashayed in toward dessert and Victoria thought she might be stealing Sandy away, her recorder in hand.

Victoria forced herself to ignore their little conference at the end of the table. When she looked up from contemplating the platter of cookies their waitress had deposited, she found Sandy standing by her chair. "Why don't we have our coffee on the porch?" he asked.

Victoria smiled agreement. Only when she rose, cup in hand, did she realize that Catherine was right behind him. "Hi," the redhead said brightly. "You don't mind if I sit with you for a minute?"

"Catherine wants to mercilessly cross-examine you on the origins and meanings of *Jumpers Creek*," Sandy said dryly. "I've explained that you and I have a serious script conference ahead of us, so we're only going to allow her three questions."

"We'll do a full-length when you have more time," Catherine said, following them from the main dining room to the small screened porch in back, where a few empty tables glimmered under waxed-glass candlelight. Victoria caught Sandy's eye as he ushered Catherine forward. He mimed a quick "Sorry, couldn't help it" at her and she flashed him a smile of understanding.

Actually, she was used to women such as Catherine. She'd met a few in her occasional talk-show sorties. They were decent journalists, but not unlike some TV news anchorwomen, they tended to dress up and glamorize themselves. There was some underlying competitiveness involved; you couldn't shake the feeling that they were trying to outshine the celebrities they interviewed.

Victoria noted the cassette recorder's blinking red light as Catherine placed it on the table. She smiled brightly at Victoria as she took her seat. "What's it about?" she asked.

"Pardon?"

"*Jumpers Creek*," Catherine said. "I read it on the plane out, so I have my own ideas, of course. But I'd like to get it from the horse's mouth."

Nice metaphor. Sandy cleared his throat, inspecting his fingernails as he hid a smile. Victoria had a feeling he was enjoying this, the imp.

"It's about learning that it's okay to not fit in," Victoria told her. "And taking your dreams seriously, against all odds."

"Nice." Catherine scribbled something on her pad. "And the title? They're talking about changing it," she added blithely, with a glance at Sandy. "But in case they don't...?"

Sandy met her gaze levelly. Victoria intuited that Catherine had purposely thrown this left curve at her, perhaps precisely to see some sparks fly between book author and screenwriter-director. So she ignored her inner flash of outrage—they're talking about *what*?! and who are *they*?!—addressing Catherine with that practiced cool she was supposed to possess.

"Jumpers Creek is a small stream on the outskirts of town, given that nickname because Tom Flanagan, the town drunk, dived into it and drowned after the war," she explained. "Some foolhardy teenagers still took that dive on a dare now and then, and didn't get badly hurt. You see, it's not really such a dangerous leap. It only looks that way."

"And your heroine, Sarah..."

"Campbell."

"...takes that leap at the end of the book. And you named the piece after the place of her suicide attempt. Why?"

"It's not a suicide attempt," Victoria explained patiently. "That's the point. She only thinks she's trying to end it all, before she jumps. It's when she survives unscathed that she realizes she did it to prove herself a survivor—with nothing left to fear."

"The book is clearly autobiographical," Catherine said. "And you sound like you had an intimate acquaintance with that jump. Is the fearless survivor really Victoria Moore?"

"That's your fourth question," Sandy interrupted. "Time's up."

Catherine met Sandy's smile with one that was more brittle. "He's such a literal man," she said, heaving a sigh as she flicked off the recording switch. "Do you have any free time tomorrow? Maybe at lunch break?"

"I'm sorry, but I won't be around for lunch," she said. She was due to see her folks again, but before the nosy Catherine could press her, she countered, "How about at the end of the day?"

"Great," Catherine said, rising from the table, her disappointment at being so easily dismissed showing beneath her casual air. "I'll look for you at the hotel. Well, talk to you later, S.O.B."

Sandy stoically endured Catherine's ruffling his hair, then began absently brushing it back from his forehead as she departed. "Well done," he told Victoria.

"She was fishing for trouble, wasn't she? Sandy, 'they' are *not* going to change the title."

He shook his head. "You and me, shweetheart," he said in mock Bogart-ese. "We'll stonewall 'em. More coffee?"

"Sure. And who's 'they,' by the way?"

"Studio hacks," he said, waving for their waitress.

"Is there anything else going on around here that I should know about?"

Sandy put his elbows on the table. Chin in hand, he gazed at her, eyes glimmering in the candlelight. "Yeah," he said. "I'm starting to like you, Victoria Moore."

That arousal she'd been working hard to ignore earlier rose within her, unbidden, as his eyes held hers. She saw more than mere amusement in their dark depths. She had to fight the subtle but strongly sensual pull. "Like?" she countered, trying to affect a casual tone. "I suppose that's high praise."

"Oh, yes," he said. "You're good. You learn fast."

"Thank you, kind sir," she returned. "I'm doing my humble best."

They were both silent as the waitress came by with a pot of coffee. Cup refilled, Victoria reached for the cream. Her hand brushed Sandy's as she passed it to him. A shiver ran up her arm from fingertip to shoulder and beyond. Stop that, she told her body. "We have some work to do," she told Sandy Baker.

"Indeed," he said. "Let's do it."

"I have a few questions," she announced, taking out her notebook. Sandy glanced at the pages of small, spidery handwriting she was flipping through and whistled low under his breath.

"A few?" He shook his head and gestured in the direction of their departed waitress with his thumb. "I have a feeling we should've asked her to leave the pot."

SANDY'S SURMISE had been all too accurate. As Victoria settled into her canvas chair bright and early the next morning she blinked blearily at the bustling activity all around her, wondering how many actual hours of sleep she'd managed to snatch.

They'd stayed at Emilio's until closing time, continuing their conference in separate armchairs in the hotel lobby a few blocks away until long after midnight. By the time one yawn too many had propelled her upstairs to her room, they'd only gotten through two-thirds of the points she wanted to discuss, but Victoria was happy to call it a night.

Sandy, astonishingly, had remained in his lobby armchair, making notes on the next day's shoot, and he'd been at the set at least an hour before she shuffled onto it. Did the man ever sleep? She wondered if his veins were full of pure caffeine, as she gratefully accepted a paper cup of coffee from a production assistant.

Today they were behind the bakery, shooting an important scene from late in the film between Sarah, Rocko and Pop Oglesby. In the book, Sarah had three main goals in life: one, to run away from home and move to Paris; two, to prove to her mother she was a writer, by winning the essay contest held by her sophomore English teacher; and three, to lose her virginity to her beloved Rocko.

Rocko was a sophomore at the local college, who was clearly on the dropout trail. Long-haired, leather-jacketed and tough-talking, he nonetheless had a soft heart—and real qualms about taking to bed a girl who was still only a high-school senior. In this pivotal scene, preceding the scene of Sarah's heart-wrenching farewell to Rocko that Victoria had watched the day before, Sarah convinced Rocko to break into the bakery. It was one of the few places they could be alone together, and there, in the back room, she hoped to cajole her reluctant boyfriend into making love to her.

As written in both book and screenplay, only Rocko's surprising self-control and a timely intervention by Pops Oglesby himself had kept the frustrated Sarah from achieving goal number three. In real life, young Victoria Moore had experienced a similar situation with Scoop, her motorcycle-riding Rocko equivalent. but it hadn't taken place at the bakery, and the untimely intervenor had been Victoria's snoopy older sister, "Prissy" Cissy. Pops Oglesby had, however, surprised Victoria and Scoop during some relatively harmless making out behind the bakery once, and had delivered a stern lecture to her in his back office.

The novel's fictionalized version of the events was more dramatic. Victoria liked what Sandy had done with it in his script, though she wasn't sure about the confrontation scene between Pop and Sarah. It had been written with minimal dialogue, depending a lot on subtle eye contact and inference. She questioned whether it would "play," and was curious to see if the actors could bring it off convincingly.

She had no questions about the casting of Rocko, however. As soon as she saw Tom Sanders on the set, Victoria knew this handsome young actor had to be playing Sarah's heartthrob. He was tall, lean, dark-haired and almost too good-looking in a very macho way, with stormy eyes, jutting chin and prominent cheekbones. Even before she saw him in his motorcycle jacket getup she was convinced Tom would be perfect for the part.

Sandy introduced them as the crew readied the first shot of the day. Tom had a slight southern twang in his surprisingly soft voice, and he instantly won Victoria's heart by making an odd but endearing request. "Ms. Moore," he said, with a lopsided grin. "Would you kiss this for me?"

Tom was holding out his copy of the script. She stared at it, momentarily nonplussed. "For good luck," he said. "Do it kinda hard, so I can get a good imprint, okay?"

Victoria laughed. "Good timing," she told him. "I just put on some fresh lipstick." She took the script and planted a firm, full lipsticked kiss on its title page, then handed it back.

"Aces," he said, nodding happily as he admired this unique autograph. "Now I know my first day of filming will go smooth as silk."

"Quite a charmer," Victoria remarked to Sandy as Tom ambled off to wardrobe, script tucked under his arm.

"That's his job, isn't it? I think Grace already has a major crush on him." Sandy smiled. "It'll read really well on camera."

Although it was early in the day, the back of the bakery was deep in shadow. This was all to the good, since the scene as written was supposed to take place after sundown. The D.P. was shooting it "day for night"—a phrase Dave, the assistant cameraman, explained to her, which meant this footage would be darkened, by both stopping down the camera's f-stop and tinkering with the film's developing process in postproduction, to make daylight "pass" for nighttime.

Victoria watched them set up, secretly pleased to see that even within these first few days, the crew was used to having her around. Some were already greeting her by name. She, in turn, was quickly developing a sense of when her presence might be intrusive. When technical foul-ups sabotaged Tom's first take, she withdrew from the filming area.

Pop Oglesby and his grandson were there in the parking lot. Victoria was glad to see that Ed Oglesby, too, had insinuated his shy presence into the company without any resistance. Snapshot camera in hand, he was clearly delighted with his role as secondary set sweeper and occasional coffee "gofer." "They said I can take as many pictures as I want, as long as they're not in the middle of filming," he told Victoria happily. She had a feeling his unofficial job was Susan Jacks's doing.

Victoria returned to the set when a good take was in the can and the tension in the air had abated. The scene's "top"—Grace convincing Tom to jimmy the lock on the bakery's back door—was now complete. The second shot was more ambitious and complex, though, and Victoria observed Sandy rehearsing both actors and crew, with great curiosity.

Pops, who was now sporting subtle makeup for his first film appearance, was to note the unlocked door, then quietly approach the window that looked into his office. The camera would "track" with him, gliding along beside him on carefully laid rails, then pause with Pop as he looked through the window, catching a glimpse of Grace and Tom. The camera was to remain at the window and slowly zoom in, as Pop appeared inside, stepping through the office doorway to silently admonish the guilty teenagers. The reactions of all three characters would be caught in a single frame.

This would require a virtuoso performance by the camera operator as well as good work on the actors' part. Sandy put Grace and Tom in position, then mapped out Pops's moves, going slowly over every juncture of what would be a very long take. It took him forty minutes to get camera, lights and actors synchronized the way he wanted them.

Victoria had never realized how much careful planning and exhaustive work could go into a single shot. There were so many variables, so many things that had to be just right, she began to wonder if Sandy was in over his head. At last he called for a full dry run. The action would be rehearsed from start to finish with the camera, but no film actually running in it.

Silence reigned on the set when Sandy called for action. Pops walked up to the back door, saw the picked lock and walked to the window, the camera following his every move. Finally stationary, it remained a mute witness at the window as Pops returned to the door and quietly stepped inside. Throughout it all, Sandy knelt to the camera's right, his eyes squinting in concentration, his wiry body as tensed as a predatory leopard.

From her vantage point Victoria couldn't see the end of the shot, with its dramatic confrontation, but after what seemed like an eternity of hushed silence, she did see the

D.P. straighten from his crouch over the camera and wave a triumphant okay with thumb and forefinger.

"Is that just okay, or is that movie history in the making?" Sandy asked wryly.

"We're talking cinematography Oscars," the D.P. said.

"Good," Sandy said, and slapped his hands together. "Let's go for take one."

"TAKE *TWELVE?*"

Victoria stared at Arlyne, incredulous. The weary production manager nodded, lips tight. The two of them were standing by the concession table set up at the far end of the parking lot, well away from the shooting area. Victoria had moved her chair down here some two hours earlier, when it became evident things were not going smooth as silk, but she was still surprised and alarmed by Arlyne's report.

"I thought Sandy never went over half a dozen takes," she said. "You told me he usually only needed two or three."

Arlyne sighed, picking moodily at one of the few remaining crullers by the concession table's oversize coffee maker. "That's right," she said.

"What's going wrong now?"

Arlyne gave her a look. She seemed to size up Victoria briefly, apparently trying to gauge how honest she could be. "Well," she said, having decided, "the truth is, nothing was wrong with the last two takes, technically. I thought the performances were fine, too. So that can only mean one thing, and it's something that rarely happens with Sandy."

"Which is—?"

"*He's* wrong," Arlyne said. "And he knows it. He's fiddling and fixing and fussing because the scene just plain doesn't work, at least not the way it's written."

"Oh." Victoria turned to gaze past the vans and trailers in the lot, her heartbeat picking up speed as she pictured

Sandy hard at work back there, but a Sandy she'd never seen, thus far. It was hard to imagine him at a loss for what to do. Funny, but his presence on the set was so commanding, it had never even occurred to her that the man might be capable of . . . well, screwing up.

It was both a disturbing thought and perversely, a reassuring one. He was a human being, after all. She'd been somewhat in awe of the way he'd taken this gigantic apparatus of people and machinery and set it to work like a finely tuned instrument that responded perfectly to his every thought and gesture. Now she had to reconceive her image of him, but in truth, she was relieved.

Relieved until the thought struck her that it was *her* movie of which he was losing control.

She turned back to Arlyne with an anxious frown. "So now what happens?"

"Well, I've done my bit," Arlyne said. "At take ten I quietly suggested to move on to a different shot and return to this one after a rethink." She tapped her neck with a rueful smile. "Maybe you can see the marks from where he handed my head back to me."

"I didn't hear a thing," Victoria murmured.

"Oh, S.O. doesn't have to raise his voice," Arlyne assured her. "He's got eyes like little buzz saws."

Victoria bit her lip, torn. She had an impulse to march right over there, into what was probably an extremely uncomfortable situation, and offer her assistance. She also had an impulse to steer clear of Sandy. Who knew how he might react to her trying to help?

She'd about made up her mind to sit this round out, even though she was inwardly squirming from the frustration of such a self-imposed exile, when she heard Sandy's voice calling out across the lot.

"Victoria!"

She turned, startled, to see Sandy striding right toward her. Strange, but he didn't look upset. In fact, his mood seemed positively sanguine as he came up to the table. "We're wrapping it up," he announced.

"You got it?" Arlyne said. "A good take?"

"No way," Sandy said, and turned back to Victoria. "This one's on you," he said. "Scene needs a rewrite."

"It—on *me*?" she spluttered.

"This is what I get from trying to stick too close to your damned book," he said mildly.

"What!"

"'Scuse me," Arlyne muttered, backing away. "I think I hear one of the techies calling."

"If you've got any plans for dinner, you better cancel 'em," Sandy continued, unfazed by Victoria's open-mouthed outrage. "I got a feeling there's a long night's work ahead of us."

"No, I DIDN'T GET A CHANCE to talk to him about it," Victoria said, head in her hand as she slumped in the hotel lobby's phone booth. "Melinda, I'm amazed I'm still talking to him at all."

"Oh?" Her friend sounded intrigued at the other end of the phone. "You're fighting?"

"No," Victoria said grimly. "We're working. That is, if you can call a couple of bulls butting heads for hours on end work. Anyway, listen." She straightened up in the booth, not wanting to give in to the exhaustion that was threatening to overtake her. "He likes the photo you gave me, and Arlyne thinks you're just what they're looking for in the part. So if Sandy and I haven't murdered each other by the dawn's early light, I'm sure we can get you a definite answer tomorrow."

"Great," Melinda said. "I mean, I can't act, it'll never happen, it was just a sweet idea of yours, but I'm really touched you went this far with it, so—"

"Stuff it, Melinda," Victoria said amiably. "You're going to be cast. I'm sure of it. So stick to that diet of yours and pick out some nice clothes. Your husband's going to find himself married to a movie star. That ought to do away with any boredom in the boudoir."

"Yeah, right," Melinda giggled. "I'll believe it when it happens."

When she was done talking to Melinda, Victoria considered giving Dad another call, but checking her watch, decided against it. When she'd phoned home earlier to apologize for having to cancel dinner with him and Mother, she'd said she'd call back later, since she'd been unable to talk with S.O.B. breathing down her neck. But now it was past eleven, they were probably in bed, and Sandy was waiting for her up in his room, undoubtedly just as impatient now as he'd been before.

"Obsessed," she said aloud. "Crazed. A lunatic. Movies are made by lunatics."

She realized she was talking to herself in a phone booth. Maybe it took a lunatic to know one. With a sigh, Victoria got up and crossed the lobby to jab a finger at the elevator button.

That was the problem, she mused, or at least part of it. Sandy and she *were* alike. They both had strong opinions and were incredibly stubborn about sticking to them. Another writer, she supposed, would have buckled under to the director's relentless attack, but she'd stood firm for, what was it, three hours now? They'd been talking since dinner, and they hadn't reached a compromise yet.

The elevator doors slid open and she stepped inside, feeling a strange mixture of both anticipation and dread. Perhaps she *was* as crazy as he was, because in a way, much as she complained, she was enjoying this battle of wills. And the thought that maybe, just maybe, she might ultimately swing him around to her point of view, kept her energy up. That kind of victory would be too sweet to lose on account of some mere hours of lost sleep.

Third floor. She marched down the carpeted hall, her package of caramel Sugar Babies an illicit but necessary glucose boost in hand. Sandy answered the door on her first knock. "Okay," he said. "I've got it."

"Oh?" Warily, she walked past him and plopped herself down in the velveteen chair by the window, her battle station since they'd begun this summit conference in his suite. "Let's hear it."

"Rocko-Sarah at the door, Rocko-Sarah inside, Caroline coming across the parking lot—"

"You mean Pops."

"Caroline."

Victoria folded her arms, glaring at him as he hovered over the paper-strewn desk. "Sandy, this is where we started. Pops is the one who finds them there. It's his bakery, isn't it? What in the world would Sarah's sister Caroline—"

"Pops isn't working," Sandy interrupted impatiently. "The scene is fine until he walks in. Because it's supposed to climax then, and instead it just stops."

"Maybe you should've cast an actor instead of the real Pops," Victoria said.

"The real Pops is great. It's not the actor's fault. It's the conception of the scene."

Victoria sighed. In the back of her mind, she knew she was fighting him for an ulterior motive that didn't have anything to do with the point they were discussing. But she brushed her vague feelings of guilt aside and doggedly continued. "Maybe the moment isn't led up to properly."

Sandy shook his head. "No. The scene never really peaks because we're missing a bigger and better opportunity here.

Caroline is the one who's most against Sarah fooling around with Rocko, and Sarah has so much more to lose if Caroline—''

"What's she doing there, then?" Victoria demanded. "Why is Caroline showing up at the bakery?"

"She saw Sarah with Rocko. She was…with some friends on Elm Street, later," Sandy improvised, pacing in a circle on the carpet. "And she sees them drive into the lot and puts two and two together, being the snoopy busybody she is—"

"Don't we want to maintain sympathy for Caroline?" she asked, shifting uncomfortably in her seat. "If we make her out to be the villain, she'll just be all bad. The stereotypical bad older sister."

"I don't write stereotypes," Sandy said, frowning. "And she's plenty sympathetic as it is. She can afford to come off out-and-out mean, for once."

Victoria could imagine Cissy seeing *Jumpers Creek* with a scene like this. Victoria would never hear the end of it, that is, if Cissy ever chose to speak to her again. No, they'd have to find a way to make the scene work without "Caroline." "Maybe you have to rethink the shot," she suggested, knowing it was heresy, but starting to feel desperate.

Sandy stopped pacing. He looked at her as she'd taken leave of her senses. "I'm not going to take offense," he told her. "I'm going to assume you're overtired. The shot is perfect. Not that you're in any position to judge such things," he added wryly.

"Add some dialogue?" she ventured.

Sandy expelled a deep breath. "We've been over this," he reminded her, the edge in his voice betraying his growing exasperation. "And I'm still convinced it doesn't matter what words you put in Pops's mouth. It would be a better scene with Caroline Campbell taking his place."

Checkmate. Victoria groaned inwardly. She didn't even want to look at her watch. She was going to have to play her trump card if she had any hopes of seeing her nice clean-sheeted hotel bed before dawn. "I haven't invoked our famous 'fidelity to the spirit of my work' clause yet," she said. "But I think I'm going to have to."

Sandy raised his fists and shook them at the ceiling. After a silent exhortation to whatever invisible gods lurked there, he turned to face Victoria. "I am *not* betraying the spirit of your work," he said. "I'm making your story stronger."

You're turning fiction into fact, she thought, but she wasn't about to say that.

"Look." He plopped down on the carpet at her feet, crossing his legs and running a weary hand through his hair. "Hear me out, just once. Let me tell you how I see this, okay? Listen, don't talk."

Victoria nodded, stifling a yawn. One thing she feared was that she might fall asleep and lose this fight by default, so she sat forward in her chair. "I'm all ears."

"We start with Caroline. She sees the motorcycle. We cut to Sarah and Rocko outside the bakery, they go in. We cut back to suspicious Caroline—"

"Why suspicious?"

"Because. . . She found something. Birth-control pills or a diaphragm Sarah was hiding."

Victoria shook her head. "No way. Sarah wouldn't have been able to get either without being found out."

Sandy waved a dismissive hand. "Something else, then. A copy of *The Joy of Sex* under her pillow."

"*Everything You've Always Wanted to Know About Sex But Were Afraid to Ask*," Victoria supplied involuntarily, since that was exactly the incriminating item, a battered paperback borrowed from a friend that Cissy had ferreted out from under young Victoria's mattress.

"Perfect," Sandy said, with a grateful look, pleased she was at least cooperating. "Okay, so we go with Caroline approaching the bakery. Cut to Sarah and Rocko inside, things starting to get steamy, and then—blam. Caroline arrives. It's the wrath of God. Caroline reads Sarah the riot act. 'What are you doing, how could you, you little tramp!' She's practically frothing at the mouth, and—"

"No, no," Victoria interrupted. "She didn't. I mean, she wouldn't," she added quickly. Oh, no! Maybe if she hurried on he wouldn't pick up on it. "Caroline would say something like . . ." Her voice trailed off. Sandy was staring at her. She could feel the blush rising in her cheeks.

"She didn't?" he said mildly. "Well, then, what *did* she do?"

Victoria was silent, feeling her face sting. Well, there was no use trying to get out of it now. "She just stood there," she said quietly, unable to meet Sandy's eyes. "Which was even worse." It had been one of the most excruciating embarrassments of her life, which was partially why she'd fiddled with it in the retelling, she realized now. She hadn't wanted to relive it on paper. She and Rocko already half-undressed on the couch in Melinda's den, and Caroline towering over them in the doorway . . .

"Didn't say a word?" Sandy prompted her softly.

Victoria looked at him now. "She said . . ." She cleared her throat, then did her best impersonation of Cissy's maddeningly singsong, dripping-with-honeyed-venom voice, "Vicki, sweetheart, it's awfully late to be out on a school night. Don't you think Mother's wondering where you are?"

Sandy gave a rueful chuckle. "Wonderful."

"It was horrible."

"But boy, would it work." He sprang to his feet. "This is exactly what I've been looking for. In fact, it's so good, I'm not even going to get mad at you for holding out on me."

"You can't use that," she said.

"Why not?" he challenged.

"It's—it's too—"

"It's the truth, you mean," he said. "Victoria, forgive me for being blunt, but what do you really want? To be satisfied that your movie turns out to be a contemporary classic, or to be relieved that you haven't ruffled your catty older sister's precious feathers?"

He was right, of course, and she hated him for it. She'd never believed that truth was necessarily *stronger* than fiction. Stranger, yes. But in this case... "All right," she said, between gritted teeth. "You can use Caroline instead of Pops. But you can't use those words. We'll have to paraphrase."

"Deal," he said, and held out his hand.

She stared at him, something in his annoyingly happy expression making her wonder. Yes, she was sure of it, instinctively. He'd known this all along. Somehow, he'd intuited the truth, that it had been Cissy and not Pops in real life. This whole argument had just been another of his famous manipulations. He'd tricked her into revealing herself.

"You're a monster," she said.

"Yes, but I'm a *good* monster," he said, withdrawing his hand. "And I'm going to make the best film that could ever be made of *Jumpers Creek*." He smiled. "The critics may even say it's better than the book."

Victoria felt like hitting him right in his handsome mug. But the fight had finally gone out of her. Instead she merely bared her teeth at him and sank in her chair. Sandy had begun another frenetic pace around the room.

"The intercuts with Caroline'll be easy to shoot," he said, and she knew he was thinking out loud rather than talking to her. "Thank goodness she was on call for tomorrow, anyway. Now we've just got to get this on paper."

"We?"

He was already drawing a chair up to the desk, throwing papers around as he looked for a pen. You wouldn't have thought he'd had less sleep than she had. He was bursting with vitality and energy, the creep, and he looked at her with surprise. "What do you think, I'm going to risk writing up this new scene alone and have you tear into me tomorrow about how wrong it is? No sir. Now, where's that pad?"

Victoria pulled up her legs. Hugging her knees, she curled into the soft chair. Visions of Cissy years ago and an equally outraged Cissy in the future merged into one disquieting image in her mind. She was going to pay for losing this little battle. What was she letting this awful man do to her, to her life? And why did she think he was the most attractive-looking monster she'd ever met? Better not to think at all, she decided, and closed her eyes.

Chapter Seven

Even with his eyes closed, Sandy couldn't conjure up the necessary images. When he was concentrating on setting up a scene this method usually worked, projecting mental pictures against the blank screen of his inner eye. But tonight his imagination's projectionist was apparently taking a nap. In fact, his whole inner-brain brigade—writer, cameraman, director—seemed to be asleep. He was afraid he knew the reason, and it had little to do with exhaustion.

No, someone else was asleep, not in his mind, but in the nearby armchair. Sandy opened his eyes again and sighed, leaning back in his chair. It irked him that Victoria Moore didn't even have to be awake to be a major distraction. And that's what she was, all right.

Don't look at her again, he told himself, but it was already too late. He stared at the sleeping woman, beautiful even with her mouth slightly open and a gentle snore emanating from it. Since when could a snoring woman look so alluring? He was definitely in deep trouble.

Sandy stretched slowly and quietly got to his feet. She looked so soft, vulnerable, with slightly rumpled clothes and somewhat unkempt hair. There was something both endearingly childlike and arousingly womanly about her surrender to sleep. His heart gave a tug as he noticed that she was still diligently clutching a notepad in her lap.

Sandy turned away again. This was bad news. He had a scene to fix on a film that was already a full day behind schedule, and he was standing around mooning over Victoria Moore. Not for the first time in the past few days he mentally kicked himself for having created a situation that might amount to self-sabotage. Shouldn't he have foreseen the consequences? Didn't he know from experience that working with a woman he was attracted to created nothing but problems?

Of course he'd foreseen it, he thought ruefully, scowling down at the blank piece of paper on his desk. He'd known what he was getting into and he'd pretended things would sort themselves out. He'd be in his director-screenwriting mode, and he'd fit time in with the author when he had the time to spare.

Right. Instead, he found that half the time his mind was full of too much author and not enough screenwriting. How annoying.

Sandy sighed again. He wasn't annoyed, he was . . . what was the word? Smitten. Sure, he'd been in love with an imagined Victoria Moore for years, but he hadn't counted on falling for the real one with quite this speed and intensity.

Well, now, wait a second. He wasn't in love with her, was he? He was infatuated, sure, attracted, absolutely, but love? Come on, he didn't have time for love, damn it! He had a movie to make.

Still . . .

Sandy stole another glance at her sleeping figure. Surely she couldn't be comfortable in that chair? She'd probably wake up with a crick in her neck and cramped muscles.

Don't do it, he told himself. Don't even think about doing it. Why drive yourself crazy?

Too late, his feet were already moving across the carpet. He stood over her, listening to some odd thumping nose that he realized, chagrined, was his own heart. What he should do was give her shoulder a gentle shake. But he couldn't. She looked too happy in the Land of Nod.

Instead he slipped the notepad from her lap, and then lifted her, as carefully and gently as he could manage, into his arms. It she woke up now, he'd probably be in for it. But no, she snuggled up to him as if it were the most natural thing in the world, her head resting against his shoulder.

Sandy inhaled the sweet scent of her hair and faintly scented skin. Heady stuff. The feel of her soft warmth against him was overpowering. He concentrated on stepping swiftly across the room to the bed. He lowered her as slowly as he could. She never batted an eye. Probably wasn't used to the sleepless schedule a shoot like this required, he mused. *Now take your arms away.*

His arms were slow to obey. They liked being right where they were. Sandy decided to view this as an extreme exercise in raw willpower. If he could step away from Victoria's warm, sexy body without bending to kiss her sleep-pursed lips, he was truly made of stern material.

Sandy hovered over her, fighting temptation. But when she snored quietly again, the gentleman in him won out. The next time he kissed Victoria Moore he wanted her wide awake. And preferably she'd be the one who was losing a battle with temptation. That would make it all the sweeter.

SHE WAS BEING CHASED through the Glen by some unseen pursuer, but she'd almost lost her way when she tripped over a tree root and went flying through the air.

Fortunately she'd only fallen about a mile or so, through fleecy white clouds that suddenly appeared in place of the woods surrounding her, when someone caught her. She couldn't see his face, but she felt safe in his arms, and didn't struggle as he whisked her to the ground. Then he was gently laying her down on a bank of soft grass, and pulling one of those white clouds up around her like a woolen shawl.

Funny to have clouds this close to the ground. But... Not clouds. Not the ground. She was— Victoria opened her eyes. It took her a moment to comprehend that she was lying on a bed with a quilt covering her, and that it wasn't her own bed. It wasn't her room. Which could only mean...

She sat up, heart pounding, then realized, relieved, that she was still fully clothed, though minus her shoes. There they were, on the carpet near the desk across the room, where one lamp illuminated the still hard at work form of Sandy Baker.

He was hunched over, writing, but must have felt her eyes upon him or heard her stir, because he turned, a sheaf of papers in his hand, and smiled. "Go back to sleep."

Victoria shook her head, yawning. She knew she should get off his bed, but for the moment couldn't move. "No," she murmured. "I have to read your scene."

He crossed the carpet and sat down on the edge of the bed. "Lie down," he directed her. "I'm not done yet."

Victoria frowned. "How did I ..."

"You went out like a light," he said softly. "But I was afraid you'd get a kink in your neck, all huddled up in that chair. So I took the liberty of depositing you here," he went on, smiling as she yawned again. "Which is where you're perfectly welcome to stay."

She shook her head. "No," she said, although the thought of standing up, let alone walking back to her room, seemed like an effort beyond comprehension. "This is your bed."

"I also have a very comfortable couch," he said. "Don't worry about it. Go back to sleep."

Victoria gazed blearily at the couch, then looked at Sandy, who was still smiling gently with—what, amusement? affection? Or...

"No," she told him. Not a good idea, staying here. It was too comfortable and therefore too dangerous. She believed his chivalrous offer about the couch, but still, she had to be on guard where Sandy Baker was concerned. She only trusted him—and herself—so far. "I'll get up," she announced, and drawing upon a reserve of strength she'd only guessed might still be there, she drew the quilt away and slid her legs over the side of the bed.

She was sitting up beside him now and he was shaking his head. "Really," he said. "There's no need—"

"Sssh," she said, and made a mental count. One, two, three—and she stood. Problem was, even though her mind was doing a good impersonation of being awake, her legs were still very much asleep. Victoria tottered, swayed, and suddenly found herself in Sandy's arms.

"Hey," she protested.

"Hey, yourself," he said, and the next thing she knew she was in the air.

"What are you doing?"

"Well," he said, one strong arm under her legs, the other wrapped around her back as he began slowly heading across the carpet, "what does it look like? If you refuse to sleep under the same roof as me, I'll take you back to your room."

The feel of his supple arms around her, his enveloping warmth and the musky mint scent of his after-shave made a heady combination. She struggled to maintain some equilibrium. "But I can walk."

"Apparently not too well," he said. "Here, lean over and pick up your bag."

"I wish you'd put me down."

"I'm having too much fun," he said. "How often do I get to carry a woman around like this?"

"I don't know," she said. He certainly seemed to have had some practice. He wasn't huffing or puffing, and she was aware that the muscles in the strong arms that held her were firm. "But this is really unnecessary."

"Necessity isn't everything," he said. "Your bag?"

He was leaning her slightly toward the desk, where she'd left her handbag. Although she knew she should keep protesting, physical comfort was winning out. In truth she didn't mind being in this position. She had a feeling she might even be able to get used to it. So she reached out and grabbed the strap of her bag.

"There you go," he said, his voice a husky rumble by her ear. "Now I'll just get your shoes."

He was turning, dipping slightly. She held on tighter as he crouched briefly, then straightened up, her shoes dangling from the hand that was deftly cradling her thighs. "Onward," he said, and they started across the room.

"I suppose this is an exercise in trust," she said. "If you drop me, all deals are off."

"I won't," he said. "Get the door, will you? Thanks." Her hand settled back around his neck as they entered the hallway. Nice hair, she noted, not for the first time. It occurred to her that they hadn't had this kind of physical contact since that kiss the other night. It occurred to her that her entire body was alive and tingling with interest in his embrace.

"You do have your room key in your bag?"

"Oh." Flustered, she opened her handbag as he walked steadily down the corridor. When was the last time *she'd* ever let a man carry her around like this? Never, that she could think of. It hadn't been Doug's style. She wouldn't have thought it would be Sandy Baker's, either, but she was beginning to realize you never knew what he might do.

At the moment he was whistling what sounded like an off-key rendition of "Raindrops Keep Falling on My Head." She stole a glance at her watch. Though there was little chance any of the crew members would be coming in or out of their rooms at two in the morning, she watched their progress down the hall with some trepidation. What would Susan Jacks, for example, think about this—or say?

"Are you sure you'll be able to carry me all the way?" she asked him. "You certainly can't carry a tune."

Sandy chuckled. "I know. But it's fun to try."

"You're just a fun-loving fella, huh," she murmured.

"I'm a prince," he told her. "Remember?"

Victoria didn't reply, her eyes still nervously watching for late night hotel guests. Fortunately no one appeared when after a few turns and one half flight of steps later, Sandy paused at her door. "Now you can put me down," she said.

"Key in door," he insisted, still gripping her firmly.

Victoria sighed and leaned forward to unlock her door. Clearly Sandy Baker was a director through and through. He had his own ideas about how every scene should be played, and in this one, the service was going to be more than door-to-door. It was going to be from bed to bed.

Victoria was no longer sleepy. She was aroused and anxious. As he carried her across the threshold she flailed for the light switch on the wall and missed it. He was carrying her across the room in near-total darkness, the only illumination a pale square of moonlight that fell upon the bed. She watched the bed loom up at her, her heartbeat accelerating as he slowly lowered her onto it.

This was where she had to take control of the situation fast, sit up, turn on a lamp and get the man out of here.

So why was she merely lying there as he sat on the side of the bed, his dark eyes glimmering in the dim light as he bent over her, an unlikely Prince Charming hovering by a no-longer-Sleeping Beauty with the promise of an illicit kiss on his lips?

NO KISS blinked a red-neon warning sign in her brain. She put an unsteady hand out as he leaned forward. "Thanks for the lift," she said, her palm resting against his shoulder.

"Anytime," he said. "My pleasure."

He seemed perfectly content to stay where he was. This wasn't a good idea. "I think I'll be getting ready for bed now," she said, her voice a trace unsteady.

"That sounds like a good idea."

"So you can go now," she suggested.

Sandy cocked his head. "You mean you don't want any more assistance?"

"I'm a big girl," she said dryly. "I can get undressed all by myself."

"But it could be so much more interesting if you had some help."

Victoria exhaled a shaky breath. She couldn't deny that she was tempted. She could still feel the phantom imprint of his arms around her, still remember the exciting warmth of his lips against hers. These were sensations she wouldn't mind exploring in greater depth. Not at all.

And it was late. And here they were on her bed, in the dark. And his fingers, playing ever so lightly with one curl of hair over her left ear were sending shivers through her tensed, anticipating body. And...

"I do have a rewrite to do," he said.

Victoria stared up at him. "That's right," she said slowly, thrown off balance. He didn't say anything else, merely looked at her. He was waiting. She realized then that his chivalrous streak ran deeper than she'd thought. He was giving her an out, letting her make the decision. Because clearly all she had to do was say the word, and their relationship would quickly take a very definite turn. For the better or worse, ultimately, she couldn't say. But she could say no, and she liked Sandy Baker even more for giving her the option.

"I guess you should get back to it," she said.

Sandy held her gaze a beat longer, letting her know with the subtlest of smiles that he understood exactly what was going on. He knew she wanted him as much as he wanted her. But there was more to it, she comprehended as he slowly shifted his weight and rose from the bed. He knew *she* knew that once again, he'd been master of the situation.

What an infuriating son of a...

"Sleep tight," he said quietly from the foot of the bed. "You should be able to get a few solid hours before you meet me on the set."

"To go over the rewrite," she surmised.

"Of course," he said. "Pleasant dreams."

Victoria lay there in the darkness after she heard the door shut softly behind him. Her heart was still beating a mile a minute and her whole body was tensed with erotic frustration. Sleep? Dream? She had about as much of a clear shot at either right now as she did at levitating into the air and turning cartwheels on the ceiling.

He really was too much. Had he engineered the whole little episode with precisely this outcome in mind? Aroused and teased her, raising the stakes, deftly manipulating her into wanting him—then making her feel that rejecting him, however right it was logically, was really wrong?

She wouldn't put it past him. Victoria clenched and unclenched her fists, staring at the ceiling. She'd never counted sheep. But now she conjured up a long row of them, each bearing Sandy Baker's face. She stood behind the first one and kicked it right in its woolly white butt. Then the second. Then the third...

CAROLINE CAMPBELL STOOD in the doorway of Pops Oglesby's bakery, her eyes two nasty bright pinpoints of light as she stared at her younger sister in the arms of Rocko DiTurro. "Mother is probably wondering where you are," she said, her voice an icy parody of concern. "If you're not home soon, someone might have to tell her."

She stepped back from the doorway with a haughty toss of her head, then disappeared from frame. Sarah and Rocko remained frozen where they were, staring in silence at the empty doorway. Then Rocko let out a breath and shook his head. Sarah bit her lip and kept staring, a number of emotions—shock, fear, anger and embarrassment—flickering over her features.

There was a pause. Then suddenly Caroline appeared in the doorway again and stuck her tongue out at Sarah. Sarah cracked up in gales of laughter. Rocko turned to the camera with a "these women are crazy" expression, as Sandy's voice could be heard calling out "cut." The screen went blank.

In the screening room there was scattered laughter mingled with applause. "That's the take!" someone called. "Oscar material."

"Yeah, it's academy all the way," Tom said. The director of photography was smiling.

"Number three?" A young woman seated behind Sandy asked, clipboard in hand.

"Number three," he agreed, and patted the shoulder of Alice Jeffries, the actress sitting next to him who'd played Caroline in these rushes, the reels of a prior day's shooting footage "rushed" to the lab in Dayton so they could be screened by the crew.

"You're a terror," Sandy told Alice.

"Thank you," Alice said.

"Really," Grace called over from a few rows back. "If I did have you for a sister, I'd run away from home."

Victoria sat some distance away, still gazing thoughtfully at the now-empty screen hung against the far wall of the hotel's dining room. The film crew had arranged with the management to convert this space into their screening room after ten o'clock every other night, since there wasn't a more formal facility available in Silver Spring. The projector was a rental from the local cinema. It was an ancient but solid piece of machinery stored in the Rialto's basement, used occasionally as their backup when either of the two more modern ones broke down.

A crew member was packing it up now, the night's viewing at an end. The buzz of voices seemed distant to Victoria. She was still deep in thought, trying to sort out the feelings that had left her physically drained, slumped in her seat, her notebook discarded with nary a note recorded.

She'd had no idea, even after being on the set for a week, how actually seeing Sarah Campbell on screen would affect her. She was overwhelmed. There were so many subjective reactions whizzing through her. Surprise at how movie-like it looked, delight at what a fine acting job Grace and the entire cast seemed to be doing, excitement at being a part of this cumbersome birthing process of the film. She was worried, too, about a myriad small details. Line readings that were problematic, shot choices she didn't entirely understand, Alice's larger-than-life and uncannily accurate portrayal of Caroline Campbell, which was almost too much like the real Cissy for comfort.

But above it all, seeping in and underlining every observation, was an awed appreciation of Sandy Baker.

He was doing it. She didn't know how, exactly, but he wasn't only getting *Jumpers Creek* on celluloid, he was getting it right. An indefinable tone was discernible even in those early reels that struck a communal chord in her. She recognized that tone because it echoed her own. There was a look to the town, a way the people acted, a pace and color to each shot's composition that was unlike anything she'd seen in another movie, a quirky playfulness in the air that was very much the world according to Sarah Campbell.

True, there were changes. Certain subtleties from her prose descriptions had fallen by the wayside, but she had to hand it to the guy. He knew what he was doing. And he knew her—the inner, unseen her that had lived then and woven this tale of many years ago. No matter what she might think of the man as a man, as a director he seemed flawless.

"Notes?"

Victoria shifted focus, startled to see Sandy himself at her side. The other crew members were milling around, some already heading for the door. He'd slid into the chair next to hers and was peering over her lap, looking toward her open notebook.

"Oh, hi," she said, closing the book. "No, I don't have any."

Sandy's eyes widened in mock shock. "That can't be. Not a single solitary quibble or nitpicking?"

"Oh, there's plenty of nits to pick," she assured him. "But nothing big."

"I'm stunned," he said, smiling. "And flattered. And badly in need of a celebratory drink. Come on, let's move to the tavern, so you can tell me everything about how much you admire my work."

Victoria shook her head. "Thanks, but I'm going to call it an early night. And besides, you've got a big enough head as it is."

"It can always expand," he said. "Praise from the mouth of the real Sarah Campbell is unique. You sure you wouldn't like just a quick light beer?"

"I'm sure," she said.

"Some decaf coffee? I could really use the company."

Victoria shot him a wry look. Company was one thing Sandy was never without. Even now she saw Arlyne and some of the other crew members lingering near the dining-room entrance, waiting for their fearless leader to rejoin the clan. But Sandy, she saw, was doing what he'd been doing ever since the other night.

Flirting.

"I'm sure you won't end up alone, Sandy."

"Funny, but I always do feel a little bit alone when you're not around," he said, the twinkle in his eyes mirroring the teasing tone in his voice.

"Give it up, S.O.," she said.

Victoria wasn't fond of game-playing, but she considered Sandy Baker a special case. To match wits with a manipulator it was best to have some kind of strategy. So although he'd been showing her in subtle ways that he was still very much intent on seduction—a lingering glance here, a too-casual pat on the shoulder there—she, on the other hand, had redoubled her efforts to feign nonchalance.

Of course, she wasn't entirely sure of her goal. Was it to put him off entirely, or to keep him interested until it was safe to give in to the attraction? But when would it ever be safe? When the shoot was over? Knowing Sandy Baker, he'd probably choose that moment to disappear from her life altogether, the master game player to the end.

"I don't give up easily," he was saying.

"I've noticed."

He glanced past her and waved at the others, miming that he'd joined them later at the Mills Tavern. The tavern was the one bar in town that stayed open past midnight, to a daring 1:00 a.m. on weeknights. Located only a few blocks from the hotel, it had become the official film crew hangout after a long day's shoot.

"Why don't we have breakfast together, then?" he asked.

"Sorry," she said. "But I'm seeing my folks. In fact, I'll probably be a little late showing up on the set."

"Ah. And how are your folks?"

"Fine," she said, guarded.

"Sister still expected?"

"Still doubtful," she told him. "Which is fine with me. I'd rather she didn't meet Alice in the flesh."

Sandy smiled. "What, you're afraid she might ask your sister for some incriminating details about her past?"

"You know, my sister isn't an ogre," Victoria said, frowning. "She's just . . . we're different, that's all."

Sandy nodded, clearly unconvinced. "Then she shouldn't be too offended by Caroline Campbell."

"Sure," Victoria muttered. She'd be offended sooner or later, regardless. Over the years Cissy had conveniently forgotten just how rocky their childhood sibling relationship had been. She tended to gloss over it, as she glossed over anything that was emotionally upsetting. But Alice's portrayal of Sarah Campbell's sister was bound to stir up all kinds of emotional upsets from the past.

"So what did you think, honestly? The scene works now, doesn't it?"

"You know it does," Victoria said.

Sandy nodded. "Yes, but I love hearing it from you," he said, smiling that insouciant smile of his. "But don't stop there, tell me more."

"Sandy . . ."

"You can at least walk me to the tavern," he cajoled, and took her notebook as hostage as she rose from her chair. "Which take did you think was best on Sarah's close-up?"

All right, she'd walk him to the tavern. "They all looked good to me," she admitted.

"Well, of course," he said, with mock pomposity. "They're all good. Sandy Owen Baker is incapable of conceiving a bad shot, you know that. But which one did *you* like best?"

"Not that it matters," she said dryly.

"Everything you say matters," he said gravely. "I mean, even though I'm always right in the end."

She couldn't help smiling as they walked across the lobby. "Were you born this egotistical? Or did it develop over time?"

"I was born with a camera in my hand," he said. "I didn't cry when I entered this world. I turned to the doctor who was hovering over my umbilical cord and said—"

"Cut?"

"That's right." He held the front door open for her. Outside the air was cool, with a hint of night-blooming jasmine. Elm Street was all but deserted at this hour. The darkness between the sparse street lamps left enough detail out of the shop windows for Victoria to imagine time had stopped in Silver Spring. This could have been a night some twenty years back, when she'd walked these streets as a teenager. Now she was a grown-up, supposedly, but it was funny how her younger self had survived. She had the odd sensation that she was out past her curfew.

"I imagine you arrived into the world already taking notes," Sandy said.

"No," she said, idly inspecting the sidewalk as they ambled onward. Hadn't she once put her initials in a newly laid slab somewhere along here? She'd have to check again in daylight. "No, I was a late-bloomer. Didn't write my first novel until I was in the third grade."

"Title?"

"'The Cat That Ate Jefferson Elementary'," she told him. "It was twenty pages of wide-ruled notebook paper, with copious crayon illustrations by the author."

Sandy chuckled. "I'd love to see that," he said. "Is it still in print?"

"Maybe," Victoria mused. "It might be up in the attic with a bunch of my old school stuff. My pack-rat Dad probably never threw any of it away."

"I'm looking forward to meeting them."

"Who? My folks?" She hadn't meant that to come out with such a clear note of alarm, but it had. Sandy slowed as she stopped, staring at him.

"Yes, your folks."

"Why do you want to meet them?"

"Why wouldn't I?" He looked genuinely puzzled.

"Well, I..." Her voice trailed off lamely. She should have expected this. Sandy Baker was obviously determined to shine the bright inquisitive light of his camera-like eyes into every corner of her personal life.

"You should invite them to the set," he said.

"Oh, I will," she said quickly, thinking she wouldn't, unless forced. Maybe he'd forget about it.

"Why don't you ask them when you see them in the morning?" he suggested.

"I'D LIKE TO MEET this Mr. Baker," Mr. Moore said.

Victoria kept her eyes on the cup of coffee in her hand. What was this, some sort of psychic conspiracy? She'd only mentioned Sandy in passing, as she sat at the family breakfast table eating her father's famous blueberry pancakes. But his response had been immediate.

"You would?"

"Sure," he said, pouring himself some extra syrup. "I've never met a genuine Hollywood movie director. Must be a pretty interesting guy."

"Oh, yes," she murmured, unable to keep an ironic edge out of her voice. "He's interesting, all right."

Her father chuckled. "Gotta have something on the ball if he's putting up with your stuff, Missy." He turned in the direction of the kitchen, where Mother was shuffling around, putting dishes away. "What do you say we have this Sandy Baker over for a home-cooked meal, Mother Moore?"

"Who, dear?" Mrs. Moore sounded distracted. She was in what Victoria and Cissy had referred to in childhood as "a mood." Victoria had tried to pay it scant attention when she arrived for breakfast this morning, but she was well aware that her mother was moving slowly and acting cranky.

She recognized the behavior not only from the past, but from her own adult experience.

Mother was acting the way anyone with a sizable hangover would.

"Sandy Baker," her father called. "The man who's directing Victoria's movie."

"If you like," Mother replied. Victoria wondered if she was really listening. She stole a look at her father. Didn't he see what was going on?

Mr. Moore was frowning faintly, absently stirring his already stirred coffee. His eyes met hers for the briefest instant. Before he looked away, Victoria felt her heart give a sickening lurch.

Yes, he knew. She could see the only half-hidden pain in his eyes. And maybe he knew that *she* knew. If so, why didn't he say something? Why wasn't he doing anything?

Why wasn't she?

Victoria looked to the kitchen doorway, listening to the water running in the sink. For a terrible moment she felt nothing but a black kind of hostility laced with despair. She hated her mother's condition, her father's passive acceptance of it and her own feigned indifference. They were all hopeless, the lot of them, including the absent older sister. Cissy was one more link in the support system that enabled her mother to keep on drinking while everyone else pretended there was nothing wrong.

Victoria had to close her eyes and grip the edge of the table with both hands to keep herself from screaming—what, she didn't know—or throwing something in abject frustration. She opened her eyes. Her father had paused in the act of forking another pancake onto her plate and was looking at her with such concern that Victoria couldn't hold on to her anger. The bad feelings abated as quickly as they'd arisen.

"What's wrong?" he asked.

"Nothing," she told him. Nothing that being airlifted right out of this house wouldn't cure. She concentrated on her pancake. It's not your problem, she told herself for the umpteenth time. For the moment, it almost worked. "Good cakes, Dad," she told him, and managed a smile.

"LUCY, YOU GET BACK here this instant! Lucille!"

Mrs. Emerson, mother of Sarah Campbell's best friend, peered over her backyard, a hand shading her furrowed brow. Standing on the rear steps of her house she folded her arms, lips set tight in exasperation. The screen door opened behind her and Mr. Emerson, a strikingly handsome man in his mid-forties, put a consoling arm around his wife's shoulder.

"Let her go, babe," he said. "She's only going over to the Campbells'. She'll come back when she cools down."

"She won't cool down if she's with Sarah," Mrs. Emerson said. "Lord knows what trouble they'll do. I mean, what trouble they'll get *into*. Damn!"

Melinda put her head in her hands, embarrassed, as Sandy called cut. "I'm sorry," she said, her Mrs. Emerson persona discarded. "I'm really sorry."

"No problem," Sandy said, ambling up to the steps.

Ted Danner, the actor playing Mr. Emerson, still had an arm around Melinda. He gave her shoulder a squeeze and murmured something in her ear before stepping back. Melinda smiled gratefully at him, then turned to Sandy. "I'm sorry," she repeated. "I had every line perfect two minutes ago. And then I just—"

"It's the first-take curse," he told her. "Almost always happens. Don't worry about it."

"I was fine yesterday," she said.

He nodded. "Yesterday you didn't have any dialogue. Hey, even the most seasoned pros flub a line or two when they do their first speaking scene. It's traditional."

"Really?"

"Really," he said, and joining her on the step, called out to Tom, who was by the camera. "Are we wide enough here with that lens? Or do you want to try the other?"

Victoria had purposely stayed off to the sidelines while they set up this shot, but now she hurried to her friend's side. She could see the crew would be taking some time out for technical adjustments, and Melinda looked as though she could use a boost.

"Hey, movie star," she said.

Melinda brightened, leaving her perch on the steps to join Victoria in the grass. "God, I was awful," she said, looking nervously towards the camera and crew.

"You were not," Victoria assured her. "Just like Sandy said, it was only first-take jitters."

"If I don't get it right on the next one I'll have to shoot myself," Melinda murmured.

"Not on *my* movie set," Victoria said, and Melinda laughed.

"All right, I'll wait until I get home." Shading her eyes in the late-afternoon sun she surveyed their surroundings. "Isn't this wild? Who would've thought you'd end up turning Mrs. Mapplethorn's yard into a movie set?"

"Certainly not Mrs. Mapplethorn," Victoria said. "Although she seems perfectly happy about it."

The elderly widow was still puttering around the periphery of the set as they watched, bringing another pitcher of her homemade lemonade out to the concession table under the shade of her backyard oak trees. The yard was covered with the mass of snaking cables, carts full of equipment, folding chairs and electrical paraphernalia that were the crew's signature. But Mrs. Mapplethorn, who'd been paid a small but, to her, impressive sum for the use of her yard and house exterior, was apparently taking it all in stride.

It did seem odd to see her familiar back steps the object of such attention, with the huge Panavision camera pointing at them from its tripod mount, surrounded by auxiliary light reflectors.

"Remember when we used to cut across here after school and she'd yell at us from her kitchen window?" Victoria said.

Melinda nodded. "Of course." She smoothed her dress nervously and gingerly touched her bangs. "Tell me the truth. I'm a mess, aren't I?"

"You're beautiful," Victoria said, and she meant it. She'd never seen Melinda look so good. It wasn't that the people in wardrobe and makeup had done anything extraordinary with her. They'd merely smoothed some wrinkles, added a little color to her cheeks and found her a dress that both matched her blue eyes and flattered her ample figure. But when Victoria had first seen her emerge from the makeup trailer, she'd been struck at how well Melinda looked. "In fact, you're practically glowing," she told her now.

Melinda smiled. "You're as bad as Ted is."

"Ted? Oh, your 'husband.'"

"He's a real flatterer," Melinda said. "He says the most outrageous things to me, and he's such a good actor I can almost believe him." She smiled. "He's cute, don't you think?"

"I suppose." Victoria glanced back toward the concession table. "And where's your real-life husband?"

"Mr. Scowl?" Melinda's features darkened. "He won't be gracing us with his presence today, thank goodness."

"Uh-oh," Victoria said. "Has it gotten that bad?"

"Worse," Melinda murmured. "Jim's really been a royal pain ever since I got this part."

"But I thought you said he was pleased for you."

"He was, initially. But as soon as I had to ask for a few favors around the house..." She shook her head. "It's been like a cold-war zone. My whole family's ganging up on me. Just because for once in my life, I'm the one who needs to be given some extra attention!" She rolled her eyes.

"They're not being helpful?"

"Hardly," she said. "Well, Jennifer's been good. She was jealous at first because *she'd* like to be in a movie, but at least she helped out with the laundry, in exchange for getting a crew pass, so she and a friend could visit the set. But Jim's impossible. We're barely speaking."

"That's terrible."

"Maybe it was only inevitable," Melinda said.

"Melinda?"

The women turned as Ted Danner came striding over. Melinda immediately dropped her troubled expression. "Hi, hon," she said, acting the wife.

He smiled. Perfect teeth, Victoria noted, and though she knew she was being paranoid and overprotective, she was already on her guard against this clearly flirtatious actor. He was giving Melinda a little hug that struck Victoria as a mite too familiar.

"I thought you might want to run through the lines once more before we go on camera again," he said.

"Good idea," Melinda said. "Are you sticking around?" she asked Victoria.

"Are you kidding? I wouldn't miss this performance for anything."

"She's going to be great," Ted said.

"She *is* great," Victoria told him.

"She's a natural," Ted agreed.

"Oh, stop," Melinda demurred.

"Yes, she is," Victoria agreed. "So watch out, Ted. She'll be upstaging you in no time."

"Oh, that's fine with me," he said. "I can take it." And taking Melinda's hand, he led her off toward the trailer that was labeled TALENT.

Melinda shot Victoria a look over her shoulder that was all too easy to translate. It was one she remembered from their high-school days, and it said: this guy is a total hunk. Victoria watched them move off with a feeling of distinct unease.

Had she done exactly the wrong thing, getting Melinda involved in this shoot? She'd wanted to help her friend save her marriage—not sabotage it!

Discomfited, she went over to try a glass of Mrs. Mapplethorn's lemonade. The gray-haired, small and wiry spinster flashed Victoria a bright dentured grin as she approached. "Victoria Moore," she said. "Who'd have thought you'd turn out to be such a somebody?"

Victoria smiled, aware that this was truly a back-handed compliment, but understanding that the old lady did mean well. "Great lemonade," she told her, and quickly moved back in the direction of the set.

She watched the next take, which went without a hitch, and she felt a surge of pride as Sandy called out an enthused "great" after his usual cut. She also noticed that Ted Danner was still being awfully effusive—and physical—in his congratulations to his costar. Victoria was watching the two of them uneasily as they horsed around on the steps, waiting for Sandy's suggested "safety take" to get underway, when she heard a familiar voice at her ear.

"So this is how they make movies, eh?"

"Dad!"

Victoria turned to face him with mixed emotions. She was surprised to see him there, relieved that Mother wasn't with him, not that she would've expected her to show up, and instantly apprehensive. Sandy would see them together, no doubt, and one thing would lead to another. Well, she supposed it was unavoidable.

"Evelyn Mapplethorn hasn't had this much fun since her husband died," he said, a twinkle in his eyes as he surveyed the scene. "Isn't that Melinda over there?"

"Yes, and she's doing really well."

Her father nodded, absently taking out his familiar bag of tobacco and a rolling paper. "She'll probably have to wear a new hat size by the time she's through."

Victoria was afraid she agreed. "How was work?"

"Can't complain." Dad was deftly rolling his cigarette, one-handed, while he felt in his shirt pocket for a match. "Sold an old rocker for twice what it's worth, to one of those college students who wouldn't know a real antique if it fell on his head."

At an age when many other men might have enjoyed retirement, Mr. Moore was still running the antique shop he'd founded in Silver Spring. After a few rough years, it had begun to turn a respectable profit, with a steady clientele made up of the collegiate crowd and people from nearby Dayton who liked to hunt through outlying towns for antique "bargains."

"You're just in time to see them do a take," Victoria told him.

Mr. Moore lit up his cigarette, flicked the match away and exhaled, nodding. "All this rigmarole, just because you wrote up a bunch of stories about our little town," he said, and then leaned in, speaking softly at her ear. "I'm proud of you, Victoria."

She knew it was silly, but she couldn't hold back the tears that welled up in her eyes as he patted her shoulder. Blinking furiously, for the Moores were not known for open displays of affection, she kept her gaze fixed on the steps a few yards away, where the cameraman was still fussing with the light reflectors.

Her father gave a sort cough and cleared his throat. Victoria restrained her habitual reflex criticism of his smoking. He was long past listening to her about it. "Got a call from your sister," he said.

"Oh?"

"Looks like she'll be joining us, after all."

"Oh."

"Maybe by the end of next week," he said, probably picking up on the subtle downward inflection in her voice, but choosing to ignore it. "So I thought maybe I'd go ahead and invite your Mr. Baker for a meal—just the four of us," he added, as Victoria turned to look at him. "Before it's a crowd at the homestead, with your little nephew there, and all."

He was good at this, she realized once again. Her father knew more than he ever let on, and had become adept at juggling the various unspoken currents of competition and ill-feeling that swept through the family network. He was letting her know, with this particular plan, that he didn't want Cissy stealing any of her limelight any more than she did, and she loved him for it.

"Okay," she said, and squeezed his arm. "That sounds like a good idea."

"Fine," he said, and took another puff at his cigarette. "How about tonight, then?"

"Tonight?!"

"Here comes your Mr. Baker now," her father said. "Why don't you ask him?"

Chapter Eight

"Some more green beans, Mr. Baker?"

"Sandy, please," he insisted. "Yes, they're delicious." He held out his plate.

Mrs. Moore smiled as she ladled the vegetables onto his plate. "They're fresh, aren't they. More corn?"

"Martha, you're turning into a food pusher," Mr. Moore said. "He's had two ears already. The poor fellow's going to bloat."

"Well, at least someone around here has a healthy appetite," Mrs. Moore said, glancing significantly at Victoria's plate.

"I'm dieting," she murmured.

"Not that she needs to," her father noted, and he gave Sandy Baker a conspiratorial wink.

Sandy smiled. Everyone seemed highly amused, even Mother. Victoria should have been happy, but she didn't know how she felt, exactly. All she knew was that she still couldn't get used to this.

Every time Victoria looked across the table and saw Sandy sitting there, she had to resist doing a double take. Everything in this room, from the familiar tablecloth, silverware and china to the faces of her mother and father was more or less the way she always remembered it. But Sandy Baker, sitting in the chair that had been Cissy's place at the dinner table, that was an element that did not compute.

He, on the other hand, seemed maddeningly at home here. He'd won Mother over almost immediately, when he arrived with a bouquet of flowers. You would've thought she'd never seen lilies before in her life. Victoria had been sure Mother would treat the young director with benign indifference. Instead, by this last round of their meal, she was relating to him more like an adopted son.

Her father was already a certified member of the S.O.B. fan club. Only minutes after she'd introduced the two men on the set that day, they'd performed an instantaneous variation on age-old male-bonding rituals by discussing the status of the American and National Leagues, agreeing that the Mets were not the team they used to be and that the Cubs looked very likely to win the pennant this year. Sandy had clinched his status by bringing over a hearty burgundy that Dad had never tried but had always wanted to.

In short, Sandy Baker had sauntered right into the Moore household with all the ease of a native of Silver Spring. Not only had he been welcomed with open arms, he seemed intent on making the Moores feel like old friends. Victoria had worried that the cosmopolitan director would find her family hopelessly dull. Instead, he evinced fascination with every anecdote her father told and every editorial comment her mother added.

The whole thing was unreal. She'd been pleased, initially, that there'd been hardly any awkwardness when he arrived. Mother had a telltale flush and brightness in her eyes that revealed she'd had a little pick-me-up while preparing dinner, but for once Victoria hadn't minded. At least she'd be in a decent mood. But by the time they were finishing second helpings and talk of dessert was in the air, the atmosphere in the Moore dining room was downright jubilant. Mother was favoring their guest of honor with the kind of pleased attention she usually only unveiled for Cissy's husband.

"I hope everyone's been cooperative downtown," she was saying now.

"We haven't had any real problems," Sandy said. "There's always a traffic jam in the late afternoon, when school's out and the kids come nosing around the set, but the police have been very helpful. So have the shop owners on Elm and Main."

"Well, of course," Mr. Moore said. "They're hoping they'll get their windows in your picture."

"And they may," Sandy said. "One of the best things about shooting here is, that even though it's a period piece, set dressing's been minimal. Most of the same stores are still in business from some twenty years back."

"No, sit, Mother, I'll do that," Victoria said, rising as her mother did, to clear the table.

"I'll take care of the coffee, then," she said. "Sandy? Are you a coffee drinker?"

"Yes, ma'am," he said.

"I know Victoria will want hers," Mother said. "Sam?"

Her father nodded, hand feeling for his tobacco pouch in the pocket of his shirt. "'Course anything you set up special now'll come down when your crew leaves town. What happens if you need to do anything over again?" he queried. "Seasons change here and your film's whole look'll be shot to blazes."

"Well, we're taking extra care with the exteriors," Sandy explained. "Tom, my director of photography, is doing some second-unit stuff, taking additional shots around town so we're more than covered . . ."

Victoria listened to the two men talk with half an ear while she cleared the table. She was trying to keep an eye on Mother without being too obvious about it. But when she lingered at the sink, starting to wash a dish, her mother shooed her away. "You go on back in," she said.

Victoria returned to the table with the percolator and coffee accoutrements. Was that the telltale click of of the kitchen cabinet behind her? It was hard to tell with the sink water running, but she thought she could hear her mother's too-familiar ritual in progress. Yes, there was the clink of a glass against the counter.

She took her seat with some foreboding. Her father, she noticed, was making a last round of their wineglasses with the remains of Sandy's burgundy. She watched him pour a splash of wine into Sandy's and her glass. He hesitated over Mother's empty one, dashed a desultory splash into it, and then finished off the bottle on his own.

"Here we are," Mother announced, reentering with a pie on a platter. Her smile was positively buoyant. Great, Victoria found herself thinking, an apple pie. It's the end of a perfect meal in a typical American home. Mom's half-crocked, but hey, let's not pay it any mind.

She stole a glance at Sandy, wondering if he'd picked up on the now-palpable glaze in Mrs. Moore's eye. He didn't seem to notice, as he smilingly accepted the duty of honorary pie cutter. Watching him, she felt a sudden, irrational surge of gratitude.

She knew that many other men in his position wouldn't have even bothered with such an innocuous domestic evening. She was well aware that he was still being deluged with the usual nonstop logistics' questions from various crew members about the ongoing shoot, that he had rewrites to work on, and storyboarding that had to be ready by morning. But he showed no signs of impatience. He hadn't glanced at his watch once, in all the time he'd been here. He'd somehow managed to put all his other preoccupations out of his mind, or was at least doing a stellar job of faking it.

He certainly had a sweet side. She smiled at him as he held the knife against the pie, offering her a gargantuan slice. "Oh, sure," she said, then gasped as he mimed actually going through with it.

"A sliver," her father prompted. "She always wants a sliver."

Sandy measured accordingly. Victoria realized she was still smiling as his eyes met hers and held them an extra beat. Her heart seemed to swell within her as he held the plate out and she looked away, concentrating on the plate as she murmured a thanks. Odd. She'd felt...

Her mind scurried away from the words that loomed up. Let's call it affection, she decided, and what was wrong with that? Sandy had some very endearing qualities, and he'd been demonstrating them amply this evening. Why shouldn't she have an affectionate feeling toward the man?

"Don't tell me this is homemade pie," he was saying, lips sticky from his first taste.

"I wish I could say it was," Mother admitted. "But it comes from Mrs. Peel's bakery on Maple Street. Scrumptious, isn't it?"

"That's the word," Sandy said.

"You know, you're awfully young to be doing what you do," Mrs. Moore said thoughtfully, watching him attack his pie slice.

"They all start young nowadays," Mr. Moore said. "Straight out of film school, isn't that right?"

"I never went to film school proper, actually," Sandy told them.

"Ah, you were a natural," Mrs. Moore surmised.

"I was making Super-8 epics when I was in junior high," Sandy said. "Great way to meet girls."

"I'll bet." Mr. Moore chuckled, puffing at his cigarette.

"Well, you can joke about it, but I know that your job isn't an easy one," Mrs. Moore said. "According to what one reads in the magazines, it takes quite a lot of effort to get one of these movies completed. Isn't that so?"

"Some are tougher than others," Sandy said. "It depends on whether you're trying to do it for love or money or a combination of the two."

He went on with a thumbnail discourse on the practical pitfalls and politics of moviemaking, but Victoria didn't really pay much attention. Instead she found herself watching her mother and fighting off a feeling of incredulity that slowly gave way to irritation.

Since when had Mother ever evinced any interest in the movies? Or any kind of artistic endeavor, for that matter? Victoria knew that her mother was extending herself, giving their guest special attention, but even as she acknowledged and appreciated that, it set her teeth on edge.

When was the last time Mother had asked her one serious question about *her* work? For all her interest or awareness of the craft of writing, you'd think that Victoria's talent was either too ephemeral or too dull to be taken seriously. But she was as attentive to Sandy Baker as if he'd been a nuclear scientist whose daily job was keeping the world safe for democracy.

"Honestly," she was saying now, shaking her head with a look of undisguised admiration. "Sam and I wouldn't ordinarily think about any of what you're saying when we go to the movies."

"Well, if a director's done his job right, you shouldn't be doing anything more than sitting and watching, laughing or crying," Sandy said.

"And buying plenty of popcorn and soda," Mr. Moore added.

"That's right," Sandy said. "If you ever do start noticing the kinds of technical things I've been talking about, then I guarantee that movie's in trouble."

"'Pay no attention to that man behind the curtain,'" Victoria said.

Sandy nodded, shooting her a grin. "Exactly."

"Excuse me?" her mother said.

"It's a quote from *The Wizard of Oz*," Sandy explained. "You know, when Dorothy discovers that the big, terrifying wizard's head is only a film projection—there's some guy pushing a lot of buttons in his curtained booth to conjure it up?"

"Oh, yes," Mr. Moore said. "And the man behind the curtain makes the wizard say, 'Pay no attention to the man behind the curtain.'" he laughed, and looked at Victoria. "I see. So that's Sandy Baker, is it—the guy pushing the buttons, whom you're not supposed to see?"

"It's really a perfect metaphor," Sandy said.

"Well put, Victoria," Mr. Moore said.

"I'm good at metaphors. I'm a writer," she said sweetly. "Remember?"

There was a moment's silence as they all looked at her, perhaps sensing the edge in her voice. Then Mrs. Moore smiled brightly. "More coffee, anyone?"

A short while later they were gathered on the front porch. "A pleasure," Sandy said, shaking Mr. Moore's hand. "And don't be a stranger on the set, all right? Any time you want to stop by, consider yourself welcome. I'll see that you're put on the permanent guest list."

"Thanks," Mr. Moore said. "I may take you up on that."

"But don't you be a stranger, either," said Mrs. Moore. "You'll have to come back again."

"Mother," Victoria said. "Sandy's a very busy man."

"No, I'd love to," Sandy said.

"Well, you must," Mrs. Moore insisted. "Victoria's older sister will absolutely pitch a fit when she hears that we had you all to ourselves for a night. I know she'll want to meet you, too."

"Good night, honey." Her father gave Victoria a smooch on the cheek. "We'll see you tomorrow?"

"I'll try," she told him, giving his shoulder a squeeze. She planted the requisite daughterly kiss on her mother's cheek and stepped back, forcing a smile. "Great dinner," she said.

"Best I've had in Silver Spring," Sandy added.

"You're an excellent liar, Sandy Baker," Mrs. Moore said, but she was beaming as her husband slipped his arm around her shoulder. "Take care!"

"Good night!" Victoria called out, and she and Sandy walked down the path toward his car. When they reached the street, she turned back to wave a goodbye again, and watched her parents move back into the house, the front door swinging shut behind them.

Once the front door closed, Victoria put a hand to her head. She could feel all the tension that had been building up inside of her threatening to bring on a major headache. Sandy, who had opened the car's passenger door for her, gave her a concerned look.

"You all right?"

Victoria nodded, willing the little throbs in her temples to abate. Relax, she commanded herself. You got through it and it's over. "It wasn't that bad," she murmured.

"No," Sandy agreed. "In fact, I had a good time. Are you sure you're okay?"

"I'm fine." She looked at the open car door, then past it to the leaves that were swirling in a windswept circle by the curb. "But you know, I feel like walking, if that's all right with you. I could use some air."

"Sure." Sandy shut the door. "Would you mind company? I should probably try to walk off some of that apple pie."

"Okay," she said, though she'd actually assumed he'd drive back into town so he could return to work. "I was just planning to take a short hike—"

"Through the Glen," he said. "I figured as much."

He joined her on the sidewalk and they walked in silence down the block, stray leaves blowing across their path. "Your father's a funny man," he commented. "In a good way, I mean. Good-humored."

"Yes, he is." Amazing that he kept up such good spirits after all these years living with— Stop it, she thought. She hugged herself as the wind rose and they crossed the street. "He liked you a lot."

"You think so?"

"Absolutely." She was surprised that he should seem to really care. "He told you some of his favorite terrible jokes. Those are reserved for favored guests, only."

"I see. Well, I'm glad I made a good impression."

"Since when is the independent-minded Sandy Baker so interested in what people think of him?"

Sandy smiled. "He's not just people. He's your father. And to tell you the truth, seeing you together made me a little nervous. You're a lucky woman."

Victoria shot him a curious glance. "Really?"

"It's obvious he truly cares about you and everything you do. He's proud of you and he's not afraid to say so."

Ah. She remembered now Sandy's earlier comments about his estrangement from his own dad, when they'd talked by the creek a week ago. Had it been that long? Here was the entrance to the Glen. Force of habit guided her feet to the same path they'd taken then, that she'd walked so many times alone in years gone by. Sandy followed without comment.

She was well aware that he was being careful around her. She intuited, by his silences, that he was giving her the room to work out whatever feelings the evening had brought up for her, and she was grateful for that, even though a part of her still resented his solicitude. She stifled a sigh as they walked down the winding path.

"Well, at least one out of two cares," she said.

"I thought your mother seemed very interested in what we were doing."

"What *you* were doing," she corrected him. "In all the times I've been there since I arrived, she's hardly asked me a single question about the shoot."

"Maybe she's a little intimidated," he suggested.

"Are you kidding?" Victoria scoffed. "Intimidated by what?"

"By your success."

"I'm not a success," she corrected him. "Not by her standards. No, she probably thinks it's only some bizarre fluke that a legitimately successfully person like yourself has taken an interest in my work."

"Do you really believe that's how she thinks?"

"I *know* how she thinks," she said.

"You don't seem to talk to each other much," he noted.

"We don't have to. We don't want to," she added, feeling her bitterness rise but feeling powerless to stop it. "What's there to say? I don't want to hear her tell me she'd have been happier with only one daughter, and she doesn't need to hear that I'd have been happier with another mother."

Sandy let out a low whistle. "It's that bad?"

Victoria sighed again, pushing a bough aside as the trail twisted around a bend. "You've read the book," she said wryly. "You're making the movie. You tell me."

"But that was adolescence," he said.

"True. And don't get me wrong, it's not like we're at war. We have a truce now, we stay out of each other's way."

"You don't sound entirely happy about it," he said quietly.

"Oh, it'll do." She kicked absently at a rock in their path, listening for the distance rush of water from the creek. She felt embarrassed now that she'd revealed such feelings. "I guess I do sound like the rebellious daughter, still," she said. "And from her point of view, I'm sure I was no picnic to raise."

"Probably not."

"Which is why I'm not in a big hurry to have any. Kids, I mean," she said. "Chances are I'd have a daughter just as resentful as I am. And I'd probably make the same mistakes she did."

"I never knew you had such a bright and optimistic outlook on life," he observed dryly.

"Oh, don't listen to me," she said. "I only get this way after I've seen too much of my family. I always come out of there feeling happy I'm not raising one."

"This is happy?"

She paused to look at him, and seeing his genuinely perplexed look in the dim moonlight, couldn't help laughing. "I'll stop talking now," she said. "Why don't you tell me about tomorrow's shoot?"

Sandy shook his head. "I'm not letting you off the hook so easily," he said. "Are you really that sure you don't want to have children?"

Victoria shrugged. "Well, here I am in my mid-thirties. And so far I'm the proud mother of five bouncing baby novels. That seems to suit me fine."

"Seems to," he murmured.

"All right," she admitted. "There are definitely times when I feel I'm missing something. Seriously? Every now and then I see one of my friends with a newborn and I have a severe attack of longing for what she has. But I'm a single woman, and I'm selfish. I like having the time to do my work."

"If you weren't single," he said, "You might have someone around who could share the time burden."

"Now we're talking fantasy."

"It could happen any day," he said.

"Oh, yes," she said. "Anything could happen."

"Well, at least you allow for the possibility," he said, and she could hear amusement in his voice. "Does this heretofore-undiscovered strain of cynicism in Victoria Moore extend to her views on marriage?"

"If you mean, do I think marriage can work, I'll have to plead ignorance," she said. "You tell me."

Sandy cleared his throat. "This conversation is certainly getting cheerier and cheerier," he said. "Maybe I should plead the Fifth."

They'd reached the fork in the path. One way led up up to the bridge above the creek, and other followed the stream's bed southward through the Glen. "High road or low?" she asked him.

"I think we'd better stay close to the ground," he said. "Any more of your grim pronouncements on marriage and family and I may join the legacy of creek jumpers."

"Go ahead, make fun of me," she muttered, setting off down the path. He followed close behind, slowing as she did when they reached the bank proper. They both stopped in their tracks to watch the moonlight turn the dancing water to silver.

"Gorgeous," he said.

"Yes."

Sandy turned to face her, his expression sober as his eyes found hers. "Look, after going through my divorce I'd hardly be the one to proselytize about how everything works out for the best in this best of all possible worlds. You think I don't have my doubts about dreams coming true, or things ever working out the way you want them to?"

"I'm sure you've had doubts," she said. "Any reasonably intelligent person would."

"Believe me, I've had my bouts with depression about all this. They'd make your mood tonight look positively gay."

"I'm sorry," she said. "I didn't mean to get on your case. It's like I said, I'm only out of sorts because of dinner. I'm not really like this, usually."

"Good," he said. "Because I know you know better."

His eyes were searching hers with an intensity that was a bit unnerving. She felt as if he was looking right down into the center of her. "Do I?" she asked softly.

"Of course. Because reasonably intelligent people, to use your terms, know that it's possible to learn from one's mistakes. We're none of us doomed to repeat the failures of our parents, or our own."

"I suppose," she said.

"You suppose?" He looked away from her at last, and shook his head with a rueful air. "Boy, I thought I was a tough cookie."

Victoria bent to pick up a long twig. She inspected it, her insides churning with mixed emotions. Somewhere within her she knew she felt the way he did. At least, she very much wanted to. But it had been easier to hide behind a veneer of detachment, to disbelieve in dreams, to not risk putting her emotional life on the line. It was a ploy that had been working for her, hadn't it? That coolness and maturity?

Not entirely. Because standing beside Sandy now, gazing at Jumpers Creek, she could feel the stirring of feelings she no longer wanted to ignore. She wasn't sure if she could, anymore. And it was all his fault.

She noticed a log a few yards away, stepped over to it and took a seat facing the bridge. "Oh, I'm not so tough," she murmured.

Sandy joined her on the log. He nodded. "I know."

Victoria smiled. "You *think* you know a lot of things."

"Well, I know people can change," he said. "I have. You have."

"Maybe I've always been like this."

He shook his head. "I read the book, remember? No, you've been working overtime to finesse the Sarah Campbell out of you. And to tell you the truth, I kind of miss that younger you."

Damn the man. Why did he always seem to get right at her, like the zoom lens of a camera swooping in for a close-up? "And which me is that?" she challenged.

"The vulnerable one," he said. "The dreamer who was unafraid to dream. The kid so full of feelings she couldn't even think about trying to control them all."

Victoria's throat felt tight as she tried to speak. "She's still around," she admitted.

"I know," he said, them smiled as she shook a fist at him.

"If you say that one more time—!"

"Sorry. I *suspected*," he corrected himself.

"Listen, that young Victoria was also hell on wheels," she said. "You should be happy I've trained her to stay put and out of trouble."

"There, you see?" He smiled again. "You're a living testament to people's ability to change."

"Okay, fine," she said. "I never said people couldn't change for the better—or the worse. I was only making a case for history repeating itself, when it came to raising a family. Hey, any psychologist would back me up on that."

"Any psychologist would tell you that the kind of family history you're citing only repeats itself if it's ignored or misunderstood. If you want to break out of a pattern, you can. You just have to see it first."

"Seeing is one thing. Doing something about it can be a lot harder than you'd think."

"Maybe you haven't tried hard enough."

Victoria looked at him, frowning, feeling her defensive hackles starting to rise. "What exactly are we talking about, here?"

"I think we're talking about you and your family."

"This is beginning to sound like a therapy session."

"That's not such a terrible thing," he said mildly. "Has she ever had any?"

"Who?"

"Your mother."

Victoria stared at him. "She'd never go in a million years," she said. "She doesn't believe in it."

"You've asked her?"

"No, but—"

"Why not?"

Victoria's stare was turning into a wary glare. "I don't even see my mother more than once a year, usually," she said evenly. "It should be pointless."

"You mean you're content to let things go on the way they are?"

"If you're referring to my mother and me and our non-relationship," she said, "I'm not entirely content, but I'm accepting of it."

"I see." He looked away, his brow furrowed. "You're more accepting than I'd be."

She could feel her earlier irritation returning, and it was getting hard to keep this conversation on an even keel. "Aren't you the one who never got around to talking to your father?"

He nodded, his face shadowed beneath the whispering boughs. "Yes, and I've regretted it for years, now."

"But then you must realize it's not the simplest thing to do," she said, "to try turning patterns around that have been going on in a certain way for your whole life. Well, maybe I'm selfish or too self-absorbed, but Sandy, I don't have the time or patience to deal with this. Not now."

"Maybe you're not being selfish enough," he said quietly.

"What do you mean?"

"I mean it has an effect on you. I've never seen you so upset, if you want to know the truth. The way you were at dinner, tense and wound-up—"

"It was a stressful situation."

"Well, sure, but you said yourself that not being able to communicate with your mother made you unhappy."

"I did?"

Sandy sighed. "Maybe not in those words, but you know it's true."

"Okay, okay," she muttered. "I know I'm being difficult."

"Not difficult. Defensive."

"All right, defensive," she said sharply.

Sandy chuckled. "Look, I'll just say this one thing and then I'll stop butting into your life and leave the whole subject alone."

"Is that a promise?"

"Yes. The point is, if you don't want to better your relationship with your mother for *her*, do it for *you*. So you don't have to wake up some awful morning years from now thinking, if only I'd tried. Or I should've done this, or could've done that." He paused, holding her troubled gaze. "And yes, I'm talking about my own mistakes. But that doesn't mean it isn't good advice."

"Are you done now? Is that it?" she asked.

"For the moment," he said.

"Honestly," she said, exasperated. "How did we get into this conversation, and why?"

"You had a psychosomatic headache," he said.

Victoria glared at him, snapping the twig she'd been absently playing with. "Yes, and it's coming back," she said.

"Sorry," he said. "I'll stop talking now."

He was true to his word. For a few minutes they sat there in silence, with only the rush of the creek and the wind in the trees as accompaniment to their thoughts. Why *was* she being so defensive? She really should be touched by his concern. Victoria cleared her throat.

"Listen, I'm sorry," she said. "I know you're only trying to help. And I appreciate it, I really do. But when it comes to my mother, I get a bit . . ."

"Sensitive?" he suggested.

She nodded. "And I don't mean to sound fatalistic, but to tell you the truth, sometimes I think the situation is beyond help."

Sandy said nothing. When he continued merely to look out at the creek, as if suddenly absorbed in its every moonlit glimmer she turned to face him again, bristling. "What?" she demanded.

"Nothing."

"Give me a break, Baker. You might as well come out and say what you're thinking. Your silence is starting to deafen me."

"I thought you wanted the subject closed."

"I want us to get *through* it," she said grimly. "So we can go back to arguing about how to make this movie. You know, the fun stuff," she said dryly.

"Okay," he said, in a don't-say-I-didn't-warn-you tone. "I was wondering about professional help."

"I told you," she began. "Mother thinks shrinks are a bunch of charlatans who—"

"No," he interrupted. "I meant A.A."

Victoria stared at him in shock, her cheeks reddening. "Did you say what I think you just said?"

"You heard me."

"You think my mother is an alcoholic?" Her voice was shaking. In fact, her whole body was trembling. Amazing what your mind and body could do when you were suddenly forced to confront an ugly truth. Her whole being was rebelling, even though not so long ago, she'd thought the same thing herself.

She'd just never said the word out loud.

"Don't you?" he said mildly.

"No!" she cried, thinking *liar*. "I mean, yes, she does drink a bit more than probably she should, but that doesn't..." Her voice trailed off. Somehow, with Sandy's steady gaze on her, she couldn't bring it off. She couldn't convince herself, let alone him. Victoria looked away, inspecting her shoes, feeling the blush still burn her cheeks. "Was it so obvious?" she asked, her voice low and tremulous. "That she'd been drinking, I mean?"

"Let's just say I've seen before what it looks like," he said quietly. "And if you must know, I could smell it on her breath, even with the mints."

"The mints, right," Victoria said dully, feeling an ache at the pit of her stomach. Funny, but the headache seemed to have transferred itself to another organ.

"To be completely honest, I had my suspicions," he went on. "It seemed a reasonable explanation for some of Mrs. Campbell's irrational behavior, in the book. You have to admit, she comes off a bit schizophrenic, the way you've written her."

"That's Sarah's mother, not mine," she said, but she knew it was a lame excuse.

"She was drinking back then?" he asked, ignoring it. "When you were in high school?"

Victoria nodded. "That was when I noticed it was...a habit."

"That's a long time ago."

She heard the implicit accusation behind the words. Possibly because her own guilt was speaking louder, she felt her defensiveness flare up again. "I was a kid," she said tightly. "I didn't think it was a—condition, I didn't know what to think. And I had enough problems of my own, without taking hers on."

"That's understandable."

Who was being schizophrenic now? A part of her was feeling relief at finally being able to talk about this openly with someone. Another part was getting more and more riled that she had to talk about it at all, and that he seemed to be confirming her worst guilty fears. "It was my fault, is that it?"

"I'm not saying that."

No, he wasn't, but a familiar inner voice was. And her spoken voice, when she heard it, was turning shrill. "Right, I should've turned it around right then and there. Hey, Mom, you're an alcoholic, get some help, will you?"

"Victoria..."

"I mean it wouldn't have been up to my *father*, or my perfect older sister, right? No, I was the one who should've blown the whistle on dear old Mother!"

"You know that isn't what I'm—"

Victoria rose abruptly from the log. "Well, what about them?" she demanded. "What about Dad? He didn't see it! Or if he did, he didn't say anything!"

"Did you talk to him about it?"

"Who talks?" She was practically yelling, but she was way past being able to control the emotions that, now unleashed, were overtaking all reason. "Who in my family ever confronted anything? Have some more pie, have another shot of whiskey, who cares?!"

"You care," he said, his voice maddeningly calm.

"Back to little Victoria," she cried. "You have no idea what it was like in those days! I was sixteen years—"

"You're not sixteen now," he interrupted.

She glared at him, lips trembling, arms folded as if to keep her body from flying into a fit. "No," she said. "And maybe I'm old enough to realize it's not my problem anymore. I suppose you think that's cowardly."

"No," he said. "I just think it might be time you let it be out in the open."

"Thanks," she snapped. "I'll take it under advisement."

"Look, I'm sorry," he began, starting to get up from the log.

"No, you're not," she said angrily. "This is so like you. Sandy Baker, the seeker of truth! Dig, dig, dig, what are you hiding, Victoria? Tell Sandy, the all-knowing!"

"Victoria—"

"He knows it anyway, but he wants to hear it from you! The director at work! Well, you've got a good scene here, Cecil B. De-Baker! If you wanted to get a rise out of me, you've done a damn good job."

His face was ashen in the dim moonlight. "I *am* sorry," he said. "I never should've started this—"

"Exactly!" she railed. "Who asked you? What gives you the right to tell me what I should or shouldn't be doing? Since when is it your personal duty to get poor Victoria-in-hiding to come into the light?"

"Since I . . ." He faltered, looking caught off guard.

"Since you hired me to make your magnificent movie? So you could get 'the good stuff' out of me? All that juicy real detail, that'll make for such interesting shots?"

He looked genuinely wounded. "Stop it."

"No, you stop it," she said. "Stop messing around with my life, okay? I'm starting to wonder if I want you in it, at all!"

She knew she was acting like a madwoman, but she couldn't do anything about it. Her feet were already taking her away from him, stalking quickly up the path. She didn't look back. She just hurried onward, seeing red and thinking that if he tried to follow her, she would push him into the river.

Sandy Baker didn't follow her, though. He stood there and watched her march off into the night, and only when she was gone from sight did he kick the log hard enough to make him grimace in pain.

He sat down on the log again and held his throbbing foot, contemplating the complete ass he'd made of himself. Worse, he'd broken a cardinal inner rule. He'd held back his own truth at a crucial point, too full of pride, too...let's face it, Baker, too scared to say what he should have said to her.

And now here he was, stuck with another dreaded ''if only,'' which was the kind of thing that drove him crazy. Why hadn't he said it? When she'd asked him what gave him the right, why he thought it was any of his business to interfere. ''Since when?,'' as she'd put it, he'd suddenly known. He'd understood in a flash what was going on, what had been going on for days.

Since when? Since he'd fallen in love with her. Because that was the truth, much as it disturbed him to admit it. He was completely in love with Victoria Moore, a woman who, judging from her exit, probably didn't want to have anything to do with him.

''Well, Baker,'' he murmured. ''What are you going to do about that?''

Chapter Nine

Her initial instinct when she first returned to her hotel room was to pack her bags and hightail it out of Silver Spring. Let him do his damned movie without her. But then she considered what that would look like, not only to her agent and the studio, but to him. Running scared.

The thought that she cared so much what *he* thought caused her to nearly rip a hotel pillow apart in aggrieved exasperation. It made her all the more angry. She was stuck, wasn't she? He'd gotten in, gotten inside, under her skin. She did care, too much. And that was scary.

But leaving was out of the question, so after a sleepless night she'd decided merely to steer clear of the set for a day or two. After a breakfast grabbed at Ernie's, gulped down minutes before she knew the crew was due to arrive, she took her rented car for a long drive into the countryside.

The leaves were starting to turn in earnest, the back roads she chose were uncrowded, and it should have been a relaxing, mind-lulling trip. But she was suffused with an uneasiness that had been seeping into her consciousness even last night. There was something worse than being stuck in this awkward situation. And that was that she might have to apologize to Sandy.

Because he'd been right, obnoxious as he'd been. And she'd practically torn the man's head off.

It was enough to make one want to scream or cry. Instead, she pulled over to side of the road when her headache from the night before threatened to return, and got out to get a breath of fresh air.

She was parked by a fence that bounded an open field. A trio of cows, gathered in the shade of a tree a dozen yards away, surveyed her with baleful eyes while their tails twitched at buzzing flies. They took in her citified heels and her skirt with benign indifference, merely staring and blinking as she leaned her elbows on the fence and gazed back at them.

"You have no idea what a good life you have," she informed them.

The closest of the three cows gave its head a shake, then lowered it, as if taking this visitor's words as a cue for napping. Victoria smiled ruefully as the other cows followed suit. "No, I wouldn't want to listen to me, either," she told them.

Self-pity had been nipping at her heels all morning like some mongrel cur. She kicked it away, stepped out of her shoes, and thankful that she had foregone stockings this morning, hitched up her skirt and climbed onto the fence. There, that felt better. Seated on the wooden fence top, surveying the green field dotted with more distant cows, she was able to get a little perspective.

Yes, she did owe Sandy an apology. She'd overreacted terribly last night, yelling at him when she was really only berating herself. On the other hand, she wasn't sure she could take much more of his relentless interest in her inner world. Why did he have to delve so deeply into her private life? Why couldn't he just leave her alone?

Maybe the solution was to leave *him* alone for a while. She trusted him enough by now to know that nothing would go awry on the set if she wasn't constantly looking over the director's shoulder. And maybe if they stopped seeing so much of each other both off and on the set, things would cool down.

Cool down, an interesting phrase. She thought about how hot-tempered she could get when that man was involved, and considered the intensity of feeling his presence usually prompted. She remembered, not for the first time, the erotic promise of his brief embraces, and that kiss. And she knew that, like it or not, she was already past the point of merely walking away from the man.

Great, Victoria. You're infatuated with another Mr. Wrong.

Infatuation, though, nothing more serious. Right?

She frowned, listening to the distant buzz of an unseen tractor. Her heart pleaded the Fifth, so her mind, always eager to try and proceed in an orderly fashion, considered her options and made a choice. The best course had to be a cooling-off period, albeit a short one.

Satisfied that there was nothing more she could do about the Sandy Baker situation, she inspected the passing clouds in the blue sky above, and turned her mind in another direction. A more important issue, in the larger scheme, was the very thing that had set her off the night before. What was she going to do about Mother?

Here her mind slowed, balking. The usual avoidance excuses rose up. Why did anything have to be done? Why should it be up to her, anyway? Victoria shifted uneasily on the fence, swatting a fly from her peripheral vision. Okay, she decided, let's just say, for argument's sake, that you really were going to attempt to deal with this problem. What would you do first?

Cissy would be here soon. Talk to her? Tricky. Talk to Dad? Possible. She could feel him out about it. And then, if he agreed that Mother shouldn't be allowed to continue as she had, with Dad involved, maybe they could talk to Mother herself.

Now, wasn't that a joy to contemplate? Victoria shivered. But wait, this had only been a hypothetical course of action, right? She realized then that in dodging the most ominous aspect, having to confront Mother, there was something easier that she could actually do in the meantime—talk to Dad.

A few minutes later she was off the fence, feeling like a great weight had been lifted from her shoulders. She knew some pragmatic things she could do, over the next few days. Talk to Dad and apologize to Sandy. Neither of them promised barrels of laughs, but at least breaking things down into manageable tasks made her feel more in control of this unwieldy life of hers.

Enough thinking for the day. She got back in her car after bidding a fond farewell to the disinterested cows, cranked the college radio station she found and tooled off down the road bopping and singing along to the Tina Turner song they were playing. Victoria had always had a weakness for Tina Turner.

She spent a good portion of the afternoon window-shopping in Xenia, then strolling around the Anteus campus, pretending she wasn't going to check the college bookstore to see if they were stocking her novels. Of course she just happened to come upon it, in the building that housed the student union, so why not drop in?

There transpired one of the greatest illicit thrills of her hometown trip. Not only did the store stock the new hardcovers of *Folly*, but they'd clearly just reordered a whole box of *Jumpers Creek*. It was on window display, and even more fantastic than that, they were selling like "a new Michael Jackson record," according to the friendly cashier.

The cashier didn't recognize her, though, so Victoria was able to experience a rare pleasure. She listened with embarrassed happiness, to this cashier's discourse on the literary merits of Victoria Moore. The girl, an Anteus student whose tanned complexion and neon-colored clothing suggested a resolutely unbookish temperament, had nonetheless recently begun *Jumpers Creek*, "since everybody else was reading it." As she started to wax philosophical on how "she could really relate to Sarah Campbell, even if she was, like, from a whole other generation," a male student who was more clearly the academic type chimed in with his opinions.

He preferred the early Moore to the late Moore. He had theories about symbolic elements in *Jumpers Creek* that Victoria couldn't have dreamed up if she'd wanted to. He was also fairly handsome for a bookworm, and by the time Victoria slipped out of the store, he had a date with the cashier.

Life was good again. She felt she'd had her ego batteries recharged, and thus energized, she returned to Silver Spring in time for dinner, not regretting a single moment of her day of playing hooky from the set. A brief encounter with Susan Jacks in the lobby was her only contact with the crew. Susan assured her that she hadn't missed anything but that they'd missed her.

Feeling that she was actually doing things right for once, she returned to her hotel room, noting that she had no messages. So "they" had missed her, but *he* had not? She refused to let this thought deflate her still-high spirits.

Fine. This would be her first totally S.O.B.-free day since her arrival. She'd deal with him tomorrow, when she returned to the set.

WELL, THIS WAS a new experience.

Victoria had never been in a situation that was comparable. Sure, there'd been times when she and Doug had had some pretty bitter fights, and circumstances had forced them to put on a good front. But she couldn't remember ever having been at war with a man and having to pretend they were the best of friends. There were millions of dollars and a dozen people's careers, as well as her own reputation, at stake.

It was a cold war. When she and Sandy did meet, he was civil but distant. She replied in kind. She knew they were doing a difficult setup, and she recognized his preoccupied air, so she didn't take his attitude personally. Still, she wondered. Was she being punished for abandoning ship without leave? Or had he decided, as she had, that distance was definitely called for now?

Either way, she didn't have much opportunity to talk to Sandy as the day progressed. He was shooting what was turning into a difficult scene, though Victoria wouldn't have envisioned there being any problem, from what was on the written page.

Sarah Campbell, at a point midway through the film, was trying to make Rocko jealous when he'd been neglectful, by taking a walk with Steve, the best friend of her older sister's fiancé, Kevin. Steve, a college senior who was to be the best man at Sarah's sister's wedding in June, had met Sarah and was intrigued by her. In this scene, Sarah was to flirt openly with Steve, thus arousing Rocko's jealousy and her sister's annoyance at the same time.

It was a two-page scene, fairly simple in Sandy's conception. The camera would track alongside Sarah and Steven as he walked her home from school. The problem, as a second take gave way to a third and then a fourth, was that Grace was overdoing her performance. And for once, Sandy didn't seem to be able to get what he wanted from her.

They were shooting on Presidents Street, an elm-lined residential block not far from the Moores' house, which had now been invaded by the usual plethora of vans, trucks, carts and crew members. Victoria hovered on the periphery of the action, growing increasingly concerned as she watched Grace fail to get at the heart of the scene.

Grace had been doing so well over the past week. She'd brought a spunky vitality and a quirky edge to Sarah Campbell that were very endearing. But today she seemed to be foundering again. She was loading up the dialogue with gestures and giggles, and Victoria could tell Sandy was unhappy. He was fiddling with the dialogue, but it wasn't until the fifth take that Victoria suddenly understood what the real problem was.

Grace, she realized, was acting as though Rocko or her sister might actually *see* her and Steven together. Thus her exaggerations. What she didn't realize, and neither did Sandy, was that this was unnecessary. How could they, it was a subtle point only alluded to in the book. Word would get back to both parties, and Victoria knew how.

She waited until the fifth take had been shot and deemed unsatisfactory, hovering near the camera until Sandy couldn't help but see her. He turned from a conference with Tom to regard her warily as the cameraman retested his light readings in preparation for another take.

"I know," he said tersely. "We're off the mark."

"I wasn't about to criticize," she said. "I just wondered..."

"If there was anything you could do?" He smiled briefly. "I appreciate the offer. But we're getting closer, don't worry. I'm going to halve the dialogue."

"That's a good idea," she said, and hesitated. They regarded each other with matching wariness. Victoria realized this was the longest conversation they'd had since the other night. There was something in his eyes she couldn't quite read. He didn't seem unfriendly, just careful.

"Did you have a good day off?" he asked.

She nodded. "I think I needed it."

"Well, it's nice to have you back."

That seemed to be an implicit truce-making remark. It was a cue for her to apologize, but a production assistant interrupted them. Victoria stood by, frustrated, while Sandy attended to a sound technicality. When he was free again, he wore that preoccupied look. She sensed their personal moment had passed, but she decided to plunge ahead with her professional suggestion.

"Sandy, I know you won't like this idea, but..." She paused uncertainly.

He shrugged. "I'm open to suggestion, if you can make it quick."

"Could I talk to Grace?"

Sandy squinted at her, adjusting the brim of his baseball cap. "To tell her what?"

Victoria had only gotten halfway into her explanation of what was missing in the script that could be confusing the actress when Sandy stopped her with a hand held up and a nod. "Talk to her," he said.

Victoria found the actress sitting in her trailer, morosely thumbing through a copy of *Vogue*. When she told Grace she had some back-plot information that might be helpful, the young woman brightened immediately.

"Good, tell me everything you know," she said. "I'm dying out there."

"Okay," Victoria said. "You don't have to play the scene for Rocko or for Caroline."

Grace arched an eyebrow. "Isn't that the whole point of it?"

Victoria shook her head. "You know that Steven's going to tell Kevin, Caroline's fiancé, everything that happened. And Rocko will find out about it from Lance."

"Who's Lance?"

"He's Rocko's buddy who works in the grocery store on the corner. He won't make an appearance in the script—" she explained "—since he was such a minor character in the original book."

"Oh, Lance!" Grace sat up. "Right, right, gooney little guy, real hood—"

"He always watches you walk home from school because he's secretly got a crush on you," Victoria told her, nodding. "And he's sure to tell Rocko he saw you with that jock, Steve."

"Ah." Grace's eyes gleamed with excited understanding. "So I'm not nervous, at all, while I'm with Steve."

"Nobody's going to see what you're doing, they'll hear about it secondhand."

"I don't even have to..." She paused. Victoria could see the actress's mental gears meshing. "Good. Great!" she said, smiling at Victoria. "Thank you! This was just the thing I needed to know."

"Anytime."

"Grace? You're wanted on the set." It was Bryce, the production assistant, with a squawking walkie-talkie on his hip. Victoria followed him out of the trailer. She went to her usual spot, a folding chair set up a few yards off the camera area where other chairs for actors and actress were set, and watched as Sandy and Grace conferred, script in hand.

A few minutes later they were ready to roll. This time as the camera tracked alongside Grace and the actor playing Steve, Grace took an entirely different tack. Instead of making big gestures, she hardly did anything. She tossed her lines off casually, and went through the dialogue as if smiling to herself, looking like a cat that was digesting a savory canary.

It was exactly what the scene called for, better than Victoria would've imagined. Grace had taken the information Victoria had given her, and put it to her own use. She was showing the camera, and the imagined audience, that she was enjoying this flirtation, that she was secure in it and was only doing it for an ulterior motive.

Not being an actress, Victoria wouldn't have made such an acting "choice," underplaying the moment and putting a spin on it by appearing secretly amused. But Grace's instincts were sharp. The dialogue that had seemed forced and contrived moments ago suddenly seemed very natural and very funny.

It was obviously a good take, and the improvement was so radical that when Sandy called "cut" the crew broke into spontaneous applause. Grace beamed as Sandy gave her a hug, then turned toward Victoria and made a point of applauding her. Many eyes turned in Victoria's direction as a second wave of applause greeted her.

She blushed, unable to keep what was undoubtedly a very silly grin from her face. Crew members she hadn't known even knew who she was were smiling at her. Best of all, Sandy himself looked very pleased. He'd led the applause, following Grace, and there didn't seem to be a trace of resentment in his expression. Maybe she was imagining it, but he actually looked proud of both Grace and her.

The clapping lasted probably all of twenty seconds, but to Victoria it felt like a half hour. She did her best to stop smiling as everyone returned to their tasks, but it was hard. Finally she felt as if she'd contributed something useful, as if she was truly a part of this shoot. She hadn't realized how badly she'd wanted to feel that.

VICTORIA SIPPED HER DECAF coffee on the porch of the inn, listening with one ear to the dwindling chatter of the crew from the dining room behind her. Notebook in hand, she gazed out on the quiet street, watching the occasional gaggle of college coeds cruise the inn. Kids from Anteus did this periodically, enroute to campus or the local cinema, to get a look at the movie people in residence.

No one seemed to recognize her, perched in her big wicker armchair at a corner of the porch, but that was fine. She was content to sit there, writing down some random journal jottings about her stay thus far, with the expectation of her first good night's sleep only an hour or so away.

Susan Jacks's smile, she wrote. *Way her eyebrows go up— use for Lynette in next chapter?*

The fact that she was actually thinking again about her formerly abandoned novel in progress was a healthy sign. She knew that this night was a rare oasis of calm. There was that problem with Mother still left to face, before Cissy got to town, and the unfinished business with Sandy Baker, and who knew what else, with the film in progress. But tonight, at least, she could rest on her laurels, however briefly.

Pop Oglesby's grandson: posture improving as he continues helping out crew; nice metaphor—weight of self-consciousness lifting off his shoulders. His camera is like a talisman that—

"I hope those aren't notes for me."

Victoria looked up, startled, automatically shutting the notebook. She wondered how long Sandy had been standing there. Not long, she immediately decided. She would've sensed him, as she always did. Her body was already doing that thing it did when he was close by—inwardly humming like a newly struck tuning fork.

"No," she said. "Just a journal."

"Oh, hell," he said, wincing as he sank into the matching wicker chair next to hers that faced the street. "You're not going to do one of those tell-all on-the-set exposés for *New York* magazine, are you?"

"Certainly not."

"Good." He looked tired, she saw, his hair sexily unkempt and beard stubble darkening his cheeks. His clipboard was a phone-book-thick mass of well-thumbed papers. She remembered all over again how much of a full-time job directing a movie was. But his smile as he looked at her was full of warmth, and those dark eyes had a lively twinkle.

A waitress from the inn was hovering nearby. Victoria saw she had a bottle of red burgundy and two glasses on a tray. "Wait," she said as the waitress set the tray down on the small wicker table beside her. "I didn't—"

"I did," Sandy said. "It's a celebratory peace offering."

"Oh." She watched as the waitress poured them each a glass of wine. This was going to be a lot easier than she'd imagined, she thought, relieved. "I'll probably fall asleep after two sips," she said. "But, thank you."

"Thanks, Cheryl." Sandy nodded at the departing waitress and handed Victoria one of the glasses. He raised his own. "To a successful collaboration," he said. "You did good today, Ms. Moore."

"Thank you." She clinked her glass with his. "I'm glad you gave me the opportunity."

"I'm glad we're still speaking," he said.

Victoria swallowed. The wine was good, but even better was the tart sweetness of his words. "Sandy," she began. "The other night—"

He held up a hand. "No, let me have my say, although that's what got me into trouble in the first place." He smiled wryly. "Victoria, I was way out of line. It was none of my business to give you unasked-for advice."

"No, I was the one who got way out of line."

"Hey, I was meddling where I shouldn't have," he said.

"I know you were only trying to help," she replied.

"By putting both feet in my overlarge mouth?" He shook his head ruefully. "No, I got my professional and private concerns totally twisted around. I owe you an apology and this—" he raised his glass again. "—is it."

"Apology accepted," she said, and sipped the wine. "Wine accepted, too. It's very good."

"I remembered you had a fondness for red."

"But as long as we're apologizing, let me get mine in," she said.

He arched a quizzical eyebrow. "For what?"

"For screaming at you like a crazy person," she said.

"You were upset. Understandably."

"Yes, but that didn't give me license for character assassination," she said dryly, remembering with chagrin some of what she'd said.

"You mean, giving me a new nickname? 'Sandy the all-knowing'?" He shrugged. "I've been called worse."

Victoria winced. "Forget it, please," she said. "I said a lot of things in anger that I didn't necessarily mean."

"Ah," he said, sitting back with a chuckle. "Now we're getting some qualifications. 'Didn't necessarily mean'—by that I should understand you meant some of what you said, but not all of it? Or that you meant it then, but don't mean it now?"

"I knew you'd needle me on this," she said. "Why don't we merely erase the whole scene—retake it, as it were? That might be easier."

"Might be, but..." He fingered his wineglass, gazing off with a thoughtful air before he turned to face her again. "There is one thing, though. Something you said that I want to clear the air about, once and for all."

"All right," she said cautiously.

"The other night you suggested that I hired you, as you put it, to 'get the good stuff out of you.' You were implying that the only reason I was getting involved in your personal life was so I could somehow use what was in it, in order to make a better movie."

"Well, I..." It was hard to hold his gaze. The softness in his eyes disarmed her. She saw now without his even saying so, that she'd hurt his feelings.

"First of all, I'm too good a director to play those sort of games," he said quietly. "I may manipulate actors and producers and yes, even writers, on occasion. But I like to think I'm perfectly capable of making good cinematic statements without digging up the skeletons in someone's closet to exploit in my work. I leave that sort of thing to the gossip rags."

"I know," she said. "I was angry. I didn't mean—"

"And second of all," he went on. "More importantly, when we had that conversation I wasn't thinking about our movie, at all, if you want to know the truth." He smiled as he saw the subtle shift in her expression. "Right, I know— Sandy Baker, the man whose mind works at twenty-four frames per second. Hard to believe I might have something else in my head."

"Can you blame me?"

"No," he said. "I can't blame you for distrusting me, because you don't know me as well as I'd like you to. But whether you choose to believe me or not, I'm telling you now that my concern about you and your family come from another place."

"Which is?" she prompted him.

"From the heart," he said simply. "Maybe you don't even want to hear this, Victoria, but I care about you. As *you*, not as another member of my crew." His earnest gaze was caressing her face. "Can you handle that?" he asked softly.

Victoria's throat felt tight. "I suppose," she said.

"I know this whole experience has been a real challenge for you," he went on. "And so far you've done a damned good job of holding your own. You've put up with all the hassles and changes and foul-ups that come with any shoot. And you've put up with me." He smiled wryly. "My respect for you has grown in leaps and bounds."

For a moment she didn't know what to say. Her heart-beat had been underscoring his words, seeming to thump louder in her ears by the time he'd stopped talking. Her hand, as if quite independent of her mind, was already stealing out to take his.

His palm was soft and warm in hers. She felt the pulse of his blood beat quietly as her own bloodstream seemed to sing with a rising warmth. "Thanks," she managed. "That's nice to hear."

"Now we don't have to talk about the other night again," he said. "Subject closed, all right?"

She nodded. "You shouldn't say these kinds of things to me, anyway," she said. "I'm liable to get a swelled head and become all the more difficult."

"I like you when you're difficult." He gave her hand a squeeze and then let it go, reaching for his wine with seeming nonchalance.

Her own hand was tingling, lying in her lap and looking oddly lonely there. All kinds of hazy and forbidden images zipped through her mind as she, too, took another sip of wine. Wait a second. Enough wine. She was liable to drift into a much too vulnerable and amenable state.

Amenable to what?

"Penny for those thoughts."

Victoria looked up to see him studying her. She straightened in her chair, putting her wineglass down with a decisive clink. "I was just thinking that I haven't gotten much sleep for the past two weeks."

"Tell me about it." He looked at his watch. "Come on, then, I'll walk you home."

Victoria laughed. "I am home."

"Door-to-door service, here at the inn," he said, rising. "A shame to leave this only half finished, though." He reached for the wine bottle and held it out. "Why don't you take it with you?"

"All right," she said impulsively. "As a token of your appreciation."

They walked together from the porch to the lobby, then slowly up the stairs. Sandy was telling her about the plans for tomorrow's shoot, but she was barely listening, her mind fuzzy with fatigue and the wine. No, it wasn't the wine. She was sober, she just didn't want to think.

His soft and husky voice close at her ear... *Don't think about it.*

The now-familiar scent of his after-shave teasing at her nose... *Don't think about it.*

His hand slipping around her back as he guided her around the corner of the stairs... *Don't think about that.*

He'd stopped talking, his hand had slipped away again, there was really nothing going on. Only two people sauntering casually down the carpeted hall, everything quiet around them, until the grandfather clock at the bottom of the stairs chimed midnight far below them.

They were standing in front of the door to Victoria's room. Sandy's head was cocked to one side as he listened to the clock chime and looked at her. She saw a questioning gaze in his eyes.

Her mind must've taken all the hints and gone off duty, because she had a very irrational thought just then. *I certainly hope he gives me a kiss good-night.*

And then she thought, *Only I hope he doesn't really mean to say good-night.*

She had a fantasy that he was listening to her thoughts. He seemed so intent on reading her expression, in that way he had that she liked so well, of peering into her eyes with a look of total absorption and anticipation. As if whatever she might be thinking could be so important. As if he cared so much.

How much did he care?

It was as though her eyes had posed the question and his answered, *I care a lot*.

I'd like to believe you, she told him.

Believe me, he was saying.

And then the last chime of midnight died away and she was struck by what a long and intense silent conversation they'd managed to have in such a short amount of time. Victoria looked at him standing there, so close. There was so little distance between them, and it suddenly seemed silly that there should be any at all.

"Is this when you turn into a pumpkin?" he asked softly, a faint smile playing over his full lips.

"Midnight? No, but I am going to turn in." She was supposed to be tired. Hadn't she been tired, only minutes ago? But now her body was doing that humming, zinging thing, as if there was palpable electricity crackling in the air between them.

Which is why it came as little surprise that when his lips touched hers she felt a shock. The softness of them merely brushed hers as he smiled, pausing, hovering. "Must be the carpet," he murmured.

"Don't let it stop you," she said.

"All right," he said, and he kissed her again.

It was better this time. This time his arms encircled her and she moved into them so easily, it was like coming home. She remembered everything about him all over again, the taste of him, the warmth of his mouth on hers, the strength in his lean, hard body gathering her softness close. It was familiar but still new.

It was very exciting.

"Was that a good-night kiss?" she asked him, when they finally came up for air. He was still holding her.

"Doesn't have to be," he said.

"This is kind of crazy, isn't it?"

"There's nothing crazy about it," he said, one of his hands slowly caressing her cheek. "What would be crazy is you sending me away now."

Victoria brushed the edge of his warm, soft palm with her lips. "That wasn't what I had in mind."

"Good," he said.

The funny thing was, it all seemed so logical and natural, she mused, as she slipped from his grasp with a little sigh and felt in her handbag for the room key. If someone had asked her even a few hours ago, Are you going to invite Sandy Baker into your room tonight?, she would have scoffed at him. They were barely getting along, right? And she'd already resolved that getting any further involved with the director of her movie would be a major mistake.

At the moment, however, it seemed that trying to pretend she didn't want to make love to this man, immediately, would have been the height of hypocrisy. And it occurred to her as he slipped into the room behind her, quietly shutting the door, that she'd been wanting this to happen for days. Neither of them even thought to turn on a light.

Now that it was happening it was happening very quickly. There was the bed. Then they were on it. Then time stopped, or rather disappeared altogether. There was too much going on, too many sensations and feelings overlapping and overtaking her, for her to take any mental notes.

First of all, there was all that clothing for them both to get out of. It was like a deliciously slow, suspended and sometimes comical dance they did, punctuated by pauses where the uncovering of some new expanse of skin would occasion shiver-inducing, pulse-racing, breathtaking exploration.

As scenes went, it was almost entirely free of dialogue. There were murmurs and sighs and inarticulate whispers, and even a few happy giggles. But most of the time it was about what a man and a woman could blissfully do with their lips and tongues besides talking.

There was one point, somewhere in the darkness, where a few words were exchanged. They were naked by then, happily, their limbs entwined among the sheets. The stiff points of her breasts were nestled in his chest hair and his taut, muscular legs were wrapped around hers. Her hands were sliding over his smooth, strong back, to stroke his tight buttocks as his hands played with her hair, and she looked up into his eyes to find her own pleasure mirrored in their velvet depths.

"You know," he said, his voice a whispery rasp, "you're even more beautiful without any clothes on than I could've imagined."

"You're not so bad yourself," she told him, smiling, the smile turning into a little *O* of appreciation as one of his hands stole from shoulder to a breast, cupping her softness, fingers gentling, teasing and tickling its taut tip. "Wait a second, did you actually imagine this?"

"Are you kidding?" She felt his chuckle resonate deep against her breast. "I've been imagining it since the first time I ever saw you."

"I'm shocked, Mr. Baker."

"No, you're not," he said. "Admit it, Ms. Moore. Our being here like this was not only inevitable, it feels like the most natural thing in the world."

"It feels good," she allowed, but knew he was right.

"It feels better than good," he said, a little gasp of pleasure escaping him as she touched him again in a way she already knew he liked. "It's..."

"Yes," she murmured, arching against him.

Then he was inside her, filling her, so full of feelings she thought she might burst. She *would* burst, she thought; they would burst together into a union of skin and soul that didn't have any words. The words were leaving her already. She clung to him, ready to be wordless, ready to let her world become the last and only important word, and that was love.

Chapter Ten

She didn't know if she'd slept. She'd closed her eyes count-
less times, but opened them again just as many. They were
adrift in some rarified space that seemed to exist outside of
time. Time was measured in the length of a caress, the width
of a smile, the depth of a kiss.

They'd made love again, and then again, she knew that,
but even now it was hard to tell where one time had ended
and another begun. She must have at least dozed, though,
because now when she opened her eyes the pillow next to
hers was empty.

Victoria sat up. The soft moonlight that had bathed their
bodies, sometimes highlighting the sweat upon their skin
with a velvet-like silver sheen, was gone. In its place was a
blue-gray light that announced a coming dawn. Sandy Baker stood by the window, nude, hands on his hips as he
gazed down at the street.

For a moment she merely sat and gazed across the room
at him. It occurred to her that it had been quite some time
since she'd last awakened to find a naked man in her room.
He wasn't aware of her yet, and she could let her eyes take
in his muscular form at leisure. She recognized places on it,
intimate planes of skin and muscle she already knew well.
She liked the feeling this gave her, studying him.

He was in good shape. Tall, still lean and trim for a man nearly forty, but with just enough give around the waist to make his belly yield to the touch. Thoughts of touching him took over this idle contemplation. Victoria swept the sheet from her and slipped from the bed.

When she came up behind him and slid her arms around him he gave a little pleased sigh in greeting. He caught one of her hands in his and nuzzled the fingertips, his eyes still intent on the vista outside the window. She followed his gaze, her chin resting on his shoulder.

There were treetops just below. From three stories up a good deal of the street itself was obscured, but the early dawn light gave glimpses of the storefronts on the other side of Elm. Over the treetops, a few blocks of Silver Spring were slowly coming into focus, like a color plate lying in a photographer's developing pan.

"What are you looking at?" she asked.

"The colors," he said. "Do you see how sharp and saturated everything is?"

She looked. He was right. The absence of any real sunlight seemed to outline every leaf, every glint of slate rooftop in clear relief. The more she looked, the more the surfaces of everything appeared to gleam with a rich luster. "The magic hour," he murmured.

She'd heard that phrase somewhere on the set recently. Tom had been talking about it, when they were wrapping up the shoot a few days back. "What do you mean?"

"It's the hour just before the sun's up in the sky at dawn," he explained, folding his arms over hers. "And just after the sun's gone down at dusk. That's the best time for filming, because the light is perfect. You have the richest colors then, and the least amount of contrast between light and shadow, so you can get wonderfully subtle effects."

"Sunrise and sunset," she mused. "Those *are* magic hours."

Sandy turned in her arms to face her. He bent to kiss the tip of her nose, both cheeks and then her lips, savoring each spot before he pulled her back again to gaze at her with affectionate eyes. "This is a magic hour. Us together like this, with nothing to hide from each other. Don't you think?"

She nodded, then nestled her head in the crook between his head and shoulder, breathing in the scent and feel of him. "I don't think, though," she murmured. "I gave that up a while ago."

"I know what you mean." His fingers traced shiver-inducing patterns through her hair, fondling her ear and the soft skin behind the lobe.

Amazing, but she wanted him again. It was as if all he had to do was that—play with her ear—and she was suddenly alive to all the other possibilities of his hands and hers. Her own hand slipped downward, over his taut belly, and she found that he was, too.

"What have we here?" she asked.

"An interested party," he said.

"Perhaps we should go back to bed. It's a little early to rise and shine."

"I've already risen and your eyes are shining," he said, smiling. "But yes, I wouldn't mind lying down again."

"Wouldn't mind?" she said, drawing back in mock offense. "Come on, aren't you supposed to whisper some fierce and tender endearments, telling me you're aflame with desire or something?"

"You know I am," he said, and his eyes glistened with arousal as his hand followed hers, caressing the soft skin of her inner thighs. He smiled as she took in a shaky breath. "You are, too," he noted. "And that bed is suddenly looking very far away."

The carpet was soft beneath her back as he joined her there. "I feel like a wanton woman," she whispered.

"Yes, you do feel like one," he said, his hands ceaselessly exploring her nudity, raising goose bumps with each deft stroke.

She laughed. "Umm," she murmured. "I am wanton. Wantin' you to hold me a little tighter..."

"Terrible," he said. "What happened to your literary respectability? Don't you know that puns are the lowest form of humor?"

"Well, considering we're on the floor—" she said, nuzzling his neck "—a low form seems only appropriate."

"You're absolutely right," he murmured. "And you're absolutely...delicious. It's a good thing I'm not due on the set for nearly an hour."

"An hour?" She stretched in his arms, smiling blissfully as his lips traced a warm, wet path between her breasts. "That sounds like a nice, long time."

"Um-hmm," he agreed. "The things we could do in an hour..."

Once again conversation ceased. She watched the morning light grow brighter over his shoulders. A little later it was as if she was rising with the sun and Sandy, merging right into that fiery ball as it ascended into the bluest sky she'd ever seen.

IT WAS ONLY WHEN she found herself alone again a few hours later that Victoria was suddenly seized with an attack of the Serious Fears.

The Fears crept up on her from behind, when she was innocently combing her hair at the mirror, humming softly to herself in the bright morning sun. She was showered, dressed, made-up and ready to rejoin the rest of the world once more, still savoring her many memories of the night before and the morning, too. Her mind and heart were full of Sandy Baker, and a happiness she hadn't felt in as long as she could remember, when the Fears pounced.

One minute she was contemplating her face and the smile on it, thinking that the night of love she'd just experienced was something she had sorely needed, and thinking about what a wondrous thing it was that she would surely have another one like it again, that very night, when the Fears' skeletal hands seized her throat. She nearly dropped her brush as she felt the Fears pin her back to the chair, an icy draft sweeping through her blood.

She'd almost forgotten about them, these terrible feelings that had come upon her at various vulnerable points in her life, but now she remembered. The Fears whispered at her ear, and the words were horribly familiar.

What makes you think there's going to be another night? said one.

What if there isn't and you're left hopelessly in love with someone who has no intention of loving you back? hissed another.

How could you have possibly let yourself be put in such a position, exposing yourself to the kind of pain you promised yourself you'd never feel again? shrieked a third.

She had to put the brush down and literally clamp her hands over her ears. As if that would do any good. The terror was inside her, alive and kicking.

"All right!" she snapped aloud, standing up abruptly, and the voices quieted. She glared at her reflection in the mirror. "That'll be enough, okay?"

The mirror-Victoria pressed her lips together, looking a bit paler than a few minutes previous, but back in control. That was the thing with the old Fears. You had to take them in hand immediately, or they'd run you ragged.

"You're being silly," she told the mirror, and both Victorias nodded assent. She puffed her cheeks, blew some air out and made a ridiculous face at herself. She gnashed her teeth, grimaced horribly, growled and then smiled a loony grin. That worked. She giggled.

Then she got up and walked over to the window. This was the very window where she'd stood with Sandy mere hours ago. She conjured up the memory in her mind and held it there until it took, and the Fears didn't have any room to operate. Look at that face, she told herself, looking at Sandy's face in her memory, hovering over her, eyes half closed in pleasure as he looked at her, lips still wet from their last kiss.

Was this a man who'd love her and leave her, like that?

No. No way...

...Probably not.

In the distance, her fears snickered. Probably? Was that the best she could do?

"ROLL SOUND—camera?"

"Rolling."

"Action!"

A bell rang. Young Sarah Campbell came around the corner of her high-school yard, late again. She look frazzled as she ran across the short grass, knowing she'd surely get detention for this, her fourth late slip in two weeks. It was all Rocko's fault, but she was the one who'd get into trouble, and that thought was easy to read on Grace's face as the actress sped by, the craning camera turning to follow her as she ran.

Victoria could relate. Men were like that, getting you into trouble and not being around when you had to deal with it. At least, most of the men she'd been involved with from Rocko onward had been that way. Which was why she'd settled for dull and dependable Doug. Which was why she'd been a fool to tangle with the Rocko-like Sandy Baker.

Stop! she commanded herself for the umpteenth time that day. She had no reason to be this paranoid. True, Sandy had maintained some distance on the set since she'd shown up, only the subtlest of hints betraying that anything momentous had passed between them. But that was only Sandy being the professional he was. She shouldn't take it personally. She knew better by now, didn't she?

Apparently not. Victoria got up from her folding chair on the location set's sidelines and paced restlessly behind the crew area. Now, come on, what had she expected? Was Sandy supposed to sweep her into his arms and kiss her passionately before the shocked eyes of the entire *Jumpers Creek* team?

No. It was enough that he'd smiled at her in that special way of his, his hand lingering with a new suggestive—and possessive—air on her arm when they'd conferred on a line of dialogue earlier. It was enough that he'd whispered a sweetly lascivious phrase in her ear when she'd gotten up from their brief script conference, enough that his eyes had followed her as she left to go out of the camera crew's path.

Well, almost enough. She'd won the first battle with the Fears, but not the war, and already some defensive troops were setting up camp. *You* make some distance, an inner voice was instructing her. Don't let him know you're in love with him. Play it cool. Back off.

That was the problem, of course. She *was* in love with him. She'd known it, not wanting to know it, for days now, but after last night, there was no more denying. That was why she'd gotten so scared. She hadn't felt such an intensity of feeling in years and years, if ever. Plus, it had happened so fast, and that was pretty scary in itself.

Now, try as she might, she couldn't get her mind off Sandy Baker and the idea that she wanted him in her life. That she suddenly couldn't imagine *not* being with him. What a disaster! After she'd worked so long and hard on being Miss Independence and the Self-Sufficient Kid. All that labor gone to naught, in the space of a single night.

Life was unfair.

Uh-oh, life was even less fair than she'd thought, because here came Catherine, the reporter, the last person in the world Victoria felt like seeing, and Catherine was heading right for her with a glossy professional smile on her brightly lipsticked lips and a gleaming tape recorder in her hand.

"There you are," she said. "You've been a hard person to track down, Victoria Moore. But I've got you now!"

Victoria found herself sitting in the shade by her old high-school bleachers, fulfilling a fantasy that the young Victoria Moore would have been tickled purple to see fulfilled. (An Interview in a National Magazine!) The adult Victoria Moore was far from tickled. She knew life was just like that sometimes, making childhood fantasies come true, only to turn them into bad dreams.

Catherine, once Victoria had obliged her with a few good quotes about books versus films and the contemporary writer's life, seemed to decide that she and Victoria were chums. Chums enough so that Catherine could confide in Victoria her observations and opinions on Sandy Baker, the man who could only love movies.

"It's not just Kathleen," Catherine said, putting her tape recorder aside with a conspiratorial air. "None of the women he was with before he married her lasted long, either. I mean, I could've told her it wouldn't work."

She sat back with a knowing, ironic smile. For a crazy moment, Victoria wondered if Catherine knew, somehow. Did she have some kind of extrasensory super-reporter's antennae, had she picked up the vibrations? Did she know that Victoria had just slept with Sandy Baker and was in love with the man, that she had sadistically chosen this exact moment for this conversation?

But no, that was impossible. It was more likely, though no more consoling a theory, that Catherine, jealous of any woman who seemed even potentially interested in Sandy, had made it a personal mission to character-assissinate the director where romance was concerned. If it was true that Sandy had never gotten involved with Catherine, much to Catherine's disappointment, then she was doing an excellent job of acting like the proverbial dog in the manger.

"The *films* are his lovers," she was saying. "I mean think about it. They come first. Women are entirely secondary."

"But he was married for a number of years, wasn't he?" Victoria hazarded, trying her best to affect an air of only the most casual interest.

"Four years," Catherine said with a smug expression. "Just a little longer than he spends on each movie. You see, that's my point. The man has a terminally short attention span, even with the things he loves most."

"I'm not sure I . . ."

"Just look at the pattern," Catherine said. "He spends, what, a year in preparation for each film? That's the courtship. Then a half a year in the actual shooting. That's the romance itself, the blaze of hot passion. Then a year in postproduction. That's the slow cooling down and process of disengaging. At last the film is released. That's the breakup," she concluded, smiling. "It's all over but the memories."

She looked immensely pleased with her metaphor. Victoria felt intensely ill.

"Even while he's in postproduction on one film, he's already looking around for the next one," Catherine continued. "Fickle as any man who can't settle down, right? Then he finds a 'hot property'—interesting phrase, isn't it?—and boom! Off and running."

She held up her hands in an "I rest my case" gesture. Victoria cleared her throat. "I didn't realize he was known as such a womanizer," she lied. Isn't that how those supermarket magazines had characterized him? The ones she'd never taken seriously before?

"Please," said Catherine. "You should have seen the wrap-up on the last shoot. You know he was involved with Debra Tyler."

"Oh, yes, I heard something about that," Victoria said vaguely.

"Well, helpful that Debra doesn't live in L.A.," Catherine said. "Because as soon as the shoot was over, that was how he ended it, in record time. 'Got to go into postproduction, Deb—we'll hook up next time I'm back East,' and you'd better believe they didn't. He goes West, she goes East, and gee, wouldn't you know it, now *Jumpers Creek* is the only love in his life."

She shook her head, gazing off toward the camera setup where Sandy was joking around with Tom and a couple of gaffers, benignly unaware that his current paramour was having her worst fears substantiated by a woman who professed to be an old friend of his. "But you have to love him," Catherine said ruefully. "He's so *good* at what he does."

Right, at finding 'em, filming 'em and forgetting 'em, Victoria thought, still feeling ill. She forced herself to favor Catherine with a winning smile. "Yes, he is, isn't he?" she said, rising unsteadily from her chair. "I've really enjoyed working with him."

Catherine got up, too, accepting this cue that their interview and its horrific follow-up dish session was at an end. "You're lucky your book was delivered into such capable hands," Catherine said. "Anyway, thanks, Vicki. I'll make sure you see a copy of the transcript of this stuff before I go to final draft."

Only the closest friends called her Vicki, Victoria thought, as she hurried away, but in this case she wasn't going to make anything of it. She didn't have the strength left.

Sandy was still in the midst of getting the afternoon's last shot in the can as she strode resolutely back to her chair on the sidelines. Victoria sat, script in hand, and watched him from a distance, doing her damnedest to objectify the man before she had to speak to him again.

Baseball cap perched backward, hair unkempt, hands gesturing all over the place, the director seemed like a miniature hurricane of energy as he exhorted his crew to get into gear. "We're losing light," she heard him say repeatedly. Yes, Sandy Baker definitely threw himself into his work. She watched his hands sketch circles in the air. She remembered how they felt on her soft skin. She remembered this was not what she was supposed to be concentrating on.

Victoria focused her attention on the other technicians, trying to see Sandy as merely one element in this panorama of people. What had happened between them, really? They'd grown close, working together, and the physical attraction that had been simmering between them had finally overtaken both of their better judgments. That was it in a nutshell, the story of their relationship thus far. Why did it have to be anything more? Why even worry about it?

Sandy was crouching in the dirt by the wire fence, animatedly framing a camera position for Tom, who knelt at his side. If I were to walk up to him right now and tell him I had to go back to New York, she mused, he'd barely bat an eye. Why would he? He had a film to shoot and that did come first, above and beyond whatever Catherine had to say.

And I have a life to live, she told herself. I was doing just fine, thanks, before I ever met Sandy Baker, and I'll do fine when this shoot is over. It occurred to her that she hadn't even let herself think about that—the end of the shoot. It was fast approaching, since they had less than a full week's location work left. Perhaps now was the best time to think about it, and think about it hard.

Twenty minutes, one cup of coffee and a quick phone call to New York later, she was feeling better. Maxanne had been happy to hear from her and she had good news. *Folly* was still climbing the bookstore charts. The studio wanted to rerelease *Jumpers* in paperback with a tie-in to the film, naturally, and there was good money involved. Her agent was pleased, predictably, that Victoria had talked to Catherine, and anxious now that Victoria get back to work on the new novel.

"It'll be your biggest yet," she'd said. "I can feel it. So get off that set and get back to your word processor already, okay?"

Victoria wasn't so sure the new book would be "big." She wasn't sure she even knew what the new book was about anymore, having spent an inordinate time away from it, but Maxanne's enthusiasm gave her a welcome lift and helped her see things in their proper light.

Back at her word processor, in her own comfortable apartment, in her own city, in her own life—yes, that was where she belonged. Wasn't this whole episode supposed to be a short vacation, period? If it had a nice dividend, like a fling with a famous and sexy film director, well, that was fine. Good material for the work in progress. But why blow everything out of proportion?

She realized that spending so much time on Sandy's turf had distorted her sense of perspective. Thoughts of how frightened she'd been this morning, how much her intimate time with Sandy had suddenly come to mean, made her think all the more seriously of putting it behind her. Who needed the angst and aggravation, anyway? When you started to love someone, your whole life was liable to turn upside down and inside out. She didn't need that now. She had a book to write.

Thus armed with a new rationale, feeling wonderfully levelheaded for the first time that day, she no longer dreaded meeting up with Sandy. The crew was breaking down the setup when she returned. When Sandy waved and mimed a casual "wait for me" at her, smiling, Victoria smiled back. She was sure he'd be as relieved as she was, to make light of their fling. That was it, a fling, a fling was what you had when you went on a vacation. Flings were fun, no more, no less, nothing to get emotional about.

Armed with this new casual definition, she didn't balk as he came over to her, calling goodbyes to Tom and his operator, and put his arm around her in clear sight of the remaining crew members.

She was aware of a few stares, but ignored them as Sandy walked her off the location set. "Grace is back in form," he was telling her. She was enjoying the feel of him so close, her senses instinctively drinking in now-familiar scents and sensations. She had to force herself to get back on the new program. Fun, she thought, wishing her heart wouldn't beat quite so fast. Fling, fun, light, easy, right? Right.

"I just hope she can recapture it when we go to L.A.," he was saying. "It would terrible to lose the rhythm of this thing during our one week off."

They were on their way across the parking lot now, and she no longer felt self-conscious. So she was a little disappointed when he removed his arm. But she realized he was having trouble carrying his clipboard. "Here, let me take that," she offered.

"Thanks."

She felt this was an even subtler level of intimacy, carrying the all-important clipboard. Stop that, she told herself, feeling herself shift into an affectionate kind of sentimentality that should have no place in what was, she'd decided, a casual non-affair. Then she caught the drift of what Sandy was saying, and she slowed, confused.

"...and we may even have to double up on her out there, if the performance is off," he was barreling on. "Besides, we may even come up with some fresh dialogue before postproduction. I was thinking about your narration idea," he said, looking at her as they paused near his car in the corner of the lot. "Maybe when we have a rough cut, we could try that out."

"We"? What was all this "we"? "Well, once you're in L.A. you can do pretty much whatever you want," she said. "I mean, as long as I get approval."

"Approval?" He looked puzzled. "But you'll be there."

"In L.A.?"

"Of course."

Of course?! Victoria cleared her throat, looking past him into some indeterminate distance. "What makes you think I'd be in Los Angeles?"

Sandy stared at her a moment, then smiled slowly. "Ah. I see. Victoria, I'm sorry to have skipped the formal invitation. You *will* be coming out for the end of the shoot. Won't you?"

"I—I hadn't thought about it," she said uneasily. This wasn't making sense. She'd assumed they'd be going their separate ways. And with what Catherine had told her... "I didn't think you'd need me after this part of the shoot."

His eyes were searching hers, narrowing slightly. When he spoke again, his voice was lower, with a quiet husky timbre she remembered from the night before. "I most definitely need you," he said softly.

Her defense system was down. Soft, warm rays of something very, very persuasive were turning all her barriers to mush. The new program was in danger of evaporating as he spoke again. "I wouldn't think of finishing the film without you," Sandy added.

The film. That was it, of course. How silly of her. Her inner defense system locked back into place with an almost audible clang. It wasn't Victoria Moore, the lover and friend, he was interested in—it was Victoria, the author-collaborator. She wondered how hard it might be for him to break pattern, actually continuing a relationship beyond the perimeter of a shoot, and if he thought he was making a sacrifice here.

"I'm sure you could manage," she said, trying to affect a light, facetious tone.

"It's not about managing," he said, brow furrowed as he looked at her. "I want you to come out there."

"I hadn't been planning on it," she told him.

His expression was hard to read. Was she imagining it, or was she seeing the hint of a hurt feeling in his eyes?

"Victoria!"

Both of them turned to see Melinda waving from the other end of the lot. Victoria waved back, glad for this timely reprieve. Melinda was hurrying their way.

"Well, let's talk about it later," Sandy said.

"All right," said Victoria.

"Meet you after dinner?"

She hesitated. Of course she wanted to see him later, but wasn't that the worst conceivable thing she could do, if she was trying to create some distance? "I promised my folks I'd visit them," she lied. "If I get done at a reasonable hour, why don't I give you a call?"

"Victoria, what's wrong?"

She saw the puzzled and concerned look on his face and her resolution faltered. But Melinda was nearly at their side. "Nothing," she said, forcing a smile. "Maybe I just need a little time . . . to recoup."

"Oh." His expression shifted. She sensed barriers not unlike her own shift into place behind his eyes. "Well, if you reconsider, do give me a call." He turned. "Hey, there, Melinda."

"Hello, Sandy." She looked from one to the other. "I hope I'm not interrupting. . . ."

"Not at all," Sandy said, and gave Victoria's shoulder a casual squeeze as he took the clipboard from her hand. "Later," he called, and strode off without looking back.

Victoria stared after him, suddenly feeling bereft and forlorn. She'd done the right thing, hadn't she? Then why did it feel so wrong?

"What's up?" Melinda said, looking curiously at her. "Are you sure I didn't come over at a bad time?"

"No, it's fine," Victoria assured her friend. "What's going on with you?"

"How much do you want to know?" She sounded more than rueful, and Victoria recognized something in the tone that made her apprehensive.

"Melinda," she said, peering closely at her. "You haven't done anything stupid, have you?"

Melinda gave a short laugh that was more like an embarrassed cough. "Well, almost," she admitted.

"Oh, no. Hold everything." Taking her friend by the arm, she marched her over to the bleachers and sat her down on the lowest step. "Let's hear it."

Melinda told her what she'd suspected. Ted, her actor "husband," had made a pass. And Melinda had very nearly succumbed to his seductive wiles. But what was worse about Melinda's confession was that although she was racked with guilt, she wasn't sure she'd done the right thing.

"Are you crazy?" Victoria cried, hands on her hips. "What about Jim? Your *real* husband, remember him?"

"He wouldn't have to know," Melinda muttered, unable to meet Victoria's eyes.

"That's not the point," Victoria said. "Honey, if you're planning to ruin your marriage, you couldn't do a better job. Is that what you really want?"

"Ted wants me to come out to California," Melinda said meekly. "He seems serious."

"Probably because he knows you'd never do such a thing," Victoria said worriedly.

"Why shouldn't I? Victoria, I've been living my whole life for Jim and the children. Now here's someone who's interested in me, just me. Can't you see—"

"Why that would be very exciting? Of course I can," Victoria said, sitting down next to Melinda. "But slow down a second. Don't you think you ought to consider what you're getting yourself into?"

Melinda sighed. "I haven't wanted to think," she said, staring at her feet. "All I know is, I've been wanting something to change in my life, and here's this sweet, cute hunk of a guy offering me the kind of opportunity I never thought I'd have in a million years..." She looked up at Victoria, tears in her eyes. "And you're going to try to talk me out of it, aren't you?"

Victoria took her hand. "I'm afraid so," she said quietly. "But you want me to, don't you?"

One tear trickled down Melinda's cheek. "I don't know what I want," she said, disconsolate. "All I know is, I've been so...happy..."

And on this last word the torrent burst in earnest. Victoria dug some tissue out of her purse and passed it over. When Melinda had calmed down a little, Victoria had a temporary solution to this crisis. "You may not know what you want, but I know what we both need," she told Melinda.

"What's that?" Melinda sniffled.

"One of Mr. Halloran's hot-fudge sundaes. Come on, let's go over to Junior's. I'm buying."

Chapter Eleven

"Oh, so sinful," Melinda said.

"Yes," Victoria agreed.

Reverent silence reigned at their corner booth while both women dipped spoons and devoured their portions of confectionery perfection. That was the thing about Halloran's hot-fudge sundaes. They weren't fancy, they weren't particularly different or special, they were merely perfect. Just enough hot fudge, just the right sprinkle of nuts, just the right consistency of vanilla ice cream.

It was enough to reaffirm the existence of pure goodness in this troubled world. By the time they'd each nearly finished theirs, Melinda was clearly in better spirits, and Victoria was able to address her situation with renewed energy.

"You're not thinking clearly, that's all," she told Melinda. "You've had a lot of excitement all at once and you can't see what you're doing."

"No, I can see it," Melinda said ruefully. "I know I'm considering doing what's absolutely the wrong thing. Ted doesn't really want me to come to California. He's not thinking about this any more realistically than I am. You know what he said when I mentioned the kids?" She shook her head with a little laugh. "He's always wanted a family. Can you believe it? As if it didn't make any difference that it was someone else's."

"Well, he's romantic, I'll give him that."

"He's out of his mind," Melinda said. "And I'm sure I am." She frowned. "Jim knows something's up, too. The funny thing is, he..."

"He what?"

Melinda's smile was sad. "He's jealous. First he was trying to act like he didn't care about the movie. Then he got very interested—right at the point I'd decided *I* didn't care, you know. And now the painful thing is that Jim is doing just what I wanted him to do, paying attention, I mean, real attention. He's worried. He's concerned. He's been more affectionate and wanting to talk more in the past week than he has in months and I..."

She bit her lip, shaking her head. Victoria gave her friend's hand a squeeze. "Sounds awful."

"It is. Because I *feel* awful. Jesse and Jennifer can feel it, too. They keep wanting to come to the set and help me with my wardrobe. And then when I *am* on the set with Ted, he looks at me in this way he has, and the cameras roll and..."

"I get the picture."

"Can't you see how tempting it all looks? A whole new life? In Hollywood, no less! Victoria, whenever I think of the kind of life you've been able to lead ever since you left here, I get absolutely green. And can you blame me?"

"What kind of a life do you think I lead?" Victoria countered.

"It's got to be more glamorous than mine."

"Glamorous? Melinda, it's not like some movie. I don't go floating around to elegant cocktail parties in beautiful dresses every night. I spend more nights at home alone in a small apartment with nothing but my word processor for company," Victoria said.

"Come on," Melinda said. "You've got all of New York City—"

"Which most New Yorkers rarely have the time or energy to take advantage of," Victoria said. "But that's not even the point. This whole conversation is ridiculous," she said, putting her spoon down after one last lingering lick. "Because I'm the one who should be green."

"Yeah, right."

"No, I'm serious." Victoria sat back in the booth, thinking as she looked at Melinda that she'd never been quite this honest with her, or with herself. Because in truth, she always had been jealous. "You can't see your life because you're living it," she said. "But the things you have that you might take for granted aren't so easily gained."

"A husband?" Melinda scoffed. "Victoria, there've been times when I've seen you beat off available men with a stick."

"And who says that was so bright? You pay a price," she said quietly. "I've finally got a flourishing career," she went on. "And to do it I made certain choices. I'm not saying I made a mistake," she added. "Don't get me wrong. But you've been able to raise two children—two exceptional kids, from the little I know them—and Melinda, my clock is ticking away."

"You're not too old to have children!"

"No," Victoria said. "I'm just old enough to miss having had them already."

Now it was Melinda's turn to look concerned. "You never said . . ."

"Maybe I never knew. Maybe I didn't want to know," Victoria said. "All I'm saying is, a husband who can still get fiercely jealous after twelve years of marriage, and two kids who dote on you—that's nothing to sneeze at. It's certainly nothing to walk away from, for what's probably only a short-lived fling."

Fling. The word was out of her mouth before she'd thought about it. Who was she really talking to, she wondered, Melinda or herself?

"I know you're right," Melinda said. "I knew it before you even said anything. But it doesn't hurt to hear it from you." She sighed again. "Yes, it does hurt."

"Because it would be easier to run away from it all?" Victoria said sympathetically.

"Sure would."

"But you won't."

Melinda stared at her empty sundae glass. "No."

"I'm glad."

Melinda shrugged. "The grass is always greener, right? I'll tell you, raising a family isn't any picnic."

"I'll bet," Victoria said. "But it has its payoffs, doesn't it?"

"Huge ones," Melinda said. She tapped her fingers on the table, a mischievous look in her eye. "Maybe I could just sleep with him once," she said. "And then return to my happy home, a somewhat fulfilled scarlet woman."

"Melinda—"

"Of course I won't," she said, and laughed. "I can't do that sort of thing, you know, be intimate with a man and then just forget about it. Still corny as Kansas out here in the boondocks," she said. "Moral as the day is long."

Melinda's tone implied that Victoria was conversely a worldly sophisticate. Funny, she mused, as they got up to pay the check, but she was still a Silver Spring girl, too. She hadn't been able to sleep with Sandy Baker and forget about it.

And if anything, her conversation with Melinda had only reaffirmed her early convictions. She should get out now, before anything deeper had a chance to develop. Because she, like Melinda, had a hard-earned life of her own to live, one that shouldn't be walked away from on account of a fling.

Did Sandy truly want *her* to come to California? He was probably as heedless of the future as Ted Danner was. They both had movie-business sensibilities, and why shouldn't they? She was different. If she was going to get involved with a man again, seriously involved, it would have to be someone who at least lived on the same coast. Someone who had a stable enough life to plan for children, if they did decide they wanted them.

Not that she did, now. Not that she wanted to deal with any of these issues! She was happy on her own and she had a book to write. Right?

Armed with these convictions, she gave Melinda a lift home. They found the Rolling Stones blasting away on the college radio station, turned it up and sang along as they drove. For about three minutes, it was like being back in school again, where the biggest problems were homework and who was going to ask you to the next dance. Thank heaven for rock'n'roll. Years flew away, like the autumn leaves dancing and spinning off her windshield.

WHATEVER YOU DO, don't touch that telephone.

Sandy Baker kept telling himself this as the evening progressed. It wasn't as if he didn't have enough other things on his mind. There were the usual ongoing union hassles, the ever-present budget disputes, and new bad news: the loss of Harry Dean Stanton, who would have been perfect to play the key role of the local sheriff.

The famous character actor was hospitalized for minor surgery and couldn't fly out as planned. Now he and Arlyne had to work with Juliet long-distance to come up with a suitable last-minute replacement, if there was such a thing. This crisis and the difficulties of booking that soundstage in the Valley for next month were enough to keep anyone preoccupied, but Sandy still found himself practically jumping out of his chair every time the phone rang.

And every time, it wasn't Victoria.

Concern was giving way to annoyance. He'd known something was up when he'd left her that afternoon, and it wasn't as if he hadn't seen something like it coming. Still, what was *with* that woman? Was he crazy, or hadn't they really connected last night?

As far as he was concerned it had been better than he'd have ever imagined. It wasn't even the sex, which even now brought a bloom to his cheeks when he thought about it. No, what had happened was more devastating. He'd discovered two things. One, that the two of them were attuned in wonderful, subtle ways that excited him no end, and two, that he couldn't conceive of not having her in his life—here, there, everywhere.

This was of course in violation of more than one personal cardinal rule. So in a way, her clear avoidance of him was a lucky thing, even as it irked and worried him. But still he couldn't shake the intuitive feeling that love had ambushed him, real honest-to-goodness love, the kind you usually only saw in a movie.

The phone rang. Sandy forced himself to let it ring again before springing from his seat by the window, where he'd been surveying Elm Street, a pile of photos and agents' listings in his lap. He cleared his throat and adopted a businesslike manner as he picked it up.

But it was only Juliet again, calling from Los Angeles. No way Dennis Hopper was available. "It was a long shot anyway," Sandy said, scowling at the pad on his desk. They went through some other names. What was bugging Sandy, he realized as he hung up again, was that he wasn't as concerned about filling this crucial role as he should've been. No, he was too busy looking at his watch and wondering where the hell Victoria Moore was.

Had she stayed over at her folks? Once again he considered calling, once again decided he had too much pride. According to his watch, it was only two minutes since he'd last looked at the time. It was still a little after midnight.

Pride, hell. He dialed Victoria's room.

Busy signal.

Just to be sure, he dialed the number again. Yes, she was there and she was on the phone.

He hung up, staring at the phone as if the instrument itself was the culprit. Sandy prided himself on being level-headed, cool to a fault, control being his middle name. He had never chased a woman who didn't want to be chased. He never pressed a romantic issue where he might lose face. So clearly he was going to forget about this for now, concentrate on the more important work at hand. If she wanted to talk to him, she'd talk to him tomorrow.

Right. Sandy strode out of his room, down the hall, down one flight of stairs and made a beeline for the door to Victoria's room. He knocked.

After a moment he heard her approach the door, sensed her looking through the little eyehole, hesitate, then unlatch the door. She didn't open it all the way. She was dressed in a bathrobe and her hair looked wet from a shower. She looked so good that for a moment he forgot to be self-righteous, and smiled.

"Hi," he said.

"Hello," she said.

She wasn't smiling and she sounded guarded. Sandy realized, looking beyond her into the quiet inn room, that she was not on the telephone, and that the telephone was off the hook. "Just happened to be in the neighborhood," he said, managing a nonchalance he no longer possessed. "So I thought I might stop by."

"Oh."

Tooth-pulling time, eh? "I hope I'm not disturbing you," he said, an edge creeping into his voice.

He could see he was. "No," she said, not meeting his eyes now. "I was just getting ready for bed."

Sandy regarded her in silence. "Got a minute?"

She shot him an embarrassed look, then nodded. "Okay. Come on in. But the place is a mess."

The place looked immaculate to his eye. Victoria hurried to the chair by her desk, took the pillow off the telephone receiver and put it back in its cradle. "I was getting ready to catch up on my sleep," she said sheepishly, when she turned back to meet his gaze.

"I don't think so," he said. "I think you were avoiding me."

Victoria sat down in the chair, the pillow in her lap. "No, I..." She stopped herself, bit her lower lip. "Yes," she said, looking up at him again. "I was."

"Why?" he asked.

Victoria frowned. He had the feeling she was finding it hard to keep looking him in the eye. "I think I needed some time," she said slowly. "Alone."

"To do some thinking?"

"That's right."

"Well, you've had some," he said, falsely flip. "And what do you think?"

She smiled wanly, still clutching the pillow to her, as if for protection. "I think I need more time."

Sandy paced across the carpet, running a hand through his hair, buying time himself so that his various conflicting emotions didn't just spill out in an explosive rush. "Let me see if we're together on this," he said. "Did you or didn't you have a good time last night?"

"Good?" She stared at him, then looked away. "Yes, it was very good," she said softly.

"That's what I thought," he told her, leaning against the windowsill to regard her in silence. She looked both radiant and tired at the same time. Nervous. "So it was too much too soon? Is that it?"

Victoria was staring at the carpet in front of her as if the answer might be written there. "In a way," she said.

He hadn't realized he'd slammed his fist against the sill quite that loudly. But judging from her startled expression and the smarting sensation in his hand, he had. "Can we jump cut?" he suggested. "Leave out any random expositional dialogue that's cluttering up this scene and get right to the meat of it?"

"Film versus literature," she said wryly.

"Right," he said. "And it's beginning to feel more like a 'Twilight Zone' episode, so maybe you could enlighten me. Have I done something wrong?"

"No," she said, eyes reading that carpet again. "But I think I have."

"Ah." Now they were getting somewhere. "And what wrong did you do?"

"Sleep with you," she said.

Okay, Sandy, you asked for it. Was that direct enough? He felt an inner shudder at her simple words. This wasn't what he'd wanted to hear. "Why was it wrong?" he asked.

Victoria tore her eyes from the carpet and rose abruptly, banging the pillow listlessly against her thigh as she walked to the foot of the bed. She hovered there, apparently realized she was staring at the bed, then turned to face him, her cheeks reddening.

"Look," she said. "I'm not saying I'm sorry I did it. It was wonderful. *You* were wonderful. But I wasn't thinking, I guess. And now that I am, I don't feel good about it."

"Because?" he prompted her, though in a way he wasn't sure he wanted to hear any more of her answers.

"Because we have to work together, for one thing."

"The shoot's almost over."

"Still, here we are," she said. "And if you weren't kidding about going to L.A..."

"Of course I wasn't kidding," he said.

"All the more reason."

"I don't get it."

Victoria sat on the edge of the bed. "I don't want this," she said. "I...I've had a hard enough time getting my life to be a way I'm comfortable living it, and this..."

"Is uncomfortable?" He couldn't keep the incredulity out of his voice and it was fueled by a hurt feeling that was threatening to attack his insides.

"Yes," she said. Now it was the edge of the bedspread that seemed to be feeding her cues. Her eyes were riveted to it. "I think we're both better off keeping some distance. We don't want the film to suffer, do we?"

He stared at her, fighting an impulse to cross the few yards between them, hop over whatever invisible wall she'd constructed and pull her into his arms. Part of him didn't believe a word she was saying. But another part, the prideful part, was already angered and ready to construct matching walls and barriers.

He'd taken a step forward without realizing it, and she was looking at him, finally. But the expression of alarm in her eyes wasn't encouraging. "Don't," she said. "Sandy, can't we just leave things where they are?"

"Which is where?"

"Which is that we've...gotten closer. And I'm—I'm happy for what we shared. But we're better off not getting into this any deeper."

Better off? His mind tried to grasp the concept, as he tasted bitter disappointment. It didn't compute. Then it struck him. He was alone in this, that was the missing piece of the puzzle. "Not getting into this any deeper"—that meant she wasn't in it, somehow. She wasn't in it the way he was. She could actually stand outside the thing and say, no, thanks, none for me.

The realization felt kind of like having a large and ugly knife slide into his too-soft skin. He forced himself to ignore the pain. Shields clicked into place. "Well, I wouldn't want to force you into something you don't want," he said coolly.

"It's not—" she began, then stopped. "I'm sure you wouldn't want it, either."

What gave her that idea? For a second confusion blurred his vision, but that only let some of the pain seep in, so he stopped the confusion by not asking questions. "You seem sure about a lot of things," he said.

Victoria looked pained now. "I'm not," she said. "This isn't easy for me. Sandy, you know I care about you—"

Good grief. He held up a hand to cut her off. "This is sounding real 'Dear John,'" he said. "So I think I'll skip the rest of that rap, if you don't mind."

Victoria stopped talking. He wondered if he'd hear anything she said now, anyway. He was too busy keeping those shields in place while he headed for the door. "We're shooting numbers twenty-seven through twenty-nine tomorrow," he said curtly, when the doorknob was in his hand. "Sarah's mother. You'll probably want to be around for that. So I'll see you then."

"Sandy..."

He turned, curious, but she was only shaking her head, looking upset. He counted to ten. "I'll see you then," he repeated, and forced a semblance of a smile. "Hey, no hard feelings," he told her. "We've got a film to finish."

Turn knob, exit fast. He'd been directing long enough to know that lingering exits were bush-league stuff. You said what you had to say and got out of there. So he was out, walking down the quiet hall, listening for the sound of a door opening, footsteps, someone running after him.

But it was only a dubbed track in his mind. All he heard was the distant slow chime of the clock downstairs and his own heartbeat, unnaturally loud. He kept seeing her face as he headed for his room, and the look in her eyes was haunting, perplexing him.

Scared. That's what it was, she'd looked like a woman who was frightened for her life. And if she was that scared, maybe she felt a lot more than she'd let on.

Maybe. Maybe not. He brooded on this as he walked toward his room and the work that awaited him before he'd ever get to sleep. He had a feeling he'd have plenty of time to brood on those maybes in the days—and sleepless nights—to come.

PATRICIA WALKER'S blond hair was already turning gray. She was tall, with piercing blue-gray eyes that matched Grace's in intensity, which was, Victoria surmised, the idea. Though the older actress only superficially resembled Grace, there was enough there to more than suggest she was the girl's mother. The two of them were relying on craft to do the rest and Victoria could see that their respective techniques were definitely paying off.

Grace had picked up Patricia's habit of cocking her head to one side slightly when she listened to someone talk. Patricia had adapted Grace's mannerism of pursing her lips when thinking. Those were the most obvious things Victoria had noticed, but there were many other tics and idiosyncrasies she was sure the camera was picking up—if, that is, they managed to get a good take in the can this afternoon without unintentional sabotage from the youth army of Silver Spring.

On this, their third day of shooting, Patricia and Grace were sitting on folding chairs outside the south entrance to the high school. Ropes had been strung up around them, signs, flags and enough fluorescent plastic highway cones to mark off the construction of a two-lane blacktop. This was to keep the always rubbernecking hordes of schoolchildren away from the camera area. For the first time since they'd started shooting in town, the film crew was experiencing major pedestrian traffic control.

Naturally they were curious, having genuine movie people making a film in what was essentially the high school's backyard. And being teenagers, they were marvelously skilled at getting past the usual barriers and infiltrating the set. Only yesterday a pair of aspiring filmmakers had been discovered sequestered in the prop truck, and this morning four teenage girls armed with cameras, had had to be forcibly removed from the background of a shot.

The wise solution this afternoon had been to shoot during classes. The school authorities had notified the student body that anyone found cutting classes to spy on the movie in progress would be subject to serious detention. So far this edict had worked. Sandy had whipped the crew into fast motion, and they were nearly back on schedule.

Victoria checked her watch as Bryce called for the actresses to take their places. Right about now, Cissy would be landing at the airport. By the end of the afternoon, she'd be happily ensconced at the old homestead, baby in tow. Victoria was figuring that her sister wouldn't visit the set today, and that was a good thing. She felt queasy about having Cissy meet the cinematic "Mom."

"Mom" was currently standing on the steps of the school's entrance, lips set tight and arms folded as she waited for daughter Sarah to follow her out the door. This shot was to follow a scene that would be actually filmed in L.A., since it was an interior. In the script, they'd just had a harrowing confrontation with the school's guidance counselor, who'd threatened Sarah with suspension. Mrs. Campbell was irate at having had to come in and talk to the woman.

Victoria remembered the matching scene from her childhood all too well. Again, she was struck by the uncanny recreation. Patricia didn't look anything like Mother, but her attitude certainly was right on the money. No loud words, no demonstrative recriminations, just a tight-lipped freeze out that made you feel even guiltier.

She fidgeted in her seat, watching Sandy talk to both actresses before they rolled camera. Sandy wasn't anything like Mother, either, but in anger, they had similar techniques. Ever since their late-night conversation at the beginning of the week, he'd frozen her out. Not with harsh words or even withering glances, just with a disconcerting blankness where before there'd been emotions.

He'd been cordial, superficially friendly even, but the only way she could describe it was the phrase she'd used in talking to Melinda. "His eyes are dead," she'd told her. "It's like when he looks at me, nobody's home."

She hated it. She hated herself, she hated him, she hated life for being so difficult, just when it had all looked so easy, for one blessed night. Four days. Four and a half. It seemed like a decade since that wonderful night and the awful one that followed it. Her only consolation was that the shoot was only two days from being over. Then she'd go back to New York and the business of putting this emotional nightmare behind her.

But in the meantime, it was like a leap from frying pan to fire. Cissy was nearly here, in time for the last weekend of Victoria's stay. Still unconfronted was Mother's Problem and Victoria's continued avoidance of dealing with it. She hadn't talked to Dad, as planned. Victoria didn't know which was worse, obsessing about her heartache over Sandy Baker, or worrying about her headache-producing family.

"Quiet on the set!"

For now, she gave over to the welcome distraction of movie magic. She watched as the camera rolled. Mrs.

Campbell came out the door, looking grim. She turned, waiting for Sarah to follow. Sarah came out, head held defiantly high. But meeting her mother's imperious, contemptuous gaze, her defiance faltered. She got a hangdog look as they walked down the steps in silence, Mrs. Campbell walking so fast that Sarah had to hurry to catch up.

The camera, mounted on a bizarre apparatus called a "steadi-cam" that completely encased the walking camera operator, moved even faster, following the two of them as they strode down the path toward the parking lot. Sarah whirled round briefly to make a symbolic obscene gesture at the school and its resident powers within, then hurried back to join her mother.

"Cut!"

Definitely a good take, Victoria judged, and she wasn't surprised when the crew starting wrapping this shot. She'd gotten pretty good at second-guessing Sandy where good takes were concerned. Something was bothering her about Patricia's performance, though. She couldn't put her finger on it. The actress had been perfect, so maybe it had to do with another element. The scene following?

She was musing on this when she heard Sandy Baker call her name. Victoria got up, surprised and apprehensive to see him hurrying toward her, clipboard billowing in his hand. "Script conference," he called, then called over his shoulder to his assistant, Carey. "Bring a coffee thermos into the *B* trailer, would you?"

Victoria steeled herself to deal with his cool demeanor, but today she barely had time to think about their personal relationship, because the director seemed to have been reading her mind again. "Something's off with Mrs. Campbell," he said, steering her into the trailer. "I'm sure we can use that take, but it's not going to match up with the following scene very well."

"I was wondering about the same thing," she told him.

"Here, let's look at it." He flipped open a copy of the shooting script that was on the table at the small dinette area in the trailer. Coffee arrived soon after. For about ten minutes there was nothing but terse comments and coffee sips as they both bent over their respective scripts, Sandy making indecipherable hieroglyphic notes to himself on his notebook's page margins.

"It's like there's a scene missing," Sandy mused, running a hand through his hair. "We've got Patricia playing Medusa here at the school, and when we cut back to the house she's a human being again. What happened in between?"

Victoria nodded, staring out the trailer's smoked window. She knew the answer. What had happened to her mother, in real life, between the scene at the guidance counselor's office and the scene in the Moore family kitchen, had been a short trip to that cabinet under the sink.

She could feel Sandy watching her. She turned back to meet his gaze, and was both pleased and apprehensive to see an expression there she'd been missing lately. He had that look of concerned interest, the one that made her feel like she was being explored, as if by some sensitive psychic doctor.

"It's not really Patricia's scene, in the kitchen," she said. "We could trim her dialogue."

Sandy didn't say anything, but merely gazed at her, as if waiting. She understood, then. He knew exactly what was missing from book and script, and was only biding time until she came up with it. The truth.

Victoria shook her head. Her stomach was churning, throat tightening. "No," she said.

Sandy raised an eyebrow. "No?"

"No, I am not going to turn Sarah Campbell's mother into a Scotch-swilling alcoholic," she said stiffly. "I don't care how some gap in continuity affects Patricia's precious performance.''

Sandy closed his script. "I wasn't suggesting that," he said quietly.

"Then what are you suggesting?" She couldn't keep the tremor out of her voice.

"That we think of something that will work. Something believable. Something that'll help us understand her character and have even more sympathy for her, not less."

More sympathy for Mother? It was an odd thought. It didn't compute with her usual mental headset where Mother was concerned. "How do you mean?"

"Well, most of the book, and our movie, is from Sarah's point of view. And for the bulk of both, Mom's an adversary, an obstacle. But we've got an opportunity here to get a glimpse of her mother's vulnerabilities, her mother's needs."

Victoria nodded, but she was already thinking beyond the movie, back into her own life. He was bringing up some volatile material here, confusing her. It was as if she was looking at her mother and Patricia, standing side by side, two characters from some story that wasn't movie or fiction, wasn't life. Could she be objective at all, anymore? Trying to analyze either one of them seemed impossible just now.

Sandy got up. She watched him pace the trailer's narrow aisle, recognizing this mode in him. He was trying to keep pace with his moving mind. He paused at her side. "What does Mrs. Campbell need?" he asked.

"She needs Sarah to straighten up and fly right."

"That's text. What's the subtext?"

Victoria frowned. "She needs..." There it was, suddenly, right in front of her. "She needs her husband's help."

"Right." He paced again. "That's what she says in the dialogue— 'You wait until your father gets home.' Only we know that when he does get home, he won't take Sarah in hand. He's much too easygoing and permissive.''

"And Caroline's useless, she's hysterical over her wedding and at war with Sarah, anyway," Victoria said. "So Mother's alone in this."

"How does she feel?"

Victoria was used to this technique by now. It was a writer's shorthand Sandy used that was not unlike putting their imaginary character on a therapist's couch. "She's angry," Victoria said.

"That's surface."

"She's upset. She's . . . I guess her own emotions are too much for her and she hates that. That's why she freezes up, it's an attempt at control. And Sarah's *out* of control, that's what scares her, so she..." Victoria's voice trailed off. Sandy was looking at her, nodding.

"So she has a drink," Victoria said.

"Yes."

"Because she's scared."

"Yes."

She stared at Sandy. "This is obvious," she said. "I mean, I knew this."

"Right."

He kept nodding. His eyes hadn't lost their look of concern. The warmth in them made her own eyes tear up. She looked away, embarrassed, her own emotions the ones that were nearly out of control. This was terrible. She was losing it. The movie had finally come too close for her to handle.

"Why did I ever agree to film this godawful . . . !"

"Here." Sandy slid into the booth beside her, a tissue in his hand. Keeping her face averted, as if that would make any difference, she dabbed at her eyes as the tears slid down her cheeks.

"I'm sorry," she murmured. "It's . . ."

"It's okay." His hand closed over hers, giving it a gentle squeeze. She had to restrain herself from leaning on him, resting her aching head on his strong shoulder. Nothing was making any sense. Why was he being so nice? He was angry at her. And why was she coming apart at the seams so easily? It was ridiculous.

"I'm sorry," she repeated, sniffling. "This is a weird time for me. Cissy's in town and I have to see her in a few hours, and I..." Her throat was too constricted.

"Blow your nose," he prompted her. She blew. He passed her another tissue.

"I'm a mess," she muttered. "Thank you."

"It's okay."

"It's not okay," she said, and punctuated this with another honk-like blowing of her nose. She looked up at Sandy through blurry eyes. "I don't want to deal with any of this," she said.

"I know." He gave her hand another squeeze. "But I also know that you can."

"Oh, sure," she said ruefully. "Why are you being so sympathetic and understanding, anyway? It's really annoying."

Sandy smiled. "Sorry." He adopted a stern demeanor. "Ms. Moore, we have a script to fix and time is money. Would you mind not letting your personal life into this purely professional endeavor?"

Victoria laughed. That felt better. Unfortunately it started the tears again, but Sandy seemed to have an inexhaustible supply of tissues on hand. "Listen," he said, after she'd soaked and shredded a few more. "Whatever's gone on between us is one thing. But I told you I'd be there for you regardless, and I am. Okay? So don't give me any heat about it."

She wanted to kiss him. She wanted to push him away and run into the woods and hide. She had absolutely no idea what she wanted anymore. She wanted to go home, but she didn't know what home was.

For a while she just sat there, lost in thought, and his hand slipped from hers. When she looked up again he was seated opposite, scribbling in his notebook. "What are you doing?"

He put his pen down. "Here's what I'd like to try, with the author's permission." He squinted at the page. "Mother and daughter are home. Daughter goes upstairs, as scripted. New material, inserted— Mother goes into the kitchen. She dials her husband at work. Busy signals. She hangs up. She looks at the ceiling. No, not ready to deal with Sarah. She goes to the cabinet and starts searching. Here's the thing. She doesn't drink, usually. When she sees her husband's Scotch she grimaces. Rejects the vodka, hates beer. Rummages around in the back of a cabinet and comes out with some sherry."

"Cooking sherry?"

"Exactly. Pours herself a stiff one and downs it in a gulp. Doesn't like it. But the drink does the trick, at least symbolically. She washes the glass and calls Sarah to come downstairs. And now we're back in the script as written." He looked across the table at her. "Well?"

"It's funny," she admitted. "We're having a private moment with her and she's doing something she ordinarily doesn't do—showing she's upset and a little desperate."

"Right," he said. "And Patricia can act the hell out of a moment like this. They'll laugh, but it'll be a very sympathetic laugh."

"So then, when they play the scene in the kitchen, Patricia's odd serenity will make sense."

"Check."

"You're good," she told him.

"I try."

Victoria considered. "No other drinking in the rest of the movie?"

"No. It'll be just what it is, a moment. People who want to make more of it may, if they want. But it's a subtle touch, that's all, something to inform her character."

"All right," she said.

"Good."

Now they were merely sitting there looking at each other. She'd missed him. Come to think of it, she'd felt horribly alone for days now, an aloneness she wasn't used to and didn't want to feel again.

"Thank you," she said.

"My pleasure."

"Really?"

Sandy shrugged. "Are you all right?"

"No," she admitted. "But I'm better than I was." She regarded him a moment. "So, what are we, friends? Is that what this is?"

"I'm not sure," he said. "But if that's what you want it to be, maybe so."

"Oh." She didn't know what to think. And she was too tired to figure him out, let alone her self. This emotional stuff was exhausting.

"Well, that takes care of one thing," he was saying.

She shot him a questioning glance. "And the other?"

"That takes care of the movie," he said quietly. "What are you going to do when you get home?"

Chapter Twelve

"He's sleeping, finally." Cissy smiled as she shut the front door quietly behind her, joining Victoria on the porch.

"I guess he was overexcited by all the traveling."

Her sister nodded. "But he'll sleep like a log, now," she said, and sank into the old armchair with a sigh. "I will, too, I'm sure."

Victoria studied her sister as Cissy gazed out on the lawn. Her blond hair was still lustrous, her skin amazingly wrinkle-free. She still had the looks of a prom queen. Victoria was past envy by now. She'd accepted her own more idiosyncratic features. But she couldn't help marveling, silently. Two children and a full-time job, but Cissy seemed to have barely aged.

Cissy looked up, feeling Victoria's eyes upon her. "It's weird to be here, isn't it?"

Victoria nodded and moved from her stance by the screen door to take the chair next to Cissy's. "Yes, it is," she said cautiously, wondering if now was the time to try to have this conversation, the one she'd been dreading for so long. She hadn't formulated any plan, she was just winging it. "So many things are still the same here."

"No kidding." Cissy smiled. "Dad's been telling the same bad jokes for what, thirty years?"

"At least," Victoria agreed. The sisters smiled at each other, then turned their gazes to the street. And this was the same, too, Victoria thought, these superficial conversations they had, like the idle chatter that had gone on through dinner. The Moore family routine had only been slightly altered by little Jordan's attempts at joining in.

Don't rock the boat, don't venture into deeper water. These were the tacit directives, and a related one was, don't notice Mother's "moods." Mother had been especially cheery tonight, delighted to have Jordan there. But even this hadn't kept her from her habitual trips to that kitchen cabinet.

Victoria had noticed that no one seemed to notice. Now for the umpteenth time she considered letting the whole issue go, since it was so clear that nobody wanted to deal with it. But what about that plate Mother had dropped and broken? What about Mother's offer to baby-sit Jordan during Cissy's projected night out? Wasn't Cissy concerned?

No, Victoria had already made up her mind that for once she wasn't going to back down. She cleared her throat, sat forward in her seat. "How do you think Mother is?" she asked.

Cissy shot her a quizzical glance. Just as quickly, she smiled again, automatically shifting into her denial mode. "Well, she just lights up when Jordan is around," she said. "I actually started to feel guilty that it's been so long since we were last out here."

Victoria nodded. "Yes, Dad's going to spoil him rotten, too," she said, and Cissy chuckled. "But that's not what I meant," she went on. "I mean..." She had to actually stop and take a breath. "I'm a little worried." She forged ahead. "About Mother's health, I mean."

Cissy looked puzzled. "Is there something wrong?" Her voice quieted in concern. "No one's said a thing to me, Victoria. What's going on?"

"Nothing that hasn't been going on for ages," Victoria said, with a sigh. "But I think it's time we...talked to her about it, at least."

For a brief instant, as Cissy stared at her, Victoria knew that her sister understood. But now, as she'd done so many times before, she chose not to. "Vicki, what are you talking about?"

"I'm talking about her—" Victoria stopped herself, aware that her voice had risen. She leaned forward. "Her drinking," she said quietly. "Come on, Cissy, you know as well as I do. Mother's had a drinking problem for years. And maybe it wasn't a health issue, when we were kids, but at her age—"

"Just wait a minute here," Cissy said, drawing herself up with a look of incredulity. "I can't believe I'm hearing this. Mother doesn't *drink*."

Victoria was momentarily speechless. She had to fend off a flare of anger that rose up in her at Cissy's tone. She recognized it from way back. It was Cissy's old, boy-is-my-kid-sister-a-wacko voice, and to Victoria it was like nails on a chalkboard. She struggled to keep her voice low and even.

"She certainly does, Cissy. What do think is in those trusty bottles she keeps in the kitchen cabinet? Lemonade? And don't tell me you don't know they're in there."

Cissy stared at her, an indignant anger flashing in her eyes. "This is silly," she said. "If Mother likes to settle her nerves now and then with a little—"

"Now and then?" Victoria interrupted, incredulous. "Cissy, she drinks every night. And if I'm not mistaken, she sometimes starts in the afternoon."

"What are you saying?" There were two red points of color in Cissy's taut cheeks.

"I'm saying she has a problem," Victoria said. "She has a drinking problem. She may be an alcoholic."

Cissy was shaking her head from side to side, as if to shake the words out of her ears. "Boy, are you . . . You are way out of line, Victoria. I mean, I understand that you and Mother have had your differences. But that's no reason to say these kinds of crazy things about—"

"She was so drunk at dinner, she broke one of her oldest good china plates and barely noticed it," Victoria said in a whisper that came out more like a hiss.

"She was *not* drunk," Cissy insisted. "We all split one bottle of red table wine and I doubt if she had more than one glass, Victoria. I think your creative imagination is working a bit too hard."

"And your denial system is in overdrive."

"'Denial system'?" Cissy echoed, with a roll of her eyes. "What is that, New York psychotherapy talk?"

She was walking a very thin line here, Victoria mused. If she gave in to her anger at Cissy, she'd never get anywhere. On the other hand, it didn't seem as though she could get anywhere with her sister if she forced herself to remain reasonable. "Mother has been drinking, primarily Scotch, for as long as Dad's been telling bad jokes, Cissy," she said, keeping her voice as deliberately even as she could. "If you haven't noticed, it means you haven't wanted to."

She could see the anger flare in her sister's eyes. Then Cissy, too, apparently decided to make an effort. "I am not denying that I've seen her have the occasional drink," Cissy said. "But I think you're making a mountain out of a molehill. It calms her nerves, that's all. She's always been a little high-strung."

Victoria sighed, trying to be grateful for at least this acknowledgement that she wasn't crazy. "High-strung? That's one way of putting it. All right, don't look at me like that. I'm not out to 'get' Mother."

"Then what *are* you doing?" Cissy asked. "What's the point of calling her names?"

"You mean, my suggesting she's an alcoholic?"

"Yes, that's the most outrageous statement I've ever heard," Cissy said huffily, sitting back in her chair. "And as far as Mother having a so-called 'problem,' how bad a problem can it be? She's been happily married for decades and she brought the two of us up without any...major mishaps."

So much in between the lines, Victoria thought. She got the message. She didn't have any trouble, with *me*, Cissy was saying, and if there were any problems with *you*, it wasn't Mother's fault.

"She's perfectly fit for a woman her age," Cissy continued. "Honestly, Vicki, what's the point of all this hysteria?"

You couldn't take those four years away, not ever. Cissy would always be four years older, four years wiser, four years a better, saner human being, constantly showing her younger, mixed-up sister the proper way to behave. "The point is, I think we could try to help her," Victoria said quietly, feeling her head start to throb.

"Oh, you're one to talk," Cissy said, with an ironic smile. "You don't visit her for years at a time. From what I hear, you barely talk to Mother. Then you come flying in here out of the blue and suddenly there's problems that have to be solved. What do you know about it, really?"

"I'm sure I haven't been the devoted daughter that you have," Victoria said, unable to keep from rising to the bait. "But that's not the point."

Cissy shrugged. "Well, if you talked to Mother nearly every week, the way I do, maybe you'd have some perspective. I mean, for heaven's sake—sometimes when Mother and I have a nice, long phone chat I like to sit down with a glass of wine. I suppose you'll say that makes me an alcoholic, too."

"I'm sure it doesn't help," Victoria said.

Cissy sat up, then rose from her chair with a look at Victoria that could have turned her to stone. "That's enough," she said tightly. "I am not going to sit here and listen to this. I came here to have a good little vacation, with every intention of getting along with *you*, fool that I am. But clearly, getting along with your family is not your idea of a good time. It never has been."

"Cissy—"

"This subject is closed," Cissy said, her voice shaky and aggrieved. "I don't want to hear another word about it again."

She turned her back and marched across the porch to the door. Victoria put her head in her hands, tears welling up in her eyes. She wanted to scream more than cry. She'd feared it would be like this, Cissy defending Mother and attacking her. She *did* want to help Mother, couldn't Cissy see that? Couldn't she understood that just indulging Mother the way Cissy did made things worse?

"Oh, hi, Dad."

Victoria looked up. Cissy had opened the door to the house and Dad was there, lighting his pipe. "I was just going in to check on Jordan."

"Think he's still out like a light," Dad said. "But you go on ahead in. I'm going to fill up this fine night air with tobacco smoke."

Cissy gave him a pat on the arm and went into the house. Victoria turned her face away, not wanting her father to see the tears on her cheeks as he slowly slid into the chair Cissy had vacated. She dabbed furtively at her cheeks with the sleeve of her sweater. He puffed noisily on his pipe. After a moment he cleared his throat.

"You two are still at it, eh?"

Victoria managed a rueful chuckle. "I'm sorry, Dad. I hope we weren't too noisy," she added nervously. How much had he overheard?

"Didn't take that long," he noted. "It's a shame, really. I'd like to see the Moore women keeping peace and harmony for one night."

Victoria smoothed her skirt over her knees. "I know," she said. "I'll try..." Her voice trailed off. Try what? Go back to the false cheer and blissful ignorance? She didn't think she was capable of it at this point. Maybe she was better off staying away from the house altogether.

"I've tried talking to her, myself," her father was saying. "Hasn't done much good."

Victoria glanced at him, curious. Dad puffed at his pipe, eyes on the trees. He looked tired, a little sad. She felt guilty for having upset him. He always did have to play peacemaker when both daughters were at home. "It's okay," she said. "I'll apologize to Cissy. It wasn't any big thing, really."

Her father shook his head, eyes still fixed on the moonlit leaves rustling past the porch eaves. "I'm talking about your mother," he said quietly.

Victoria stared at him, her throat tightening. "What do you mean?"

"Don't think I haven't made any attempts, over the years," he said. "But your mother can be a very stubborn woman to reckon with. Maybe I'm too close to her in some ways... and too far away in others," he said, with a rueful grimace. "We've had our battles over this thing, believe you me. But I've never made any real headway."

Tears were blurring her vision again. She blinked, staring at him, almost afraid to believe she was hearing this. An age-old taboo was being broken. Walls were crumbling, the floor unsteady underneath her feet. "You ... you did, you heard ..."

"You and your sister?" He shrugged. "Enough to know what's going on." He shifted in his seat, looking at her directly for the first time. "Enough to see *you* know what's been going on," he said, and the sadness in his voice made her heart ache.

"Yes," she said. She put a hand on his knee and saw the dark material of his corduroys stained with a teardrop fallen from her cheek. "Oh, Daddy ..."

"Hey, hey," he murmured, stroking her hair. "I guess it's about time we did talk about it. To tell you the truth, I was wondering if one of you gals ever would."

"I was ... scared," she blurted, crying in earnest now. His arm moved around her shoulder.

"I don't blame you," he whispered, his hand still gently smoothing her curls. "It's scary stuff. Your mother's never been very good at confronting people, and I'm no champ in that department, either. Maybe it's a family weakness."

"Why does she do it?" she asked. "When did it start?"

Her father sighed. "According to your mother, she doesn't and she never did."

"It can't be good for her," Victoria murmured, sniffling.

"I know," Mr. Moore said. "I've been trying to convince her to get a physical from Doc Hauser. I know he'd say something to her, not that she'd listen, necessarily. But your mother won't go."

"But if nobody ever says anything ..."

"I worry about it all the time," her father said.

"She'll never listen to me."

"I'm not so sure."

She looked up at him through a mist of tears. "Do you think I should even try?"

He smiled ruefully. "I wish you would. Somebody's got to stand up to that woman, and you seem to have been bucking to get elected."

"I guess so." Victoria sniffled, leaning her head against his warm shoulder, gratefully accepting the folded handkerchief he pushed into her hand. "Thank you." She sat up again, blew her nose loudly, then smiled at him in embarrassment. "I didn't mean to mess up your favorite corduroys."

He waved a dismissive hand. "I'll tell you one or two things, though," he said. "One is, anything you want to say to your mother, you should know I'll be right there behind you if the going gets rough. She starts laying in the heavy artillery, I'll back you up, sweetheart."

"Dad..."

"And I'm going to have a little talk with your big sister, too," he said. "We've all of us got to get together on this thing. It's been too long coming."

"I think so," she said. "Maybe Cissy will listen to you. With me it's hopeless."

"Well, we can't do everything at once, can we? Turn this whole family upside down..." He gazed off, shaking his head. "But I'll try to bring her around."

"I should've talked to you first."

"Should've, could've." He chuckled ruefully. "Don't get *me* started on those kinds of thoughts. Besides, I've got some bad habits of my own," he added, eyeing the pipe in his hand.

"We'll tackle you next," she said, dabbing at her eyes with his handkerchief. It smelled like his tobacco. She loved him more in that moment than she knew how to say.

"I'll tell you one other thing," her father said, exhaling smoke. "You may find it hard to believe, but when it comes to confronting the big stuff—matters of the heart and soul—your mother's just as scared as you are, honey." He smiled. "Maybe even more so."

She stared at him. "You're kidding, right?"

He shook his head. "Honey, you're the one person in this brood who's had the gall to do something a little adventurous with her life."

"And Mother's never approved of it."

"It's not that simple," he said.

"She disregards every accomplishment I've ever achieved, Dad."

"Not exactly." He gave her a wry smile. "To tell you the truth, I think you intimidate the hell out of her. You always have."

"What?" Even as she squinted at him in disbelief, a part of her registered a resonance of truth in what he said. It reminded her of what Sandy had said, just that afternoon. Maybe it wasn't entirely preposterous that her mother's attitude was rooted in more than mere dislike.

"You're even more independent, stubborn and bullheaded than she is," Dad said, and chuckled. "You gave her more of a hard time around here, back in the old days, than anyone ever had the nerve to. And to top it off, you went out and became a certified author. Now, that's not too shabby."

"She doesn't even read my books."

"I think the first one shocked her silly," Dad said, placing his pipe in the ashtray on the end table. "If she hasn't read the others, it wasn't from lack of interest. I think it's more like she's afraid to.''

Afraid? Mother? It was still a difficult concept for her to get her mind around. But even as she grappled with it, Victoria could feel something shift inside her. Maybe things could change. Maybe, given a chance, she could just make a little difference here. If she was willing to take the risk.

"QUIET ON THE SET!''

The silence in the Silver Spring woods this afternoon as the camera got ready to roll seemed more electric than it had ever been, and Victoria knew why. If they got this take in the can successfully, that was it. It would be a wrap, as they said in the movie biz, the location shoot would be over.

Grace-as-Sarah was in position, standing on the bridge over Jumpers Creek. Carey, the A.D., was going over details on the retake with Ted, the sound man. Kathy, from makeup, sprinted to Grace's side to fuss with her hair. Dave was bent over the camera as Tom watched his every move.

Victoria took in each and every member of the crew, realizing she knew most everyone by now. She knew their names and some of their idiosyncrasies, knew that Bryce was the resident party animal and Scott the super-film buff, that Shelley, from wardrobe, was having an affair with Jonathan, the line producer, that Tom's perfectionism drove Dave crazy, that Susan Jacks and Arlyne had been at war but were now fast friends.

Friends. In a way, she felt she'd made some friends here, but knew it was all so fleeting. This whole intensive pressure cooker of people would soon evaporate into mere memory. For a moment she regretted not having been able to spend more time with the crew. Should've, could've...her father's least favorite words—and Sandy Baker's, too. Funny, but the two men were alike in some ways. That wasn't something she wanted to dwell on just now. Grace was ready for her take.

"Camera?"

"Rolling."

Victoria watched Grace "get into character," looking down at the creek, where she herself had stood so many times, staring at the same water below. She saw the emotions flicker over her alter ego's face, reliving them in an instant, her mind intertwining past and present.

"Action!"

She would jump. She'd jump not to die but to live, to prove to herself that she could survive. She'd take that all-important risk so that she could continue to risk for the rest of her life—risk loving, losing, hurting and learning. *Not* to jump, that was the real danger.

Victoria found her eyes seeking Sandy. He was crouched by the camera at the foot of the bridge as the D.P. zoomed slowly in, his wiry body as tensed as an alarm clock's spring. Had she forgotten this lesson? she mused. Not taking the risk with Sandy Baker—was that going back on the most essential thing she'd learned at Jumpers Creek?

It was a sobering thought. She turned back to watch Sarah as the camera came in close to study her face. Victoria imagined her thinking about the risk, seeing it, feeling it in the moments before flight, before that awesome leap into the unknown. Grace's eyes gleamed, reflecting the last rays of sunshine glittering in the quiet rush of water below. She pursed her lips, took a breath, then stepped resolutely to the railing.

"Cut!"

Victoria had been so caught up in the moment she was startled by the sudden interruption. Then the sound of the entire crew erupting in a spontaneous cheer brought her back to reality. That was it. They were done. The Silver Spring location shoot had ended.

As Susan Jacks whirled by with a bottle of champagne held in each hand and the other crew members' voices rose in a tumult of talk and laughter, Victoria remained staring at the bridge above them. Through the magic of cinema, Sarah's actual jump would be done on a carefully constructed set in Hollywood, then seamlessly cut together with these exteriors to make the scene complete. This was both for safety purposes and to give the camera crew more control over the jump and the footage to be shot in the water.

Victoria trusted that Sandy would bring it off. She trusted that the rest of the shoot would go just fine without her. What she didn't trust was that she'd be able to live with herself if she returned to New York, the risk of Sandy Baker untaken.

He was surrounded by crew now. She didn't even try to catch his eye. She didn't feel celebratory, only pensive and apprehensive. Tonight she was going to talk to Mother. And then she'd have to say goodbye to Sandy. Neither task was anything to look forward to."

"Congratulations!" Arlyne was there, with a smile and a plastic cup of champagne for her. Victoria smiled and congratulated her back. For the next twenty minutes, while the crew packed up their gear in high spirits, she did her best to be the professional, the teammate, the happy collaborator. She joined in the anecdotes recounted, exchanged addresses, made the promises that most understood didn't have to be kept.

No one was actually leaving Silver Spring immediately. There would be all of tomorrow and the next day for the massive amounts of equipment and people to be gathered and shipped out. The official wrap party wasn't until later tonight, and even after that, most of these people would be reunited out in California. But for Victoria, it was the beginning of a long goodbye. It didn't feel good. She began to seek an opening for a graceful exit.

"Victoria!"

It was Melinda, with husband Jim on her arm. She was relieved to see that the two of them looked genuinely happy together. Jim deluged her with questions about the shoot, bemoaning the fact that he'd only finally made it to the set in time to see the filming end. Victoria didn't have a chance to ask her friend any direct questions about what was going on with them, but she could see that the crisis had been dealt with. Ted, the actor, was gone, and Jim was here. And Melinda, she noted, was making no mention of leaving Silver Spring.

Most of the equipment was already dismantled, the crew in a slow exodus from the creek location when Victoria finally disengaged herself from the casual pre-party party and headed out of the woods. Once out of the Glen, she made a beeline for the phone booth at the edge of the parking lot.

This was a hard part. For about five minutes she dawdled around its periphery, pretending to inspect the contents of her pocketbook, while across the lot, various crew members straggled out of the woods with boxes of equipment in tow. Finally the procrastinating seemed to absurd. She went into the booth, deposited her quarter and dialed. Mother picked up on the third ring.

"Oh, hello, Victoria. Cissy said you might be calling."

So far so good. Victoria's heart was beating in double time, but she felt a surge of relief. So Dad had talked to Cissy. This was, in a sense, their prearranged signal. If Cissy had actually agreed to pave the way for a family discussion, she was supposed to have told Mother that Victoria would be coming by that evening for a visit.

"Yes, I'm hoping to stop by and see you after dinner, if that's okay."

"It's fine, dear," Mother said, and Victoria could hear the questioning tone in her voice.

"I just..." She faltered, then clenched the receiver, determined to stick to the script she'd been mentally preparing all afternoon. "The shoot's pretty much wrapped up and I'll be leaving Sunday, and I thought... Well, you and I haven't had a chance to really sit down and talk."

"Is something wrong?"

Again, she knew her mother well enough to recognize the subtleties. This question had resonances of Mother's old, What trouble have you stirred up now? tone in it. "Nothing's wrong," she hastened to assure her. "I mean, I'm fine, really, but..."

She expected her mother to say something in the momentary silence, to fill it in as she usually did, to keep the conversation smooth, the surface unruffled. Instead she could feel her mother waiting, actually listening. And in that moment, she had a sudden intuition that Dad was right. Victoria was the one in charge here. Her mother was more apprehensive than she was.

"I'd just like us to be able to talk," she blurted. "I worry about you. I worry about us ever being honest with each other."

"Victoria—"

"No, Mother, let me finish. I know we've always had a hard time communicating, and maybe it seems strange to you that I'd bring it up now, but..." She sighed. "Life's too short, isn't it? I'd like to leave Silver Spring with a feeling we really did at least make the effort. Can you understand that?"

"I..." She heard a catch in Mother's voice. And when she continued, there was a softer tone in it, one she'd never thought she'd hear. "Yes, dear. I think I do."

"Good." Victoria smiled, even as she felt her throat choking up. Good grief, how much was she going to cry? She'd shed more tears in this one trip than she had in the past five years. "So I'll come by around nine or so. Would that be all right?"

"That would be fine." She sounded uncertain, flustered, a little—what was the word? Vulnerable. That was shocking in itself, but it made her feel a hope that was even more uplifting. If Mother could be at all open, if she gave Victoria a way in...who knew what might happen?

"So I'll see you in a little while, then," Victoria said.

"All right, Victoria. Bye-bye."

"Bye-bye," she echoed, and hung up. She stood staring at her hand still on the receiver, her mind whirling, her emotions in tumult.

That wasn't so hard, was it?

No. It was a beginning. The Fears were clamoring for attention in the recesses of her mind, as they had been for the duration of her phone call. But she could ignore them. True, the whole thing might blow up in her face. Yes, even if Dad had talked to Cissy, that didn't mean Cissy wouldn't be as difficult as she'd always been. It didn't mean that she and Cissy would ever get along any better than they did. No problems were really solved, yet.

But she was taking the plunge.

Victoria slowly lifted her hand from the receiver and turned from the phone to stare at the entrance to the Glen. There was really only one person in the world who would truly understand what was happening, what she was going through. It struck her as criminally absurd that he was the one person she'd been afraid to talk to.

Victoria started walking. She had to tell him, all about this, and more. She wanted to thank him, first, for being the friend he'd said he would be. For putting his own hurt feelings aside to help her get in touch with *her* real feelings. She started walking faster.

Thank him? That wasn't really the point. She wanted to share it with him, the moment, the everything that was going on. She didn't want to be alone with it, but more than that, she wanted to know if he'd be there now. Had he changed, too? Was he still the same guy who'd explained so calmly how he had problems being partners with a woman? Hadn't they been partners? Or hadn't they been together as a man and woman, could, should be, if they really...

... loved each other?

She'd broken into a trot before she realized it. Don't hesitate, don't think, she thought with every step. She was still in midair, still taking that awesome leap.

If he's there, I'll tell him the truth. I'll tell him what I've known without admitting I know: that I want him, whatever the consequences. I don't want to say goodbye. And she knew, somehow, that he would be there on the ground, ready to snatch her.

She nearly did stumble right into Sandy Baker's arms as she came careening down the path toward the foot of the Jumpers Creek bridge. He was standing there, the sole person left in the darkening dusk, a strange expression on his face as he looked up to see her running toward him. Almost as if he'd been expecting her.

Don't think, she thought one final time, and she let herself jump the final jump, into Sandy's arms. It was like coming home. His arms enfolded her so naturally, the kisses he covered her face with were all she needed, that she was halfway into her umpteenth cry of the day before she started laughing. This confused him completely.

"What? What?" he kept asking, as he cradled her in his arms.

"You," she managed, burrowing her face in his neck, kissing his chin.

"I look funny?"

"Yes," she said, wiping her tearstained cheek against his ticklishly unshaven one.

"Thanks," he said. "Well, I was feeling funny, standing around here after everyone else was gone, pretending I was lingering for no particular reason while I waited for you to come back."

"You knew I would?"

"No. But I wanted you to." He held her head in both hands, gazing into her eyes. "I wrote, rewrote and redirected the scene a number of ways. You version—with that kind of flying leap in it?—was even better than mine."

"High praise."

"I'm glad you came." His voice had a tiny catch in it. "It would've been terrible to miss the wrap party while I hung out in the dark with a bunch of squirrels."

"Truly terrible. Sandy, can we talk?"

"I wish we would."

"*Real* talk," she said, and took a deep breath. "Now don't say another word until I confess that I'm in love with you."

His eyes sparkled with renewed excitement. "Are you?"

"You know I am," she said. "I just haven't wanted to be. Can you understand that?"

"Absolutely," he said, hugging her even more tightly to his chest. "I didn't want to love you as much as I do, but it's way too late."

She clung to him, letting the good feeling wash over her like a warm bath as he gently kissed her forehead, stroked her hair. "But what's the point?" she murmured. "We can't stop loving each other, can we?"

"No," he said, and kissed her again. "All I want to know is, what's made you suddenly come to your senses?"

"You," she said. "Me. Everything. I talked to my mother and I think we're really going to be able to *talk*, you know?"

"That's fantastic."

"I talked to my father about it. There's even an A.A. group in town, an informal one that meets in the church once a week. We figure if all of us talk to her and bring it all out in the open, maybe we can bring her around. In fact, I know we can!" she cried. "And it's partially because of you, putting all these ideas in my head."

"I didn't do anything."

"You cared. You asked the right questions. And you gave me the right kind of hard time," she added, smiling at him.

"Me give *you* a hard time?" He gave her a look of mock incredulity. "You're the one who—"

"Tell me one thing," she interrupted impatiently. "What will you do if I actually do come out to Los Angeles?"

His face turned grave. "I think I'll be happier than I've ever been," he said. "I think I'll lock you in my house with me and not let you out until you agree to never leave again."

"That's a very provocative threat," she murmured.

"I'll probably end up spoiling you rotten," he said. "Buying you things. Expensive clothes, gold rings. It'll be awful."

She stared into the velvet darkness of his eyes, almost afraid to believe him. "Do you have any idea what you're getting into?"

"I do," he said. "Which is why I am."

"And this has nothing to do with the movie?"

He laughed. "Oh, that's right. I can't collaborate with a woman I love. Well, let's lay that old line to rest, okay? I want to collaborate with you in every possible way, shape and form there is.''

''*Every* way?''

''Oh, yeah. You don't believe in marriage and kids.''

''I didn't before,'' she admitted.

''Before you met me,'' he prompted her. ''Only now you're going to suspend disbelief. Like they do in the movies.''

''Something like that,'' she said. ''We're nuts, right? This is an insane conversation.''

''No, it's an attack of sanity,'' he told her. ''We've been struck smart.''

He kissed her again, this time full on the lips, and a fullness she remembered from their one night of love swelled up inside her again, so huge it left her breathless. It also left her wanting to feel that again.

''I'm sorry I was bad to you,'' she whispered.

''It was the last defense of a woman running scared,'' he said, smiling. ''I figured that out, all on my own.''

''Aren't you smart,'' she said. ''And arrogant.''

''Aren't you brave,'' he said.

''I'm trying,'' she told him. ''I'm trying to believe this is the right thing to do, that you're the right guy for me to do it with. That I'm not my mother. That I can have the things I was afraid to have.''

''You're not going to have to try very hard,'' he told her, cupping her chin in his hand. ''I'm here to help.''

''Sandy, we have so much to talk about.''

''Yes, love. But we're going to have plenty of time.'' He kissed her lightly on the tip of her nose. She stepped back to drink in his smiling features, the love she could see shining in his dark eyes. It was a face she couldn't imagine tiring of.

But what if he . . . ?

Stop. Say it. Exorcise the demons, instead of hiding them. Wasn't that what she'd been learning to do?

Victoria exhaled a deep breath. "I feel like I'm jumping off that bridge again."

Sandy nodded. "Only this time, somebody's going with you," he said, and he took her hand.

HARLEQUIN
American Romance®

RELIVE THE MEMORIES....

From New York's immigrant experience to San Francisco's Great Quake of '06. From the western front of World War I to the Roaring Twenties. From the indomitable spirit of the thirties to the home front of the Fabulous Forties to the baby-boom fifties... A CENTURY OF AMERICAN ROMANCE takes you on a nostalgic journey.

From the turn of the century to the dawn of the year 2000, you'll revel in the romance of a time gone by and sneak a peek at romance in an exciting future.

Watch for all the CENTURY OF AMERICAN ROMANCE titles coming to you one per month over the next four months in Harlequin American Romance.

Don't miss a day of A CENTURY OF AMERICAN ROMANCE.

A CENTURY OF
AMERICAN ROMANCE
1960s

The women... the men... the passions... the memories...

Coming soon
to an easy chair near you.

FIRST CLASS is Harlequin's armchair travel plan for the incurably romantic. You'll visit a different dreamy destination every month from January through December without ever packing a bag. No jet lag, no expensive air fares and *no* lost luggage. Just First Class Harlequin Romance reading, featuring exotic settings from Tasmania to Thailand, from Egypt to Australia, and more.

FIRST CLASS romantic excursions guaranteed! Start your world tour in January. Look for the special **FIRST CLASS** destination on selected Harlequin Romance titles—there's a new one every month.

NEXT DESTINATION:
THAILAND

 Harlequin Books

JTR2

You'll flip . . . your pages won't!
Read paperbacks *hands-free* with

Book Mate • I

The perfect "mate" for all your romance paperbacks
Traveling • Vacationing • At Work • In Bed • Studying
• Cooking • Eating

Perfect size for
all standard
paperbacks,
this wonderful
invention
makes reading
a pure pleasure!
Ingenious
design holds
paperback
books OPEN
and FLAT so
even wind can't
ruffle pages —
leaves your
hands free to do
other things.
Reinforced,
wipe-clean vinyl-
covered holder flexes to let you
turn pages without undoing the
strap . . . supports paperbacks so
well, they have the strength of
hardcovers!

Pages turn WITHOUT
opening the strap

SEE-THROUGH STRAP

Reinforced back stays flat

Built in bookmark

BOOK MARK

BACK COVER
HOLDING STRIP

10˝ x 7¼˝ . opened.
Snaps closed for easy carrying, too.

Harlequin Intrigue®

REBECCA YORK

Labeled a "true master of intrigue" by *Rave Reviews*, best-selling author Rebecca York makes her Harlequin Intrigue debut with an exciting suspenseful new series.

It looks like a charming old building near the renovated Baltimore waterfront, but inside 43 Light Street lurks danger . . . and romance.

Let Rebecca York introduce you to:

> *Abby Franklin*—a psychologist who risks everything to save a tough adventurer determined to find the truth about his sister's death. . . .
>
> *Jo O'Malley*—a private detective who finds herself matching wits with a serial killer who makes her his next target. . . .
>
> *Laura Roswell*—a lawyer whose inherited share in a development deal lands her in the middle of a murder. And she's the chief suspect. . . .

These are just a few of the occupants of 43 Light Street you'll meet in Harlequin Intrigue's new ongoing series. Don't miss any of the 43 LIGHT STREET books, beginning with #143 LIFE LINE.

And watch for future LIGHT STREET titles, including #155 SHATTERED VOWS (February 1991) and #167 WHISPERS IN THE NIGHT (August 1991).

HI-143-1

Harlequin Superromance®

A powerful restaurant conglomerate that draws the best and brightest to its executive ranks. Now almost eighty years old, Vanessa Hamilton, the founder of Hamilton House, must choose a successor. Who will it be?

Matt Logan: He's always been the company man, the quintessential team player. But tragedy in his daughter's life and a passionate love affair force him to make some hard choices....

Paula Steele: Thoroughly accomplished, with a sharp mind, perfect breeding and looks to die for, Paula thrives on challenges and wants to have it all...but is this right for her?

Grady O'Connor: Working for Hamilton House was his salvation after Vietnam. The war had messed him up but good and had killed his storybook marriage. He's been given a second chance—only he doesn't know what the hell he's supposed to do with it....

Harlequin Superromance invites you to enjoy Barbara Kaye's dramatic and emotionally resonant miniseries about mature men and women making life-changing decisions. Don't miss:

- CHOICE OF A LIFETIME—a July 1990 release.
- CHALLENGE OF A LIFETIME—a December 1990 release.
- CHANCE OF A LIFETIME—an April 1991 release.

SR-HH-1R

Sadie raised an eyebrow. "No?"